❧ CIRCLE OF LIGHT 2 ❧

Faragon
Fairingay

D0712027

Don't get left behind!

STARSCAPE

Let the journey begin . . .

From the Two Rivers
The Eye of the World: Part 1
by Robert Jordan

To the Blight
The Eye of the World: Part 2
by Robert Jordan

Ender's Game
by Orson Scott Card

The Cockatrice Boys
by Joan Aiken

Mairelon the Magician
by Patricia C. Wrede

Ender's Shadow
by Orson Scott Card

The Whispering Mountain
by Joan Aiken

Orvis
by H. M. Hoover

The Garden Behind the Moon
by Howard Pyle

The Dark Side of Nowhere
by Neal Shusterman

Prince Ombra
by Roderick MacLeish

The Magician's Ward
by Patricia C. Wrede

A College of Magics
by Caroline Stevermer

Deep Secret
by Diana Wynne Jones

Pinocchio
by Carlo Collodi

Another Heaven,
Another Earth
by H. M. Hoover

Hidden Talents
by David Lubar

The Wonder Clock
by Howard Pyle

Obernewtyn
by Isobelle Carmody

The Shadow Guests
by Joan Aiken

This Time of Darkness
by H. M. Hoover

Song in the Silence
by Elizabeth Kerner

Red Unicorn
by Tanith Lee

Putting Up Roots
by Charles Sheffield

The Billion Dollar Boy
by Charles Sheffield

In the Land of the
Lawn Weenies
by David Lubar

The Farseekers
by Isobelle Carmody

Starswarm
by Jerry Pournells

A School for Sorcery
by E. Rose Sabin

The Eye of the Heron
by Ursula K. Le Guin

Ashling
by Isobelle Carmody

The Cyborg from Earth
by Charles Sheffield

Peter Pan
by J. M. Barrie

The Hunt Begins
The Great Hunt: Part 1
by Robert Jordan

New Threads in the Pattern
The Great Hunt: Part 2
by Robert Jordan

Greyfax Grimwald
by Niel Hancock

Dragon and Thief
by Timothy Zahn

❧ CIRCLE OF LIGHT 2 ❧

Faragon Fairingay

NIEL HANCOCK

STARSCAPE

A TOM DOHERTY ASSOCIATES BOOK
NEW YORK

FARAGON FAIRINGAY: CIRCLE OF LIGHT #2

Copyright © 1977, 2002 by Niel Hancock

Originally published by Warner Books in 1982.

Map by Ellisa Mitchell

A Starscape Book
Published by Tom Doherty Associates, LLC
175 Fifth Avenue
New York, NY 10010

www.starscapebooks.com

ISBN 0-765-34616-8
EAN 978-0765-34616-2

First Starscape edition: April 2004

Printed in the United States of America

0 9 8 7 6 5 4 3 2 1

For the prodigal's mother and his lady, Beth.

NTON
TH

FALLOW HILLS

BATTLE of
SEVEN HILLS

WORLUGH-HELD
HILL

FOURTH WAITE

CROWN of HAVAMAL
RUINS

ANCIENT COUNCIL
HILL

MELODIAS
STARSON'S
FORCES

GORGOLAC
ARMIES

HEL HAVAMAL

ASHGNAZI
WORLUGHS

RUINS of
CODA

of CYPHER

NORTH REALM GATE
of CYPHER

Alis Mitchell
2003

New Hope's Rise

Safe Haven

Ned Thinvoice awakened with a start. The room, fair
and high, and solid white, spun dizzily down until he
could hold his vision steady. A long, white bed stretched before him, and beyond, another bed, where lay a bandaged
form, still peacefully sleeping, and far from this waking dream
Ned had fallen into. He tried recounting to himself what had
happened, but the images blurred, and events crossed and re-
crossed his memory at such a startling rate he lost control and
lapsed into a vision-haunted half hour, filled with bear witches
and dwarfs, chased about a roaring battle fire by aging wizards
and countless misshapen Gorgolac and Worlugh warriors, all
carrying horrible weapons and shouting his name in their
hoarse, crude tongues.

"Ned, Ned Thinvoice."

Ned half bolted from his bed, his hand seeking his weapons.

"What is it?" he cried, again surrounded by galloping Urinine cavalry, singing their black death song.

"Easy, old fellow, easy. You're safe enough now," assured the calm, soft voice.

Thinvoice looked up into the kindly face of a gray-haired man who was dressed in a simple riding cloak. The dust of miles settled over his shoulders like a soft sand-brown mantle.

"Who is you, sir? And what lot has I fallen in with now?" asked Ned, fearing the worst.

"My name is Dr. Greenlawn, and you've fallen into the lot of the 47th Field Evacuation Station. Your friends brought you here almost six nights ago. We thought you were going to leave us for a while, but you're as tough as a boot, and mending fast. And young Cranfallow there is expected to have the happiness of doing us the same honor."

"Cranny? Where?"

"Across the aisle, there."

Ned looked anxiously over at his sleeping friend.

"He's not short nothing, is he, sir? I mean he's all together?"

"He's fine, Ned. We received instructions from a certain fellow that you were to be spared nothing to get you well again."

Ned frowned, trying to place his wandering memory of the six nights together.

"Where was it I was brought from, sir? I remember a fight, and being sore hurt, and overrun, but I can't reckon what's happened to six whole days."

"You were wounded at the Battle of Seven Hills. General Greymouse won a brilliant victory there the day you were wounded."

"Was there a dwarf witch there too, sir? A short sort of

fellow, dressed up sort of funny, and could call up demons out of his hat? He called himself Broco, Dwarflord, or some such?"

"If he was there, he wasn't wounded, Ned, so I don't know. Four tall, fair warriors from some battalion unknown to me brought you and the other fellow in and waited until we had said you'd be all right. Their helms were of some cavalry squadron, and they carried no firearms, but were outfitted with great shields with markings such as I've never seen before. One of my orderlies asked what parade dress was doing among a battle, but they laughed and said they served well in that gear, and were in the service of Faragon Fairingay, or a name close to that."

"Fairingay? The dwarf witch called out the name once in his sleep upon the road here. And I seems to remember something, the sky all golden and red and green, and that name, maybe, spelled out across the sky. Must have been my wound, I reckon."

"More than likely. At any rate, you shall be out of here soon, and fit as before."

Ned looked sheepishly down at his sheet-covered toes.

"Do you believe in dwarf witches, sir?"

"I don't think so, Ned. I'm a doctor, and as such, a man dedicated to science. Why do you ask?"

"I was just wondering, sir. I was scared half out of my wits while I was with him, or dreamed I was, but there was something else I liked about him. Something that made me feel as I was doing good. I never has been too much on learning, although I read and write a bit, but the things he knew, and told us. I was hoping maybe it was more than a gourd fancy."

The gray-haired figure of the doctor halted a moment at the door.

"It might have happened, Ned. I'm not one to say you were wrong. Perhaps it was so."

The door softly shut, and Ned lay back upon his pillow.

"I hope it were so, too," he said, and fell into a long, sea-green misty tunnel spiraling away into that bright darkness. He dreamed again, and there was the dwarf, spinning his hat about his hand, and smiling at him from a great, smooth white tower, shaped in the form of a huge flying swan.

Flewingam, from the other side of the wall, groaned, and a white swan unleashed powerful wings and the wind from that rushing pale dream eased the burning fever of his wounds, and he awakened with a cry.

A Nightmare Ends

"They've breached us," rang Flewingam's desperate warning. The constant stillness of the clean, bright room sounded like a din of a thousand small arms roaring. A white-coated orderly entered, and tried to calm the stricken Flewingam, who saw only the dark black tunics of a hundred Worlughs shrieking in their dark tongue, long fangs drooling behind the hard, cruel, leathery lips.

Flewingam leaped upon the orderly, trying to strangle the life from him, and only his weakened condition saved the man's life. Hearing the cries and the struggle, two more men entered and helped the gasping man hold Flewingam down until he at last quietened, and at length his eyes cleared, and the black Worlugh soldiers dimmed and passed.

"I'm sorry, friend, but you went out on us for a while." The orderlies released Flewingam, and stood about the bed, pity for the wounded man shining in their eyes.

"How long have I been bedded here?" asked Flewingam, struggling to regain control of his reeling senses.

"Six days and nights, taking today into count."

"What of the three who were with me? General Greymouse, and two others?"

"There was only yourself brought here, friend. But there are other hospital stations about. Maybe they were taken elsewhere, or perhaps they weren't wounded at all. I'm sure we would have heard if the general were hurt, and we've heard no news to that effect."

"That eases me, but I still know nothing more of my two friends."

"I've heard tell of an elfin host who saved the day at the darkest hour, and that they brought two wounded to us here. I saw the soldiers with my own eyes, fair and tall they were, with no weapons at all, but shields and swords, as long as a man's body, and I spoke to one. He told me he was in the service of Faracorn Farthingclay, or some such bloody rot. But they could have been, for all I know. They sure weren't of any battalion that I know."

Flewingam raised himself to an elbow.

"Could the name have been Froghorn Fairingay, friend?"

"That was the first one all right. Froghorn. I've never heard such a bloody fool name before."

"You'd be wiser to remember it, friend, and make no jest about it. His warriors carried the day when it was lost to us."

"I meant no harm, friend. I thought they was some fancy headquarters bunch, to look at them. If they're as brave and powerful as they looks, I'd be most glad to call them friend."

"They're the best allies you'll ever hope to find upon this world, friend, or in the next, to boot."

Flewingam stiffened with pain and lay back. "But what are

the names of the other two you have here, friend? Be quick,
for I'm heavy of heart at the loss of two such good comrades."

"I'll find out," offered the second orderly, eager to make
amends with the strange warrior upon the bed.

"My thanks, friend. I know you meant no harm." Flewingam smiled up at the blushing man.

The first orderly brought a tall pitcher filled with cool water
to Flewingam's bedside.

"Here, drink this, and I'll see if I can bring some staples
for your hunger."

"I could eat a horse," laughed Flewingam, discovering at
the mention of food the great hunger that had grown within
him since his awakening.

"Six days," he said aloud, musing, trying to remember what
had happened before he fainted from his wounds at General
Greymouse's side on the embattled hill.

The door opened, and the second orderly returned.

"Corporal Cranfallow and Ned Thinvoice are the two next
door. They were brought in the same time as you." Flewingam
turned the names over in his mind.

"I know of no one by the names you speak. You say the
fair warriors brought them here?"

"Yes sir, them what said they were in service of Fairin-
bloom or whatever."

"Then they must have been of the elfin host. I have heard
much of their general. I had begun to think perhaps I had
gone mad."

"I think the whole bloody world has gone off its hinges,"
replied the orderly bitterly. "But I've never seen the likes
before of those warriors. If I wasn't a man with a sharp head,

I'd think some other power than reason had blinded everyone. Fancy as parade, they were, but grim as a bloody hatchet."

"Could I speak with the two next door?" asked Flewingam, an uneasy shadow of doubt troubling his mind.

"I guess there wouldn't be no harm to that. Only one is awake, though."

Flewingam raised himself painfully, and wrapped the bedcover about him.

"I feel like a thousand horses kicked me all night," he said, his bruised face awkwardly smiling.

"Here, go easy, and take my shoulder. But I can't let you stay long. Regulations."

"I won't need long for my errand," said Flewingam, and he placed a hand upon the man's shoulder, and passed through into the long, dim hallway into Cranfallow's room.

New Comrades

"You've got a visitor here, one that was brought in by those that brought you," said the orderly, pulling a chair near the bed where Ned Thinvoice lay.

"Now you two can have a few minutes to yourselves. I've rounds to make, then I'm putting you back to bed where you belong."

"And don't forget the supper you promised," Flewingam reminded the man, then turned his attention to the pale, huddled form on the bed.

"Flewingam, friend, lately of the battalion of Greymouse, wounded at Seven Hills six nights past."

The figure on the bed shuddered once, his eyes clouded with a shining film that seemed to reflect a long-extinguished battle fire.

"Ned Thinvoice, friend," he croaked, holding out a feeble hand.

"I hear you were wounded in the Battle of Seven Hills, Ned."

"Aye, we was. Cranny and me was fool enough to get ourselves run afoul of a bunch of Urinines. Plumb near kilt us
both, they did."

"I think I saw part of that skirmish from our hill, friend. It
was close upon you."

"If it hadn't been for the dwarf, I doubts if we would have
won the lines. He spun his hat like he was always about, and
the next thing I knows is I'm hanging onto my horse, and
there was shooting all around us. Then we was under a
wagon, and they was singing that bloody awful song they
sings, but that's all I can remembers, till now."

"Was his name Broco, friend? The dwarf?"

Flewingam's features had cleared, and the doubt he had
hidden within himself slowly vanished.

Thinvoice looked sharply at Flewingam.

"Who has told you a thing like that?"

"Just guessing, old fellow. I thought when they told me
you two were brought here by Froghorn's elves that you
might be the two comrades I lost at Seven Hills. They often
spoke of their dwarf in passing, and I was surprised to hear
you mention that you also rode with a dwarf. They aren't so
common as traveling companions in these times."

"Was you with those that call themselves Otter and Bear?"

Flewingam laughed, then cut it short as the pain trickled
down his sore body.

"The same. They spun me such yarns as I never heard, and
I wouldn't have believed a word if I hadn't seen them work
their spells with my own two eyes."

"Then they is the same ones, friend. Long ago, no, not so
long, I gets confused in my head, they was passing through

a town we were guarding. A smaller bloke with a big mustache that put us all to sleep with a pipe tune, and a bloody big fellow that turned out to be a bear witch. Then we was tangled up with the dwarf witch. And nones the better for any of it."

Ned lowered his head, and whispered so low Flewingam could barely make it out.

"Lord help us, but I felt kind of good inside when I was with the little bloke. I know he has them powers, and that men isn't supposed to be mixed with them as does, but there was something down deep inside me that knew it was all right, like."

"I don't think you've run to bad company, Ned. Worse for you if you had, with General Greymouse and Fairingay for enemies."

Flewingam felt a deep inner sense of relief, which quickly passed.

"But what of the dwarf? Was he hurt, or worse?"

"I doesn't know," said Ned sadly. "The last I seen of him, he was all bloody and then them scums of Urinines was all over us. I don't remembers nothing else till I waked up here." Ned's rough hands gripped his blanket, and he turned his head aside into the pillow. "I was hoping the dwarf witch was real, and that he got out without hurt, but I doesn't knows."

Flewingam reached out and patted Ned's thin shoulders.

"I'm sure he got out safely, Ned. I don't know what happened to Bear or Otter either, but I'm sure they are all safe somewhere. And look at how we got here. Elves, Ned. It couldn't have been any other way. I'm sure they were of

Fairingay's hosts. And I'm sure our friends were taken care of by them, too."

Ned turned a hopeful face to Flewingam.

"You thinks they is all right somewheres with the elves?" he asked, then frowned, thinking hard. "Well, it would seems so, him being with them powers and all, with that hat of his, and having powerful friends. I guess they wouldn't brings them to someplace like where they broughts us."

"I'm sure that's so, Ned. And I know we'll find them again."

Ned grew silent a moment.

"I don't knows if I rightly wants to, friend. I ain't so bad a soldier, as soldiers go, but when I starts getting caught up with the likes of witches and dwarfs and such, I'd just as soons keep to my own." He fell silent, kneading the blanket in his hand back and forth. "But I guess I'd likes to see the little fellow again. He was brimful of good tales at table. Kind of scary, too, if you takes my meaning."

"I know, friend," laughed Flewingam. "I had my share of surprises, too."

"You really thinks they is all right and all? I mean about being wherever them elves is?"

"I'm sure of it. There was more to our friends than perhaps meets the eye, Ned. Anyone whose friends include wizards and such are no ordinary fellows."

"They wasn't ordinary, for sure. Why, I about dropped my teeth whenever he'd start spinning his hat and calling out all sorts of funny-sounding words and such. And right out of thin air would come a bunch of marching dwarfs, with terrible red eyes that would like to drill holes plumb near through your soul."

A soft knock interrupted the friends, and the tall orderly peered around the door.

"Your food is ready, and I think you've talked enough for now."

"Just a little longer, friend, then I'll be along."

The orderly nodded.

"Two more minutes, then."

Flewingam turned to Ned as the door edged shut.

"What is your plan after you're mended, friend?"

"I hadn't thought nothing abouts that. And I doesn't rightly know how bad old Cranny is. We always goes together. Always has."

"Then when we get out, what do you and Cranny plan to do?"

"Why, the only thing we knows, friend. We has been soldiering for so long, that's all we knows how to do. We'll finds us an outfit what needs men, I guess."

"Then let's all three find General Greymouse, Ned. You, Cranny, and myself. We'll most likely find our friends there, too. Or at least discover their whereabouts."

Ned's drawn, pale face furrowed in thought, and the shadows of years lined his eyes with a heaviness that was more than age. "I can't says what Cranny will wants," he said, "but if he fancies going out to hunt for General Greymouse, then I guess that's what we'll does."

"Don't no one ever ask old Cranfallow what it is he's wanting?" Cranfallow's voice cracked, and he made a feeble attempt to sit up in bed.

"Cranny," bellowed Ned, "you possum, you old rum sot. You isn't dead on me. How long has you been awake there?"

"Long enough to hear you two goes on so long my head's full."

"This here's my friend, Cranny, name of Flewingam."

"I still has my ears, Ned."

"And they is still big enough to box, if I was able to get up."

Cranfallow laughed weakly.

"Well, here we is, Ned, squabbling like always. Fetch me the water jug, will you?"

Flewingam broke up the friends' reunion.

"Then we'll do it, the three of us. Agreed?"

"I feels like Ned, friend. I somehow doesn't know if it's right to be going about with those with them kind of powers. But I always felt sort of good, too, if you gets what I mean."

"Cranny, I has already told him we stays together. And he wants to find the general again. What does you say?"

"I says yes, I does. I can't think of being with no one else."

"Good," said Flewingam, rising unsteadily to his feet.

"Then we shall hurry our mending, and be on our way."

"We'll mend as it happens, friend, but there's time enough for our plans and such. Right now I is going to sleep another two days, I thinks."

The tall orderly returned, putting an arm around Flewingam to steady him. "Here we go, old fellow, just lean on me."

Flewingam turned to the two friends. "Our plans are laid, then. You have my hand on it."

He raised a faint farewell arm, and was gone.

In his room alone, he began to outline to himself what they

must do in order to find General Greymouse once more. But first, they must heal and rest, for the road would be long and hard, ending in a shadowy land he only dreamed without dreams. Yet in his secret heart, he was sure he would find his old comrades once more, for somewhere, somehow, he felt he had another part to play, as in his dreams of the shadow lands.

Vaguely, he could see the outlines, like figures before a great fire, gray against the darker lines of darkness, and there seemed to be yet another battle.

His mind wearied at last, and he ate and slept, all the while remembering Ned and Cranfallow in the next room, and their promise.

An Awakening in Cypher

Otter's mind reeled with blurry visions of stars flashing past his whiskers so fast he heard the wind rushing close in his ears, leaving them ringing and numb, and at times he thought he could make out the hazy features of an old man, cloaked in gray, leaning near him.

A brilliant red-orange flame seared his sight, and he screamed aloud, struggling, but his limbs would not respond, and the form of Bear toppled beside him, so still he knew he must be dead.

"General Greymouse," croaked Otter, brandishing what he thought to be his firearm, but it turned into a golden snake that smiled secrets into his fevered brain.

The stars slowed, then stopped, and Otter felt a cool hand upon his brow.

"I fear he is gravely hurt, my lady. I risked the ire of the Circle in bringing them here, but I felt only your hands could heal them."

"You have done rightly, Cairngarme. They will best rest with me in Cypher for a time."

Otter's eyes cleared of the hazy veil that had cloaked them, and he peered uncertainly about his surroundings.

A tall, fair lady, robed in pale silver gray, stood by his bed, her fine features clouded with concern. At her side stood General Greymouse, now Mithramuse Cairngarme, in his stained and torn battle garb.

Otter tried to speak, but his throat was so dry he merely chuckled once, and a pain tore through his jaw, so hot and terrible he thought he would faint again.

Froghorn knelt by his side.

"Here, old fellow, take this now. Up you go, there."

He helped Otter hold his head up long enough to sip at a flower-smelling wine in a small goblet.

His pain receded, then dimmed, and a feeling of weariness swept over him, carrying him away down long avenues of riverbanks and mudslides, in bright golden waters he could touch and feel, and there far below was a shining green eye that peered up from the depths like a sun he had seen often before, when he looked up at the sky from below his deep weir in his old valley.

"He'll sleep now, I think," came the lilting, soothing voice of the lady.

"We must look to Bear and Dwarf," drifted General Greymouse's voice. "They have suffered graver wounds, I think."

Otter felt a hand touch his paw before he went completely into his golden world, and he heard the murmured thanks from the great general.

"Do you think they are beyond help, my lady?"

Froghorn's voice was strained as he studied the gaunt features of Bear and Dwarf. "Dwarf looks so cold."

"He is in the most danger, for he has another wound more deadly than a rifle shot or bomb burst."

"You mean his capture by the Dark Queen?"

"Shush, Faragon, out with you. I'll need to be left alone if I am to help."

"And Bear?" pressed the young wizard.

"Run along with you both. I'll tend their hurts as best I can, but I don't need you gaping about like a gang of magpies."

Greymouse and Fairingay closed the door gently behind them. The older man put a hand upon his young friend's shoulder.

"If anyone can help, it is Lorini, old fellow. Cheer up. We've brought them to the only help in Windameir that might save them."

Froghorn strode angrily to the long table that stood in the hallway of the twilight wing of Cypher.

"It's certainly no thanks they owe us, my friend. I managed to let Dwarf be taken right from under my nose, and even coming with the elfin host, I timed myself tardy once more."

"That's hardly so, and you know it. You can't blame yourself for this foul blow."

"I certainly can't pat my back over it, either."

The older man walked slowly to the sunbright window that overlooked a garden blooming in a rainbow shower of water from a tall white fountain.

"You know, when I was younger, and a lot wiser, at least

by my own way of thinking then, I ranted about being able to do so little in the struggle against the Darkness. Felt myself held in check by old men who doddered in their wine and thought a game of whist was high enough excitement. And my friend thought so, too. That was your father, Fairenaus. We were very young, and so eager. We struggled then against the dragon hordes of the Dark Queen, not here, but upon Maldan and Origin, and we almost lost. Those worlds are gone now, forever. Cold and lifeless they circle the heavens as epitaphs for headstrong young men who thought they could move time and replace evil with good at a moment's whim."

Froghorn ceased his nervous arranging of books upon the table. "You mean, sir, you and my father were on Maldan and Origin?"

"That's exactly what I was saying, Faragon. Your father and I suffered a great, perhaps our greatest defeat there. Melodias and Cephus Starkeeper had put us in charge of the defenses of those two worlds, for the rest of the Circle were away on other, more urgent matters at the time."

"What could be more urgent than the dark sister of Lorini?" shot the young wizard, closing a heavy volume with a loud thump.

"Nothing, yet there are various degrees to which a thing may go. Maldan and Origin were already lost before we took up the fray, yet we did not know that then. Her Dark Highness had so undermined those worlds they were lost from the start. The Circle was away preparing the other worlds against just what had happened there, under our very noses. We merely fought a losing battle to give them time, Faragon, important time."

Froghorn paced uneasily to the window.

"Did you know that you were going to lose, then?"

"No. Your father and I did exactly as we were instructed, with every hope of winning through. It did not enter our minds that perhaps sometimes you must lose something to gain something more precious in its stead. And we asked the same questions of Melodias that you have asked me. We thought we had somehow failed to such an extent that we were forever doomed, had lost the Light, and betrayed the Circle." The old man smiled. "That was when your father and I were very young."

Lorini came out of Bear's sickroom and walked quickly to the old wizard.

"He's asking for you, Cairngarme. And you, my young pup. I can't get him to sleep until he knows you're safe and beyond harm."

"And our good Dwarf, my lady?" Mithramuse inquired, taking Lorini's hand in his own.

"His physical wounds shall heal. I only worry now about the ones we cannot see."

"But there is hope, isn't there?" came Froghorn's low reply.

Lorini smiled at the young man. "Hope? The light of the world, Master Fairingay. As long as we hold the Arkenchest against the tide, there is, shall always be, hope."

A drowsy growl-rumble came from Bear's room, turning to a low-pitched whine.

"You must go in to see him now. He's almost as hard-headed as someone else of my acquaintance."

Lorini turned and led the two into the dimness where Bear lay.

"By the crown of Bruinthor," said Bear, in a muffled, subdued voice when he saw his friends standing by his bed. "Well, I never," he began, then drifted away into the sleep he had struggled against for so long.

Froghorn placed a hand on his stout friend's paw.

"Rest well, old comrade. You have served faithfully and true."

"It's rather like the old times," mused Mithramuse, "to have animal kings at our side, and dwarflords bearing arms for the light."

"It must be drawing nearer, my faithful old Cairngarme. To be as it once was, the Circle completed, the line unbroken."

Lorini withdrew from the room as she spoke.

"Indeed, my lady, it draws closer still. Our hours come inevitably to their beginnings."

The three walked together from the soft blue night of the twilight wing of Cypher, down white-gold hallways with their tapestries of spun gauze winds, past the great hall, and on to Lorini's sitting room, where the afternoon sunlight made golden circles on the floor, and Cybelle waited at the high arched window, smiling at Froghorn as he strode into the room.

"Have we houseguests now, Mother, or do they still lie abed?"

"We have three very tired, hurt servants of the Light, my dear, who need all the powers of healing I may find to give them."

"Oh, then are they badly off?"

"Bad enough, pet. Now see if you can find me Urien Typhon. I must see him at once."

Froghorn touched her hand briefly at the door, then she was gone.

"Are you off, Cairngarme?" asked Lorini, seating herself at the small desk near the window.

"I am, my lady. I must return at once."

"Then good speed, and stout heart, my dear old friend. I know you are needed, and will detain you no longer."

Mithramuse Cairngarme made a motion upon the wind, turned suddenly into the image of General Greymouse, and faded slowly, until at last with a brief blaze of startling white light, he was gone.

"And now, young master, I find an errand for you. Urien Typhon is the last High Elfin King in Cypher, and I shall dispatch him and his lady to the Last Home beyond Calix Stay. There he will muster what strength he can. And you are to follow soon after, to bring that strength to our defenses as needed."

As Lorini spoke, a tall, golden-haired elf appeared at her study door. His deep blue-gray eyes twinkled, and an agelessness hung lightly over his fair head like a crown, yet he looked saddened by some ancient grief.

"Here, Urien, is the seal of the High Council. Gather to you who you may. I'm afraid some of your kindred won't answer the summons after what happened in the last days of the dragons, but do what you can."

"They will come, my lady. It seems there is no choice this time."

"Still, they need not become part of it. It was granted to them that they might leave if they chose, to seek Calix Stay."

"My lady, those days you speak of are long gone over. My

father told me once of the strife that came to be between Melodias Starson and Eiorn of Woodsend, but he and most of his court have long ago passed on to the Meadows of Windameir. Not many are left that still hold that grudge valid."

"Is that Eiorn who would not give up the One he held of the Five?" asked Froghorn, moving closer to the elf.

"The same, my lord," answered the elf.

"It was an old feud, Fairingay, one that began before my sister held half of Atlanton Earth. The Circle had separated the Five Secrets of the Arkenchest, giving each High Elder one to hold, to make sure none of them were captured in those dark times. Eiorn, good sort that he was, was convinced that they called back the Secrets prematurely, and he wished to hold his safe in Woodsend. Melodias, of course, would not hear of it. After all, the Circle was quite sure my sister would cease her attacks after her conquest of Origin and Maldan. Eiorn took his Secret with him, and none know where it lies, whether still with Eiorn in the Meadows of Windameir, or elsewhere. It is said to have fallen to the hands of Tyron the Green, who yet remains across Calix Stay."

"Why has Greyfax never bothered to mention this little tidbit?" snapped Froghorn. "I thought only the Circle held the Five."

"Greyfax never mentioned it because it has not become a matter of importance until recently, my patience. Now you know the other part of your errand across the River." Lorini looked sternly at the young wizard.

"I thought it a lot of kite talk, my going simply to lead Urien back. Now we reach the heart of the pie, and I detect it is not so sweet as it looked."

Urien Typhon sat in one of the high-backed chairs before
Lorini. "You see, old fellow, I have had recent intelligence to
the effect that Tyron the Green is moving his host across
Gilden Far. Not three hours hence, an archer from Tyron's
party arrived here, with news that is not very encouraging."

"What he is saying, Fairingay, is that we fear Tyron may
have had ideas of his own about how we are waging our war
against my sister. He is massing an army across the River,
preparing to strike out on his own."

Froghorn slapped his riding quirt hard against his boot top.
His face had gone the color of old ashes.

"The fool, the bloody fool. And what if he does indeed
carry one of the Five?"

"It is Urien's belief that he carries Eiron's burden."

"Then plans must be laid. We must reach the fool before
he misfires." Froghorn paced angrily about the quiet study,
his hands tightly locked behind his back. "The miserable fool,
the bloody, miserable fool. Doesn't he realize he may endan-
ger the Circle if he's taken and the One lost?"

Urien had risen, and stood facing Froghorn as he spoke.
"I'm afraid he doesn't hold much faith with the Circle, my
lord. He is one of the very few I mentioned before who still
hold ill faith with Melodias. Eiorn coached his sons well in
diplomacy with Mankind. Stay away. And that included the
Masters of the Council. And Tyron, like Eiorn, is a brilliant
mind, as shrewd in those dealings as any. But Eiorn's single
fault lay in his pride. He was for destroying Dorini when the
Circle had captured her, knowing even so that if she were
utterly destroyed, then Lorini would perish too. He argued at
the meeting halls, and right up to Cephus Starkeeper himself,

and would have argued with Erophin, had it been allowed. Once, for all, he said, and have done with it."

Froghorn stopped his pacing, looking drawn and frail.

"You mean he would have destroyed both the Darkness and the Light as well?"

"Eiorn was a strange being, Fairingay," interrupted Lorini, "one who served faithfully and well during the troubles before. His high standards did not include a single compromise. If he himself would have had to be destroyed, then he would not have flinched a degree from his decision. You must understand that he was of those who had been from the First Beginning, and who had seen the harmony of those years."

"Elves," snorted the young wizard, "forever clever, forever taken with their own power. Always elusive, but count on them being elusive, and they're in your hair like spring molasses."

"Like certain among the Circle, I might add," shot the fair elf, "who meddle where they had better left alone."

The young wizard whirled, his cloak flashing about him. "Better meddling somewhere than sitting about Cypher drinking mint tea with the ladies, or singing sad old songs about your sires who had sense enough to get out."

Urien flushed, his fists clenched, but Lorini broke the angry silence first.

"You see, my young friends, how well you carry on your sitting room conversation. You've each managed to insult the other, which is exactly what my dark sister would delight in. Fighting among ourselves."

Cybelle entered the room, glancing from one face to an-

other. "I heard voices, Mother. I thought perhaps we had another guest."

"What you heard were two young hotheads busily engaged
in trying to see who could be the biggest ass."

"Mother," cried Cybelle, shocked to see her usually calm
mother so flushed and angry.

"It was not my idea to accuse anyone of deeds done or
undone," offered Froghorn, uneasy with the new Lorini, and
he dared go no further.

"Nor mine," replied Urien, unable to meet the stern glance
of the lady.

"Now, gentlemen, if I may stretch the meaning of the word
that far, shall we get back to business?"

Lorini sat once more at her pearl-gray desk.

"Cybelle, please bring us something to cool our tempers.
We all have need of it."

"Yes, Mother," she said, bowing and leaving reluctantly.

Lorini turned to the elf. "Urien, I want you to find Tyron,
and deter him from his plan of crossing Calix Stay without
my order, or order of the Circle. We shall have need enough
of him somewhere that it will be useful. There are armies
enough carrying on their little independent wars, but they
merely feed the dark forces weapons and stores. If we are to
defeat my sister, we have great need of strength and courage,
and more than a little luck. And it would be a grave injury
to our chances if she were to capture even One of the Five.
That is your mission, Urien. Simple, and to the point. You
must hold Tyron the Green in check across Calix Stay."

The fair elf bowed low.

"My lady."

"And you, my fresh-tongued young magician, you are to travel after Urien, and treat with Tyron, and deliver him the Circle's battle plans. If he must join the fighting, then at least let him join it where he is most needed."

"And what of that he holds, my lady?"

"You will say nothing of it, Master Fairingay. Is that clear? Mention it, and he will be convinced we are merely trying to trick him out of what he feels he rightfully holds. If he moves, you are to move with him. If he crosses Calix Stay against my order, then you are to stay with him, no matter what."

Froghorn nodded, then bowed.

"I shall hasten my departure, my lady," said Urien softly, "for I fear even now I may tarry too long."

"You know I'm hotheaded, Urien. Let it not be cause for me to mourn the loss of a dear friend," said Froghorn gently.

Urien Typhon studied the contrite young wizard a moment before answering.

"What's a dagger between brothers, my lord, if not to be used to sharpen their senses?"

He held out a firm hand to Froghorn, who clasped it tightly.

"I have a feeling we shall need our two senses together in dealing with your kindred across the River, my friend."

"Ha, well said, my fire-tongued fellow," said Urien, clapping Froghorn heartily on the back. "For as you say, we're clever, shrewd folk, we elves, and as elusive as a smell of heather on a spring day."

He bowed once more to Lorini.

"I shall do my best, my lady. Adieu."

"Good speed, fair Urien, and to your lady. May the Light ever brighten."

Urien Typhon passed through the tall doorway, waved once, then moved deftly along the corridors until Froghorn could no longer see him.

"And now, my good Fairingay, that we have patched the rift once more between elf and Circle, we shall study our histories a bit, and then you shall have your time with Cybelle."

"But my lady," complained Froghorn.

"And then we shall look in on our patients."

The young wizard started to protest again, saw it was useless, sighed, and sat down next to Lorini as she spread out a thick volume before her. She turned swiftly to the pages Greyfax had marked for her on his last visit.

"A schoolboy," he mumbled half aloud, "at my lessons once more."

Then his eyes came to rest on the first page of the book, and his anger left him, for there was the Sacred Sign of Windameir, its broad seal embossed on the stiff, glowing parchment, and beyond that was the Eye of Cephus Starkeeper, looking out into all the worlds as they were born, or passed.

Lorini studied the young man at her side, read his amazement, and said, "Yes, dear Faragon, you have come to this at last. Greyfax gave me strict instructions as to when this step should be taken. And I think now is the time."

He looked up at her with eyes full of wonder and awe, and then silently returned to the Sacred Book.

Lorini quietly left him, stopping Cybelle in the hall as she returned from her errand.

"Here, leave that, dear. Your young master has found something else of greater interest than my wine."

* * *

As Lorini left and her voice faded, there came a low, steady call of a faint and faraway conch being blown, and the faintest echo of an answer. Froghorn Fairingay disappeared into the golden pages of the book spread before him. Cypher and all its beauty faded, with the sparkling towers of the swan and turtle and dove and all the others falling away below him as he soared upward on that Sound, conch and bell, and as he rose higher, lute and flute, and sweeter sound than any, the pipe, so beautifully smooth and rough at once it threatened to destroy his senses.

As he spun away into the lessons Greyfax had left him (for lessons these were, ones he must study to make any further progress on the Path he had been given when he was taken into the Circle) he saw visions of all that had gone before.

Years unfolded upon themselves as the Music went on, and Froghorn saw the beginnings of the lower worlds, and the creation of the two sisters, Lorini and Dorini, and the Masters who reigned over each of the lower worlds. Origen and Maldan, two of the worlds which were taken by the Dark Queen, had been wrested from the hands of their lords, who had gone against the Law of Windameir, and now that Law was righting itself, in the struggle of the Circle against the Queen of Darkness, who had gone against her lord and was determined to put herself on equal footing with the Lord of All.

There came scenes in the long and weary years of the Wars of the Dragon, when Lorini's husband and Cybelle's father had given himself to the Fields of Light, and in doing so had taken the most dreaded and fearful dragon lord into those realms where all was returned to the All.

That had occurred in the first beginnings of Atlanton Earth, which was three lifetimes ago for Froghorn, who was young in the Circle, although like all other living things, he had been from the very Creation. The difference now was that he was ready for his journey back.

Flashing and sputtering, there came scenes from the Great River, Calix Stay, and there stood he and Greyfax, beside Pe'lon and An'yim, their swift steeds, talking to Bear and Otter and Dwarf on the very day when those three had crossed. He watched the visions whirl and dance, and saw the fall of the last dwarf hall in Atlanton, and the friends long years in their peaceful valley. Then there came Cakgor, who stole Dwarf away and laid ruin to the countryside. Bear and Otter began their journey to find Greymouse, as he had told them, and at last Dwarf had escaped Dorini with the innocent singing of one of the Secrets, which had freed him from her power.

Then there was Bear and Otter beside Greymouse at Seven Hills, and Dwarf, beset with Urinine cavalry, and himself, leading the Elfin host to carry the day.

Amid crashing blue and green and red-flashing stars, the trip was made that brought Bear, Otter, and Dwarf to Cypher, where the lady Lorini now worked her magic in the healing of the three friends.

And from there, Froghorn flashed onward and upward, catching glimpses of a confrontation with Tyron the Green, and the wounding of Greyfax, and a dim, icy vision of something that appeared to be Cybelle, covered with frozen sleet and snow.

Before he could go farther, a flashing silver light caught

his eye, and he found himself in the presence of Greyfax, his own teacher, and together they went on, farther upward, toward the farthest reaches of the plains of Windameir.

In another part of Windameir, in Cypher's starlit twilight wing, a tiny gray form wobbled into the shining corridor and collapsed, chittering weakly.

"It's Otter," cried Lorini, rushing to the small animal's side. She picked up his gray head and smoothed the fever wrinkles from his brow.

Cybelle sat quickly beside her mother, and took the little animal in her arms.

Otter opened one brown eye and peered carefully at his captor.

"Is this the place we go?" he asked, his other eye opening upon the splendor of Cypher.

"No, this is where you are now, little friend. This is where heroes of the Circle are brought," said Lorini.

Otter, in a great deal of pain, but suffering more curiosity than hurt, struggled up, saw Cybelle, and fell helplessly in love.

His whiskers curled, and he shyly burrowed back into the comfort of the warm arms.

"Come. Your friends are sleeping, and that's where you would be, too."

Cybelle took the small animal and carefully put him back into the huge bed.

Otter immediately crawled to a snug place in the center, where only a small lump marked where he lay.

"Thank you," he said politely, remembering his manners,

then curled upon himself to dream of the fair lady he had seen, who had stolen his heart away.

"So this is where wizards go," he said drowsily, smiling and feeling somehow proud that he had at least unraveled one of the great secrets.

Bear, burning with a raging fever, awakened in a fright, which quickly went away, to be replaced by a waking dream of thick clover honey from an old tree, where the bees were as thick and round as sparrows, and he lay snugly burrowed in his warm winter bed, sighed, smiled to himself, turned over and went back to sleep, knowing he had yet a few more months of winter left to nap.

Broco writhed in a slumber nearer to death, only the warmth of the lady Lorini keeping his small heart from that winter of eternal darkness, and so she sat, her life given to the tormented dwarf through the hand she placed on his forehead. He tossed and turned in mad efforts to escape his deadly pursuer, the Dark Queen, and the two sisters struggled savagely for control of the dwarf's soul, but at length Lorini, in her warm halls of Cypher, threw down her dark sister, and that icy darkness was banished from the little man's heart, leaving only the faintest memory of a frozen splinter lodged where even the great love of Lorini could not remove it.

She felt the cold fingers that clutched her hand grow suddenly warm, and the terror that was frozen upon his face slowly lifted. A veil in the room's soft light seemed to open, and she knew she had pulled Broco back from that final darkness.

Broco opened his eyes, and seeing Lorini, clasped her hand to his heart and wept.

A Reunion

A soothing, golden stillness hushed the room where Broco lay, his still, pale features worried into the beginning of terror.

"Aieeeee," wailed Dwarf, eyes wide at once with despair and hopelessness. "The Darkness is upon us." And struggling to his unsteady legs, he held the tall white carven bedpost, his hands freezing, remembering another touch, and with the other arm he reached out to strike a feeble blow with the mithra-worked image of Atlanton Earth, a fine, thin base with the globe held in place by no more than sunlight over silver.

"The Circle," cried Dwarf, falling again into a fear-making dream of the frozen halls, and the harsh, cancerous laughter of Dorini covered his soul with doom.

Outside, in the high, sun-bright rooms of the wing of the swan, quick footsteps approached Broco's healing room.

"It sounds as if he's awake, Bear. I'd know that voice anywhere."

"I think the silly ass must have fallen out of bed, the way he's carrying on."

"We mustn't stay long. Our lady said his wounds were worsened by the memory of his stay in that place. Even her wonderful magic had a time healing him, what with all the things that were done to him."

"Brrr. From what the elves told me, I chatter everytime I think of our dear Dwarf frozen like that. But he's in wonderful hands now. The lady is so beautiful and kind."

"Shhh," hushed Otter, paused at the door listening.

"On Cranny, ride on. We must make the lines," shrieked Broco, struggling about on the floor with unseen adversaries.

Bear, hearing Dwarf's desperate cry, bolted into the room, fangs and claws unsheathed. Otter tumbled in behind, ready to nip any who dared enter the sacred halls of Cypher.

Dwarf stared up at Bear from beneath the wide, enchanted bed. Their eyes met and held, and slowly the grim mist clouds that covered Broco's sight cleared, and after a few moments, Dwarf assumed a small half huff, and muttered, "Well, by the beard of Co'in, it's about time."

Storm Tide

As Broco awakened in Cypher, Greyfax Grimwald looked gravely across the low ridge of hills that bordered Amarigin, the northern region of Lorini's realms upon Atlanton Earth. Melodias Starson and his armies had journeyed forth two days before to cut the escape routes of the hordes of Gorgolacs that were now in retreat from the advancing elfin hosts, but the Northerland hung heavy with the tall black pillars of battle fires, and across that land the flames of war devoured the sky, and the invaders hung grimly on. Victory for either the mighty forces of the White Light or the cruel, powerful hordes of Dorini was still upon the balance, and Greyfax was worried, for he had had no word from Melodias for a day. Away in the direction of the Starson's march, the clouds hung low and dark blood-gray, and a distant rumble disturbed the late afternoon air, as if some great tide were breaking upon a storm-beaten shore.

Greyfax sat down heavily upon the high rock that served as a command post, and tried to reach Melodias through thought. Only rising thick columns of dark smoke filled his eyes, and the mind of Melodias was elsewhere, directing a desperate struggle for survival against a fresh wave of Worlugh attackers who had come upon the battle in the night, and who brought with them Fireslayer, the oozing black many-headed wife of the dreadful Suneater. This new addition to the swelling ranks of the dark forces fell upon the warriors of Melodias in a vicious day-long, savage attack that had driven the defenders into a tight circle upon the top of two hills called Hel and Havamal, a crossroads at the very realm's edge of Lorini, and an important crossing point for those with powers to go or return from Cypher.

Of Elves

Lorini, at the moment, sat in deep talk with Broco, who for the first time sat at the long banquet table, in the place of honor. Bear, in his own form, and Otter, tiny gray ears barely clearing the edge of the table, sat upon either side of Dwarf, who was blushingly accepting a compliment from the lady.

"We are most fortunate and honored, Sir Broco, to have among us a dwarflord of old, such as used to bless our table before the Fifth Age. Long have our halls suffered the absence of dwarf wit and wisdom."

"Thank you, my lady. I fear all I bring our troubled times is confusion, and I daresay the likes of those dwarflords of old are, alas, long gone over. But I am most deeply honored and grateful, my lady, to sit at table with the fairest of all that yet dwell in any sphere, and whatever service I have done, or may do, is pledged to the lady Lorini."

A mutter of approval from the many elves and others guests at table greeted Dwarf's speech.

"The dwarf speaks well for himself, my lord," whispered Cybelle to Froghorn, "and he knows such interesting tales," she continued, smiling across at Broco, who went crimson to his toes and coughed suddenly into his cuff.

"Tell me, Sir Dwarf," said a tall, golden-crowned elf, "did you know of elves across the Swift River?"

"None there were so fair, nor I so lucky, my lord. But the Beginen Mountains where I dwelt were deep and fast, and I ventured not out while I stayed there."

"The only sensible thing, I might add, our dear Dwarf has done," growled Bear good-humoredly. "But living in a cave certainly gave him appetite for travel."

"Well spoken, Bear," huffed Dwarf, "although I'd go so far as to say earth dwelling has done nothing for your table manners."

Bear hastily put down the bowl of honey he had put to his mouth to drain.

"Harrumph," and grumbling he cast a quick look about to see if any there had noticed him.

"Bears are supposed to eat that way," chirped Otter, "and I think the journey must have swelled your head another length or two from your talk."

"Hold your tongue, you undersized water dog, or I'll pull your whiskers."

"You've not finished, Sir Dwarf. I take it then you know nothing of my kindred who have sought haven beyond the River?"

"The Endin River spoke once of a passing of fairfolk, and sang a few of the songs he had heard away at the end of his roots, but of them I saw nor heard no more than what he sang."

Dwarf stood politely, and began to hum, then fell into a half-remembered song he had heard the river sing him so long ago.

"Across the wide river
        now we are bound
            our home has long been awaiting.
Our ships have all gone
        the golden world by
            and the dark stars above us are waving.
In fields full of light
        we fly now tonight
            to the last long day
                of Endin.
            His back does us bear
                to carry us there
                to our homelands now
                    so long awaiting."

Dwarf bowed, and sat down.

To his surprise, the elflord had joined him in the last stanza, and now smiled sadly, his fair features pale and old.

"There are other verses you might have sung that would not have stung me so," he said at last.

"My pardon, my lord, I did not wish to sadden you," spoke Dwarf, upset and cross with himself for having sung the song.

"Nay, Sir Dwarf, you have given me much pleasure, and news of the certainty that my kindred did in truth reach their destination. My sorrow comes only from absence, I fear, although I am gladdened of heart to have heard the song."

Bear shuffled up from his chair, cleared his throat loudly, and bursting with eagerness, announced that he, too, had news of the elfin folk.

"Ahem, if I may speak, I heard something or other upon my long travels down toward the Meadows of the Sun that might lead me to believe I may have news of your folk, too, sir. I passed through a wood that glowed like a sun ray, and there was music coming from the very ground as I walked. It was a tune I had never chanced across before, so I stopped to listen to see if I could learn it, but the more I listened, the sleepier I grew, and when I had awakened, the glowing and singing were both gone, and I never knew till I reached here about elfin singing, and all, but it's like the same sort of music I've heard so often in these lovely halls."

The tall, fair elf across from Cybelle addressed himself to Otter. "It seems both your friends have chanced upon acquaintance with our kindred, Otter, but of yourself you have spoken nothing. Have you, too, met with news of an elfin nature?"

Otter blushed, twisting the smooth silver spoon about in his small lap. His eyes were barely visible over the soft white expanse of table where they sat, and his voice trembled as he blurted out, "None but those fairest who share this table, although my mother taught me songs she had heard from them of their travels, long before the River was as closely shielded as it is in these times. There are some among you who are waterfolk, too, I think, and mighty boatmen with ships as light as air, or so I've heard."

"Friends of old have long been Olther and his merry ways," laughed the elf, "and I, too, have learned a tune or two from the river dwellers when I was not quite so ancient as I am now."

"Instead of speaking of these songs, let us hear them from Cybelle's harp," said the lady Lorini, rising to lead her dinner guests to the long, high room where there were about a hundred pale blue cushions that relieved the weary traveler his journeys, or the heavy heart its sorrows. After all were seated, Cybelle raised her dazzling smoke-colored instrument and began to play.

Pen and Ink

I n the starlit twilight wing of Cypher, Faragon Fairingay paced uneasily about in his sleeping chamber. A high, canopied bed stood at one wall, which was covered with glyphs and charts of Atlanton Earth at its birth, and near the center of the dark floor, a deep night shade of rare blue which reflected the twinkling eyes of the stars, stood an ivory-colored desk. Its legs were carved in replica of a rowan tree whose topmost branches supported the heavy figure of a great seashell, which formed the writing surface and provided shelves and drawers where the user could keep a large number of papers or other items.

An inkstand stood open, and a pen with the bright silver likeness of a feather was left unused upon the thick stack of parchment. It was to this desk the young wizard paced at intervals, after having stood at the arched window for a time, gazing out upon the gauze blue night that lay dimly over the twilight wing. Music from soft harps and reed flutes drifted on the scented air, joined by the faintest murmur of fountains, and it was this part of Lorini's halls that all returned to when sleep was heavy in mind or body. But Froghorn was far from sleep. After having tossed about upon the bed for some time, he had finally risen, thrown on his riding cloak, and taken up the pacing that led him first to the window, then to the blank parchment upon the desk, then to the window again.

His mind went over the hushed whispers of his meeting with Greyfax as they had left the far reaches of Windameir, and he shuddered inwardly at the visions there, and the urgency of his next errands that would take him so soon away from Cypher and his enchanting Cybelle.

These thoughts reoccurred as he stood before the desk once more, his chin resting fitfully upon his fist, and with a quick, jerking movement he pulled out the chair and sat heavily down, taking up the pen and ink, and began to write in his handsome flowing hand.

The fine parchment came to life as he worked, and the slender glyphs of the mother tongue of Windameir formed breathing signs in a pale bright halo over the page. At last, exhausted, he sealed the missive, cleared away the desk, and fell upon the sleep-giving bed without having paused to throw off the journey-stained riding cloak. He found a troubled, dream-haunted rest after a time, and drifted fitfully above the war-torn-lands of Amalnath, past the ruined valley of Otter, Bear, and Dwarf, across the Great River. Then he traveled back farther to a time when as a very young apprentice he had met Greyfax, and the two of them had traveled far and wide over Atlanton Earth, and farther still to other stars, ever seeking to play out their part to put an end to the menace that was loosed upon the spheres of Windameir. Between these disturbing dreams the lovely face of Cybelle crept smiling down upon him, and the light of that fair lady's eyes filled even his fears with a faint hope of their passing. The darkness where he half slept slowly vanished, and a sweet, soft edge of rest came upon him, and he neither heard, nor saw, nor dreamed again for a time.

Ladies of Cypher

"He has gone, then?" asked Cybelle of the elf who handed her the thick, sealed parchment missive that Froghorn had spent so long in penning.

"I fear so, my lady. He gave me this even as he was at his stirrup, and charged me with delivery to none but you."

"Thank you," she said, smiling quickly at the nervous elf, and returned into the bright morning chamber, eagerly breaking the message open, and sat down at a low ivory-wrought table near the window.

My fairest, light of Cypher:
I shall be upon my way as you read this, charged with an errand of the lady Lorini. I am bound beyond Calix Stay, and cannot say for how long your absence shall pain my heart, but I fear the hour is upon us that perhaps shall keep me long away from Cypher, and from your lovely company. Your mother will be able to tell you more of this, and I have not time, nor desire to sadden

you by my own hand, in going into it here. It has gone beyond our power to do what we will, and choices now are directed by the Darkness, and all of us must face the possibilities of many farewells, and long partings. I knew all this, and willingly consented to it when it fell my lot to take the mantle of my father and to fill his place in the Council, but it weighs heavily upon me at times, and the burden of leaving you is great, and the office I fill does not ease the sorrow of goodbyes.

Yet I am heartened, for if we succeed this time, then the cause of much grieving shall be erased, and perhaps we all shall have need no longer to part with those dear to us.

Now I have gone on too long, and shall make you unhappy, so I shall cease this self-pity and set out that I might hasten my return.

Forever in your service,
Faragon Fairingay

Her heart contracted in the news of his parting, and she flew from the room in tears, running through the gilded archway that led into the twilight wing of Cypher. There she found Froghorn's room, and threw herself with a great sob onto the barely rumpled bed the young wizard had so recently slept upon. A noise, faint yet persistent, announced someone knocking softly on the chamber door, and Cybelle cried out to enter, her voice muffled by her tears and drowned in the depths of Froghorn's pillow. Lorini entered in silence and went at once to her daughter.

"What's this, my child? Tears so early in the morning?" she gently chided, stroking the golden hair from the smooth forehead of Cybelle, and holding the sobbing girl close to her bosom.

"Why ever must all this take him away from me? It isn't fair." She fell into a new fit of weeping. "He's barely arrived, and now he writes that he doesn't know when he'll be back again."

Lorini waited until the crying subsided, then began gently.

"Your young Fairingay has much to do, and the very fate of Cypher upon his hands. I don't think it would make him any easier if he knew how you are taking this. We each have our part to play, for good or ill, and tears won't change it. If that were so, I would have spent my life in weeping." She smiled tenderly down into her daughter's strained face, her eyes old, yet timeless, and Cybelle embraced her mother tightly.

"Oh, I'm so sorry, Mother. I'm so much weaker than you, and so unwise."

"He shall be back, dearest heart, for he is truly his father's son. Greyfax complains of him constantly, but it's only his gruff way of hiding concern. I honestly don't think Grimwald could go on without the fresh thing."

Cybelle's features cleared, then grew puzzled.

"How long have you loved Greyfax, Mother?"

The candidness of her daughter startled Lorini into laughter. "How long," she said, tossing her fair hair back, laughing again. "It's been longer than I can sometimes remember, and then I don't think I ever admitted it until you said it just then." Her face lost its humor, but her eyes still smiled as she went

on, remembering aloud things from the first beginnings of
Atlanton Earth. "Your father and I were very much in love,
and so happy for so long."

"Did Greyfax know my father?" Cybelle studied the soft
bedspread carefully, avoiding her mother's sad gaze.

"They were Elders of Windameir in those ages, and Trianion
Starseeker was sent here to Cypher, along with Greyfax, to
keep watch upon Atlanton Earth, and to serve as Guides to the
Light. Not long after you were born to us, just before the First
Battle of the Dragon Beasts, your father slew the first sire of
Fireslayer, and in so doing, was returned to the Fields of
Light. It was Grimwald that bore me that news, and since that
day he has taken it upon himself to watch over us." Lorini
fell silent, gazing again into that distant time.

"Then you do love him?" questioned Cybelle.

"Yes, I love the scoundrel," she laughed, "and I think at
the bottom of his heart, he's found time to love me, in his
way."

Remembering her own misgivings, Cybelle took her
mother's hand in her own. "Is this errand you've sent Fairingay upon very dangerous?"

"To set foot beyond Cypher's walls is dangerous in these
times." She patted her daughter's hand. "But he has long been
Grimwald's student, and well able to take care of himself. He
has gone across the River to gather the kindred of Urien Typhon, High Elfin King, to aid us against my dark sister."

"And then to return here?"

"And then to return here," said Lorini reassuringly. "So you
see it is not as bad as you thought."

"But he is still gone," corrected Cybelle, still finding an ache born of his absence within her heart.

"Come, let us entertain our guests now. We have much work to do to heal our good Dwarf and his companions, and I'm sure your music would do much to make us all feel in better spirits." Lorini rose and went to the door, followed by her daughter, who quickly dried her eyes and smiled gratefully at her beautiful mother.

As they entered the high halls that were used as common sitting rooms by all, they saw Bear parading about with a tall silk hat upon his head, juggling a great number of ripened, bright red apples, urged on by great gales of laughter from all those sitting about on soft crimson cushions.

"No more, good Bruinlen," cried a tall, fairhaired elf, who leapt up as Bear pranced by and stole the high silk hat and put it on himself. As Bear bowed low and sat down, the elf whirled the hat soaring away into the rafters, and as it reached its apex, it exploded into a half a hundred bright tin birds that turned and wheeled into the bright sunlight, and a muted, gentle rush of sound swelled until all manner of instruments were heard, brass and strings and 'reeds, and the song grew on in its fullness until all within danced and sang along with it, led by the tall, handsome elf, who seeing Lorini, captured her for his partner, and took her spinning on his arm about the long hall, making her golden hair fly behind her like a flowing gold-yellow river, and the floor hardly felt the feet of those that spun and turned on its clear smooth face. Otter, walking to greet Cybelle, bowed solemnly to that fairest of ladies, and politely asked her for her hand in the dance. She, as solemnly, bowed to the tiny creature, and before his eyes

whirled a gray-silver mist, and when it had been blown away
by the wind of the many spinning dancers, she stepped to
greet him in the form of the most beautiful silver-gray otter
he had ever seen, and whistling to him in his own ancient
tongue, joined him in a wild, free otter reel, and the entire
company laughed and clapped and danced until at last they
all wearied, and yet still laughing, they found their way to the
singing fountains, and there listened as the sparkling waters
sang and lulled them into a waking dream of a dream of time
not passing or passed, but standing still, and the blazing White
Light of Windameir flared into dazzling bright sunlight, covering the dimming lands of Atlanton Earth with almost unbearable beauty, of a sort that is all the more so because it
stays but a moment, and is gone again.

Dwarf Discovers
a Library

"Where ever is our Dwarf?" cried Bear good-naturedly as they sat down to table. "Our morose, huffing comrade who is so free with his cheery nature?"

"Yes, where is the good fellow?" laughed Cybelle. "For he promised to finish me the tale he was telling."

"I'll fetch him," cried Otter, chirping and darting away beneath the table. "He won't escape us tonight, and we shall have a laugh from him yet, if I have to swim in his soup."

Scampering on, Otter climbed the sweeping, curved white stairway that led up to the tower shaped like a great winged turtle, and hurried on to find his friend.

At Broco's door, Otter knocked loudly, then went in to the little man's chambers, a compartment high and airy, as all rooms in Cypher, and with three windows overlooking an inner courtyard that held many flowing fountains of all colors, making the water in some brilliant green, in others a deep ruby color, or gold or blue, until looking at all the sparkling spendor of them, it seemed one was caught up in a constant rainbow. At the low window seat of the first opening Dwarf sat, looking at the ancient silver-white tree that spread until it shaded the first of the fountains, and its leaves and limbs reflected the bright colors of it like a mirror. He held a thick book bound in scarlet leather on his lap, the pages crossed with a print Otter couldn't make out.

"Whatever are you doing brooding about here, Dwarf? We're all waiting for you, and the lady Cybelle says you have promised her the end of a tale."

Dwarf remained seated, gazing out the window a moment longer, then turned, a wistful smile upon his still pale features.

"I've been reading," said Dwarf, a forlorn touch to his voice, "about the dwarflords who once came here."

Otter took up the heavy volume, turning it first one way, then another, and finally exclaiming, "I can't make fruit from fish of it, Dwarf. Is it dwarf tongue?"

"High Dwarfish, as my father taught me. But even then, I don't think many of our kindred left about could read or speak it. I only took it up because I come of a lore-master family." Broco paused, then went on in a soft, wondering voice, "What glorious times those must have been." Dwarf turned, eyes wide. "And Brion Brandagore himself was here, and Tubal, and all the other dwarflords I ever read or heard about."

Otter looked long at his friend, and it seemed Broco's eyes filled with misty visions of dwarf-lords in resplendent cloaks and fine, shining helms, or bright cloth-wrought caps with runes that wound about over them. Then the histories seemed to pass, and Dwarf's eyes grew dim, and he looked dully at Otter, as if he didn't see him there.

"And now they've all gone, all the wise and noble kings, gone forever."

"Not forever, Dwarf. And all things pass, you know as well as I. Although it seems to me that we've been about and gone, and back again, too, but I get confused when I think of it."

A small frown wrinkled his whiskers until Broco was forced to laugh. "And besides, maybe you were here then, too, and just don't remember right."

Dwarf got down from the window seat and paced to a wall that was filled with the heavy volumes, all tooled in gilt edge and polished to vibrant gloss.

"There are books here of your folk, too, Otter, and Bear, and elfin kind." And pointing to a huge tome at the very top of the tall shelves, "And there's one there that tells of the Council, and Greyfax and Froghorn and the others."

"What does it say, Dwarf? Have you read it? Maybe we'd know more if we studied it a bit."

"It's in a tongue unknown to me," said Dwarf. "And even if we could read it, I doubt we'd learn any more than we know." He placed the volume he had been reading back in its place. "When the time comes that we shall need to know more, I'm sure Greyfax will tell us."

Otter lay upon his back on the floor, and began rolling a piece of smooth marble used as a paperweight back and forth across his stomach. "I wonder," he began, the question he was about to ask vague in his mind. "Do you remember when we started, Dwarf? And you found me in my old river? And Bear came with us too, and when we crossed Calix Stay, Greyfax and Froghorn were there, just like they'd been waiting for us?" He let the smooth rock balance delicately upon his nose. "Do you think they were, Dwarf?"

Broco looked thoughtfully at his small friend for a moment.

"No or yes? Perhaps they were. In a way it seems so."

"But if they hadn't been there," said Otter, rolling the piece of marble down until he held it in both tiny paws, "we might still be in our valley."

Broco laughed grimly, remembering Cakgor and his capture. "I think it's more likely we all would have been in someone's stewpot if they had not been waiting. And we would never have come here, for that matter."

Placing his toy back where he had found it, Otter turned to the window, and after gazing out for a time, he spoke in a different tone. "Then it was well worth it, I think. Even if we never see it again, it was worth it, and I'd do the same a thousand times over just to see it, and the lady, and Cybelle, and all the elves."

"So would I, old water dog, so would I." Dwarf grasped Otter's paw and led him to the door. "But come, we keep that fair company waiting upon the moroseness of a stiff-necked dwarf and the wonderment of an overgrown river pup." And so saying, he laughed and clapped Otter so heartily upon his back the little animal almost fell nose first, and recovering, chased Dwarf down the broad, winding stairway nipping at his heels and chittering until they came, breathless and full of contagious laughter, to the feast hall, and Bear, upon discovering them, cried out in a wounded tone, "They wouldn't begin without you, and I'm starved to the point of fainting."

To make up to their injured friend, the two leapt upon him and poured an entire flagon of the magic wine of Cypher into his stuffed mouth, and at last, mollified and forgiving, he shook paw and hand, and they turned in earnest to the vast table, bubbling with a joy born of comradeship and the wonderful spell of Cypher.

In The Balance

A Shadow of Partings

In the small east garden, Broco sat deep in thought, hands on either side of his head and a deep frown darkening the sense of peace that hung gently over his fair retreat. He was happy now, and the frozen ghost of the memory of Dorini's halls had mellowed and held no terror here, but something in his heart told him he was not through yet, that he had still many things left undone. The whereabouts of Greyfax Grimwald had not once been mentioned by the lady or any others of her realm, and no one had spoken of his journey. Dwarf huffed a bit, and filled with self-importance, decided it was time he was treated no longer as an invalid, and resolved to ask the lady Lorini at once all the questions that had been weighing heavily upon him since his awakening in Cypher. As he rose and turned to go, Otter and Bear entered the garden, pausing beneath the silver-arched gate that led into the flower-guarded hedges.

"Oh, Dwarf, we've been searching everywhere for you. Come on, let's go down to the singing pond and listen to those beautiful words." Otter clapped his hands, whistling with bursting joy.

"Don't be so morose, Dwarf. You'll have that frown of yours spread all over everyone's face if you don't cheer up a bit." Bear drew down his mouth and wrinkled his brow, reflecting the expression upon Broco's face.

"There's not much, as I see it, to be cheery about. And if you two ninnies would stop to think a moment, you'd see we've about stayed out our time here lolling around like a bunch of baggage. "I'm on my way now to find news of Greyfax and if you've any wits left about you at all, you'll come along, too." Broco brushed past his two friends indignantly. "And if you're not too busy playing about, you might see if you can find the lady Cybelle, for I think she has had news of Froghorn."

Bear and Otter exchanged startled glances.

"I think, Bear, that our dear Dwarf has made a full recovery."

"If you mean he's growing more like himself, I find you're right. It was so lovely, though, without his eternal huffing."

"Now, Bear, you know he's never happy until he can worry. Let's go and find Cybelle. Perhaps she can cheer him up a little. And I've been wondering if it were all right to speak of that other . . ." His voice softened, then trailed off.

"It seems a shame to bring up anything unpleasant here, but I am anxious about Greyfax, so I suppose now is as good a time as any."

"And the lady seems sadder somehow. Perhaps we should know, that we might be of help."

"If helping concerns going back *there*," Bear said, raising his eyes, "then I'd as soon rest a bit longer before we have to think of it."

Otter looked long at his friend. The memory of before crept like a dark shadow across his eyes, and he began a whistle deep in his throat.

"I don't want to, Bear, but I think Dwarf is right. Somehow we must go on before we can ever stay anywhere, even here. It makes me afraid to think of leaving, but worse to think of staying. We've something yet to do, although I can't think what, but I feel it."

Bear looked back across the quiet garden, perfumed with elfin blossoms, and shining in the golden light.

"I suppose you're right, friend, but I shall miss this place. I don't often take to living outside my own digs, yet this place reminds me of something long ago, before I crossed Calix Stay." Bear shook his head sadly. "If all these wars were only done with, then we might find time to do as we used to in our own valley."

Otter's mind returned to his green door and the warm hole beyond it, far behind now, and his old river, and the early morning trips to his favorite weirs, and the sparkling silver fish as they darted and turned beneath that underwater sun.

"I wonder, Bear, if we shall ever see our own homes again?"

The sound of singing floated gently over the hedge wall, voices of the elves carrying a song of fireflies and still, dark nights, and Otter and Bear went out of the garden, leaving their troubled thoughts, to find the lady Cybelle, for her voice led the rest in soft, smooth motions, rising like crystal bubbles into the cool air of Cypher.

If there was to be a parting, as they feared, the friends decided not to dwell on it until it came to pass.

Greyfax

I n the long silver-gray hall that led to Lorini's chambers, Broco turned a sudden corner and bumped into a tall figure dressed in riding clothes that had seen much wear, and dirt and mud from the journey masked the stranger's face like a scarf.

Broco bowed low.

"Many pardons, sir, it is only the clumsy feet of a dwarf that has almost toppled you." Raising his eyes to the gaunt figure, he added, "But whatever else a dwarf may be that might be of service to you, is yours."

Unbelievably, the stranger broke into loud laughter, at once enraging, yet somehow vaguely familiar.

Dwarf huffed up to his full height.

"This house is sacred, sir, and much is overlooked, or never asked, but your breach of common manners is too much to pardon." Broco backed away, bobbing, dealing horrible blows to the stillness of the golden light as it played through the high windows.

"I see Lorini's healing is what it always was," came the words, faintly edged with laughter, "even with so thick a hide as a dwarf has."

The stained cloak fell away from the stranger's throat as he spoke, and Dwarf stood in startled disbelief.

"Greyfax," was all he could manage across the faint murmur of his own heart pounding.

Greyfax Grimwald, worn and thinner than Broco remembered, reached out and clasped Dwarf's arm.

"It's long since we've spoken, eh, friend? And many journeys between us since. But come. I'm on my way to our lady, and we can exchange our tales over some refreshment."

"But," stammered Dwarf, unable to put all his questions into words at once.

"Greyfax," shouted Otter, coming from a side passage that led back to the great dining hall. "Greyfax," and he began a fast scamper that ended in a quick turn through the wizard's legs, almost bowling him over, and another rapid run back toward the now emerging, lumbering Bear.

"He's here, Bear, he's here," squealed Otter, bolting back.

"Harrumph, I shouldn't wonder," mumbled Bear, ever alert for the least sign of trouble, and the sudden appearance of Greyfax only confirmed what he had been dreading since their talk with Dwarf, that indeed their parting was imminent.

"Harrumph," growled Bear again, and hurried on to offer his paw to the long-departed wizard who had on that faraway day brought them all into this unpleasant business, and was, as likely as not, going to lead them farther away before all was said and done, or before they could all enjoy a long evening before the fire, spinning the whole nasty mess into the more pleasant task of weaving a good yarn to swap, or perhaps during the long, lazy winter put into a chapter or two in the book of bearlore he had carried so long. Then the thought of good bark tea struck him, and he cheered a bit, and thinking of the tingling brew over his tongue, he followed Broco and Greyfax and Otter into the outer chambers of Lorini's rooms, to find out the news, and just how quickly they would have to say their farewells.

Councils, Visions, and Farewells

"It's good you've come, Greyfax," said Lorini. Her voice was drawn with emotion, and the wizard noticed as he turned to where she stood at the door to the inner hall that she looked older now, although her beauty to the three friends was unchanged.

"My lady," spoke Greyfax, bowing, "I have just this moment reached Cypher, and was on my way to you when I found these villains lurking about."

"It is as well, for I was on the point of sending for them. But come, we haven't time to spare. Melodias is in the gravest danger, and Fireslayer has been abroad, and I fear her underlord is thrown against Starson at this very moment."

Broco's heart froze at the mention of the Dark Queen, and even though the chill which numbed his body had been healed by the hand of Lorini, small, frozen chains enveloped him, and for a moment his eyes dimmed, and he saw with horror the tall green throne in the frozen blackness of that dark realm, and Dorini, suffocating him with her icy laughter, beckoned to him with a long, slender finger of her awesome will. His mind was numbed, and he almost spoke her name, but Greyfax, standing beside him, saw what was occurring, and touched Dwarf gently on the shoulder.

"Oh, Greyfax, I saw her, and my heart was stopped within me. I was going to call out to her." Broco broke out in a long sob, hiding his face with his hands.

Bear lumbered over and clumsily patted his stricken friend with a huge paw.

"Here, here, this will never do, Dwarf, we're with you." And so saying, he looked down at Otter, who was clutching the little man's leg, whistling encouragingly.

"That part I can never heal until she has been taken to the Fields of Light," said Lorini quietly. "I have seen it but few times before, but all who have been taken to that dreadful realm and looked upon the face of my dark sister seem to carry an icy sliver of memory about that no amount of my power can rid them of."

Greyfax's features seemed to cloud over as he nodded agreement.

"You mean even you, my lady, can't make him forget?" asked Otter. He could not believe there was anything the beautiful Lorini could not do.

Lorini smiled kindly down at the small gray fellow.

"No, my dear Otter, for she is a part of me that I cannot destroy. We are as one breath, she and I. But she has desires to hold these lower worlds for herself, and there is the difference. Long ago, before the first ages of Atlanton Earth, we traveled the great distances across Windameir, and were happy, as all souls were then. Then, after a long reign on one of the worlds, she began to crave more power than she had by the Law. It was never enough to be a part of the scheme of things. She soon wanted more than merely to govern wisely, as a channel for the High Lord of Windameir. She wanted the power to rule alone. I entreated her to mend her ways, but she ignored my concern and went further in her demands. After a time, she refused the Lord of Windameir, and created her own worlds, which are but mirrors of our own, although lifeless, as you know, my stout-hearted friend." She touched Dwarf gently, then continued. "And so, on through all the evolution of the Creation, she goes on creating the likeness of that which is real, with her own creation, which is flawed and imperfect. You saw the heart of her realm, which is but a copy of Cypher."

"But how could that be?" questioned Bear, his great brow furrowed. Understanding bear lore was one thing, and he thought himself quite well versed in it, but other creatures even as powerful as wizards, or those like the fair lady, left him confused and lost.

Greyfax moved to the long table and poured out a cup of golden-colored liquid, and handing it to Broco, continued. "A quick explanation will have to do, for we're short of time as it is, but you've been in the dark for a long while now, and perhaps before we go on, it would be best for you to know some of what we had hoped to spare you." Greyfax studied the faces of the three friends, then went on sadly. "You three have given great service, although you may not have been aware, and reaped but small reward, except for injuries and narrow escapes with your very lives." Here Greyfax paused, then turned to Lorini. He took from her desk a small hand mirror, and held it in front of Bear. "There, my friend, you see what looks to be a bear, but it's cold, and merely glass."

Bear looked at the wizard blankly.

"Now, have you the Chest, my lady?"

Without speaking, Lorini withdrew from her desk the small, faintly glowing object, and handed it to Greyfax.

As he held it to the light, a fainter light within began to show, then grew stronger, and the room was filled with a brilliance so great the friends had to shield their eyes, but that light swept over them, and even by closing their eyes they could not escape its blinding fire.

Dwarf, crying out in pain, felt the room spin dizzily about him, and a long, spiraling tunnel of the most intense white light opened to him, and he fell forward into the whirling, blazing flames. He hovered over an abyss that dropped away from his feet so far he almost fell headlong into it, and the temptation to do so was great, but an invisible arm held him back, and slowly the mists receded, and he found himself before his father's fire of so long ago, and watched himself as a small spanner sitting on the knee of a tall, powerful man he knew, but could not place. The man and his father were repeating words to a song, and he repeated the song after them, and the man was smiling at him, and in the smile, he recognized Greyfax Grimwald, but a different Greyfax, much younger-looking, and wearing a different-colored cloak. Upon the table beside them was the Chest, unchanged, but then only giving off a pale silver-gold light, as if reflecting the fire upon the hearth before them.

The Greyfax of old spoke, and the words seemed to echo within his own head.

"Someday I shall seek you, and ask for the song back, and you must give it without question."

"But it is a nice song, and all songs are the same. Why must I return it?" spoke the dwarf spanner.

"That you will understand then," said the man, bouncing him once, then placing him on the floor. When Broco approached the table, the small box began to shower dazzling rainbow colors about the room, spinning and turning its light across his eyes, and shadowing the room with its brilliant flashes and bursts of sparkling hues.

"And now I must leave you, friend; for how long, I can't say."

"But," said Dwarf's father, "how shall I guard this thing, Greyfax? I am but a simple lore master, and this comes from the White Light."

"That's why I leave it with you. No one would suspect it here so unprotected, and where one does not think a thing, that is exactly the place they shall never seek it."

Suddenly the light flared, then went out, and Dwarf stood blinking at the faces about him.

"And that, my dear friend, is the answer to the questions you may have wanted to ask. You have carried one of the Five about all these years, and kept it safe." Greyfax placed the Arkenchest carefully beneath the folds of his cloak.

Otter's eyes were wide, and he turned to Lorini.

"But what were you saying before, my lady?" he asked, "about mirrors and the Dark Queen and all?"

Greyfax answered before Lorini could speak.

"Too many questions at one time, my friend, tend to take the mind away from important matters at hand. But what I alluded to with the story of the mirror was that that is how the Darkness creates a likeness of life. It is merely a reflection of what is real, just as the image in the mirror looks like Bear, but is not. And now I fear our hour grows near to depart." Greyfax turned. "Is Greymouse within call, my lady?"

"If he but were, matters would not be as grave as they are. But he is upon the borders of the Dragon Wastes to secure Thirdwaite from attack there."

"And Fairingay?" Greyfax's face grew clouded, eyes dimming, as if he were trying to see something far away.

"Across Calix Stay to gather an elfin host. He is with Urien Typhon, and together they shall try to hold Tyron's hand from misstriking. And there is that other matter of trying to secure the Secret that Eiorn held, and which Tyron now keeps. I fear it would take too long for him to reach Melodias."

Lorini studied Greyfax silently, until at last he sighed and sat down at the long table.

"Then it is only me," he said, looking around, "and any who choose to go with me."

Otter approached the sitting wizard and bowed low.

"If it is allowed, I'll accompany you," and raising himself up, added, "for whatever worth my help may be."

Greyfax smiled quickly and patted the small animal gently.

"You are small and unobtrusive, and I shall have need of someone who can go unnoticed. I welcome your offer, and accept it gratefully."

Bear, against all his common sense, and smelling more trouble, could not remain quiet, much less let his small friend go alone. He stepped forward grumbling.

"For all that, he's not able to move a whisker without mischief coming to someone, so I'd best go to keep an eye out for him."

Bear flushed a bright crimson when Lorini smiled and took his huge paw in her small, fair hand.

"I have known no greater knight than you, Bruinlen, and of none who have rendered the Light greater loyalty."

"Oh, grumpty fie," huffed Dwarf, recovered now somewhat. "Whatever has to be done, I'll do it. Upon my beard, I've never seen such goings-on about a trifle. If we must save Melodias, let's be off, or if not, let's have tea and talk about it."

Greyfax had turned, looking at Dwarf disapprovingly, ready to reproach the little man, then noticed that Dwarf, in his bluster, had blushed a fiery red up to his large ears, and stood staring down at the elaborately worked pointed slippers.

"Besides," he went on in a mumble, "it seems that my work, as I see it, is carrying the Secret safely and what use would it be simply to wait here until something worse happened?"

"But Dwarf," wailed Otter, "if you go, then there might be a chance of them getting you again. It would be better if you stay here, and let Bear and I do what we can to help Greyfax."

"Ummmph, I'll have to agree," grumped Bear, already sure in his mind that he'd best get as much to ease his already rebelling stomach as he might before they were off again on some errand that would take him still farther from his own fire.

"I'm afraid this time you shall have to come, Dwarf, for we have yet a long journey to make afterwards." Greyfax looked at the two animals. "There is some truth to what you say, friends, but I fear the day has arrived that calls for desperate action, and if anything is spared, I feel perhaps we shall have tarried too long. No, Dwarf, if you're willing, I must ask you to accompany me upon this task. And, regrettably, if you're not, I shall have to ask you to come all the same."

"A fine lot we'll be to save Melodias," complained Bear. "Two silly animals and a dwarf. It seems that if that's all that's required to rescue Melodias, we might just as well send a blue jay with a sunbonnet."

"Yet you underrate yourself, friend Bruinlth," said Greyfax quietly, and as he spoke he spun his cloak about him, revealing a single white pillar that rose upward until the top was beyond height, and as Bear watched dumbfounded, the pillar curled into a haze of white smoke, and as it furled and circled, Bear saw a vast army of men behind, tiny at first, then brought closer, until he saw two mighty men seated upon stallions taller than houses, and upon the head of each man sat the silvermithra crown with five jewels that blazed in the misty light, and beyond, the armies cheered, and held many-sided shields aloft and beat them with savage blows from dreadful, gleaming swords. Bear saw with awe and wonder the ancient king and prince of his race, in the time before time when his kind were in league with all those who dwelled upon Atlanton Earth, before the ages of trouble, and a terrible doubt swept over him as the king lowered his glance to meet the eyes of Bear. There were no words, no motion or sign, but their eyes locked, and Bear's mind filled with a thousand thousand lives, glory and treachery, sorrow and joy, passing in layer upon layer of years flown and those yet before, and Bear, unable to tear his eyes from the face of the king, fell into a swoon. One vision passed away to be followed by another, and like some terrible echo from another time, battles raged through him, old and new, and for a moment he stood beside General Greymouse at Seven Hills, then before that had gone, he saw himself armored in shining helm and breastplate, watching fires blaze along a coast that held back a burning blue sea, upon which floated an endless array of battleships with stark red sails and many men upon their decks turned to salute him. Noises, colors, all whirled into a mass of light so bright he shuddered even in his faint, and then came a clear, cool morning with dew-like silver bells across a wide, sleeping meadow, and a deep, clear stream ran peacefully through the dark, rich green grass past a small bolt sheltered against the creek bank, on beyond the windows of a tidy, neat house with a living roof of red and yellow flowers, and at last on past the very door of a deep, sweet-smelling cave, such as he had lived in of old, bordered by lush berry thickets, and untroubled except by the soft drone of the floating yellow honeybees.

When Bear at last forced himself away from this dream, only he and Otter were in the hall of Lorini, and Otter quickly patted his paw reassuringly.

"Well, Bear, you've had a nice nap, I must say. The others have gone to make ready a quick meal, and Greyfax asked me to stay and bring you along when you woke."

"I've just seen so many troubling things, Otter," moaned Bear. "But at the end I think I saw our old valley, or what must have been, or will be, our valley."

"Greyfax said that it was the easiest way to explain things, although I can't see how, because I still don't know any more than I did."

Otter paused a moment.

"You say you saw our old valley?"

"It must have been, or a valley that will be, sometime. Our dwellings were there, or dwellings like we had. But that was at the last. The rest was awful, all wars, and ships, and armies, and such, and filled up with Mankind."

Otter looked at his friend a long moment, then his eyes clouded, and he asked in a dreamy, faraway voice, "Was the water very nice, Bear?"

Bear started to scold his small friend for thinking of play when they were in such a fix, and on the point of leaving Cypher again, but the look in Otter's eyes made Bear feel suddenly old and sad, and selfish, and taking the little animal's paw to lead him to the great hall, he answered. "It was very fine, old friend, and filled with cat reeds, and rushes, and just outside your door there was an elderberry patch, and a slide so long it would take you a day to climb it."

Otter looked quickly up at Bear and sighed.

"Well, if we're ever going to get there, I suppose we must do whatever it is we're supposed to, and if that means leaving Cypher, we might just as well say our farewells."

Bear and Otter trotted down the long hall that led through the tower of the swan, to join the others in the great hall, where already Lorini and Greyfax were seated, heads together, making plans for the aid of Melodias Starson.

Greyfax Grimwald looked older, and his fine high brow was crossed with many new wrinkles that Otter had never noticed, and the tall figure seemed somehow drawn upon it-

self. But the eyes, clear and pale gray, still twinkled and shone
when they fell on the two friends as they entered, and Otter
felt that this parting from Cypher, however long it would be,
would not be forever. Full of this thought, as soon as he was
seated he picked up the tiny cup at his place and stood cer-
emoniously up on his stool so that he might be seen and heard
by all.

"To the fairest lady Lorini, our pledge that this sad parting
shall only make our returning a more joyous meeting."

"Hear, hear," came the voices of the hall as one, and all
stood to drink Otter's toast.

He flushed and sat down suddenly when Cybelle smiled at
him from across the table.

The meal was better than either Dwarf or Bear could remember, and Otter, stuffed with mountain berries from the
Secret Beginning, could not ever think of when he had had a
more delightful dish.

Only toward the last, when at length Greyfax stood to bid
the lady Lorini farewell, did they remember their journey, and
the sadness of having to leave Cypher, which had been their
home now for what seemed to the three friends forever.

At the tall carven archway at the end of the north gardens,
Greyfax took Lorini's hand in his own, and without further
sign, turned and was gone. Otter, Bear, and Dwarf, each in
his turn, bowed low and hurried away to cover their distress,
and at the very North Realm gate, Greyfax halted, and beckoned the three to him.

"From here we shall travel through the Forest of Cypher
toward Havamal. Stay close, for it is easy to stray in these
woods. I don't think we need worry about the enemy, but it's

as well to be safe. I cannot show myself until we are ready, for the dark underling of Dorini is too strong upon these planes at the moment, but we shall have a nice surprise for him soon. Now come, let's off."

Before the friends could ask him of his plan, the tall, gray-cloaked figure had disappeared beneath the high archway of trees, and they had to hurry to keep from losing sight of the quick-striding wizard.

A Darkness at Dawn

Great ugly red pyres filled the night with a foul stench of death and battle, and all about the besieged encampment of Melodias Starson, hoarse, leathery voices broke the night with a terrible victory cry.

> "Bones and blood and
> Broken head
>   Skewered meat
> And splintered limb
> With fire to roast the dead."

The dreadful Gorgolac armies, now thousands strong, roamed about the frail pickets of Melodias, shrieking their crackling triumph, gorged on the rotten flesh of those slain in the battle of the day before.

Gorgolacs, led by their gigantic General Donark, reinforced by two full armies of Worlughs, with their bloody leader, Thiazi, had ambushed the legions of Melodias and trapped them upon the larger of two hills known as Hel and Havamal, which stood almost at the beginning of the Forest of Cypher, where any mortals, if they entered, and did not know the Secrets, would wander lost forever. Thiazi held Hel, and Donark's Gorgolacs crawled over the foot of Havamal, leaving pale brown earth blackened, and slowly moved upward where the remnants of Melodias' army now prepared to make their last desperate stand upon the crown of Havamal, in ages past the once beautiful summer palace of Lorini.

Fireslayer, having driven Melodias at last from the fastness at Fourthwaite, had already been recalled by Dorini, to be thrown into battle against General Greymouse's army to the south. Melodias watched the fires brighten as they were fed new victims, and withdrew within himself to see if he could contact Greyfax, or any of those of the Circle, to let them know of the dark treachery that now threatened even the very realms of Lorini.

Harsh blue-black flames enveloped him as he struggled to see Cypher, and an ominous cloud, bloodred about the edges, began to grow across his sight, and the more he struggled to pierce this new menace, the stronger it grew, as if searching out the mind whose power sought to go beyond its will. A faint green light began to crackle and dart about the center of the cloud, and soon Melodias plunged through into this blackish mass, and saw with dismay it was Doraki, an icy crown about the thick head, his narrowed eyes blazing with such hatred they were nothing but smoking, staring sockets. Melodias withdrew quickly, for he was not strong enough now to pit himself against the powerful underlord, and weakening steadily while the enemy grew bolder and more daring with each hour that brought them closer to an inevitable victory for their Dark Queen.

Melodias wearily drew himself up, and walked down among his captains to encourage them, and thought quickly that without aid before the end of the coming day, there would be no army between the halls of Cypher and Doraki.

A thin shaft of muddy red light crept slowly over the dirty orange eye of the fires, and another, perhaps the last, day dawned over the embattled hillside of Havamal. The struggling troops of Melodias Starson looked hopefully to the sunrise, but saw only more black-uniformed shadows moving about hastily below them, and hope faded slowly in their eyes and hearts. A great icy wind sprang up from a long, low, threatening black shroud that hung low over the east. Their arms and legs were numbed with this cold, and their heads lowered slowly in the swift knowledge that they were alone in defeat. Not even the brilliant light beginning to glow about Melodias Starson warmed them. With a growing terror they watched as the black hordes below gathered force and flowed swarming and calling fiercely upward to where they waited in silence for their terrible enemies to sweep them all into the cold, frozen tomb of death.

The Forests of Cypher

Barely away from the North Realm gate, Dwarf turned quickly, but even from so short a distance there was no sign of the high green archway they had just passed through. Dark shadows fell silently about them and the sun, early in its morning voyage, was yet an hour from noon. Below, thick carpets of ancient leaf and needle dampened the sounds of footfalls, and Bear thought it odd that he heard no forest creature or bird break the almost threatening silence. Ahead, Greyfax strode on unerringly, changing directions here and there to avoid some obstruction, but never faltering or having to check his course. The three friends followed blindly on, having to trot rapidly at times to keep pace with their guide.

All about them great gnarled oaks and ash grew, their trunks many yards thick, and the dark green canopy only let the barest trace of light through to smaller trees many feet below the tops of those moss-bearded giants. Dwarf watched for signs of a beaten trail, but all looked eerily the same, no

matter which direction one turned, and the silence of the place
added a more ominous note. Only those who knew these time-
worn woods could ever find their way about, and only those
who knew the secret words of Cypher ever dared to journey
beneath this dark glass green roof that blocked the sun and
sky and held at bay even the most unrelenting enemies of the
Light.

Bear and Otter trotted along in silence, as if by some law
that forbade noise in the stifling, gloomy place. Otter turned
to Bear once with a question, but the big fellow shushed him
with a scowl, and no one spoke until long after what must
have been midday.

Bear, ducking sharply about to avoid a huge rambling
thicket of undergrowth, bumped nose-first into a motionless
Greyfax.

"Umph," muttered Bear, and Dwarf, hard on Otter's heels,
fell over the small animal, landing with a grunt at the wizard's
feet.

Greyfax glowered down at the friends, his features suddenly drawn and clouded with anger. He looked away quickly
as Dwarf regained his feet, and seemed to be studying a great
green wall of foliage before him.

And then the friends heard it.

"A fine mess you's made, slime of a filthy liar. Now we's
stuck and good." A voice cold with rage sounded even louder
over the awesome silence about them.

"It wasn't me what said it, Cap'n, it was them filthy pris-
oners of them that told the lie." Harsh, guttural sounds, unused
to the common tongue.

A faint swishing hiss through what sounded to be a melon broken open by a blow, followed by an oath.

"Ing your barbarth," then groans from more voices. "Which of you dogs marked the trail?" came the first voice, a piercing, icy shriek.

"Az is what knows. Az knows," whimpered a voice.

"Then on with it. I wants to rid my sight of this foul place." A kick was placed upon some part of a body, and amid growls, snarls, and curses from the first voice, the invisible company noisily departed, going on, however, deeper into the forest.

After a long while, and after the silence had become unbroken again, the four friends moved cautiously ahead.

"Just as I suspected," mused Greyfax to himself almost. "A scouting party."

In the small clearing, the broad head of a Worlugh warrior lay beside his hideous body, ugly yellow teeth showing behind the thick, swollen lips. An oozing stench filled the hot afternoon air.

"That's not the first of his likes to foul the forest, nor is it likely the last," said Greyfax, bending over the black-clad figure, removing a small black disk from the thing's leather collar.

"What is it?" asked Dwarf, moving nearer, but avoiding the leering, pale yellow eyes of the ghastly head.

"Ashgnazi" said Greyfax, holding the disk out to Dwarf.

It was round, and solid black except for the very edge, where a small line of green sketched a flaming tower.

"What does it mean, then?" asked Otter.

"I've not seen these legions abroad for quite a few lifetimes," replied Greyfax, turning to the others. "They are among the elite of the Dark Queen. Palace guards, if you could call them that. They are only brought forth under Doraki, and usually it means that vile beast is with them." Greyfax looked away toward the south.

"But come. We must hurry now. Melodias is in more danger than I realized."

The small company once more took up the march at an even greater pace, so that at last Dwarf had to ride upon Bear's great back, with Otter holding on behind.

In the distance, barely audible above the tremendous stillness, a new sound awoke another fear in them that had slept through their rest at Cypher: the rattle of rifle fire so thick it sounded like ominous thunder, coming from beyond the forest where Melodias Starson battled for his life upon Havamal.

The Coda Pool

Almost at the forest's edge, the small troop came across what appeared to be the ruins of an old roadway, for broad paving stones, once a gleaming white, lay scattered and broken by the roots of the huge trees. Off to one side, in a clearing knotted with low thornbushes choked with tiny plants resembling a creepy vine with small brown flowers, a low wall stood, circular in shape, and tumbled now in many places.

"Whatever was this?" asked Otter, suspecting that whatever it was, it must once have been a well of some sort, and the longing for water in large enough amounts to swim in caused his caution in risking the wizard's anger to disappear momentarily.

Greyfax stood slightly in front of the others, his back turned as if studying the ruined clearing, and Otter asked again, thinking his question had not been heard.

"Is it very old?" Taking a quick step forward, Otter saw that the wizard's eyes were of a pale, smoky gray and older.

Yet the careworn face seemed to lose its lines, and the little animal saw for a fleeting instant the young Greyfax Grimwald, handsome and fair, in a time before Time when Atlanton Earth lay fresh and new, untouched by the ugly face of wars or trouble.

"It is very old, Otter," said Greyfax sadly, "so old that Othlinden, the sire of your kind, had not yet ventured abroad for more than one lifetime, nor yours, Bruinlth, and the spanners of Dwarfdom were only beginning to delve the earth. There was a great highway here that ran from all parts of Atlanton Earth to Cypher's doors, built with the secret powers of the Elders of Windameir, and this was one of the Coda Pools."

"I've heard that somewhere in my studies," broke in Dwarf, " 'and upon the gates of the kingdom stood the Pools of Coda, where all could drink the wisdom of the Universes.' " quoted Dwarf.

Otter moved to the edge of the pool and stood upon the crumbling wall. To his great disappointment, the floor of the pond was grown over with great thistle bushes, and the powerful clear water that had long ago shone there in its pure shimmering light was no more, and only pointed, barbed thorns were left to fill the emptiness.

"This was before the great forests were planted by the elves, and this forest is young compared to the age when this highway was used, for the elves did not move upon Atlanton Earth until after the first terrible war of the dragon beasts had swept over the world, when the Darkness sought to overcome the Light on these spheres," Greyfax turned to Broco. "That was about the time I met your father first, Dwarf, or had any cause to seek out the help of Animalkind."

Otter whistled noisily, then disappeared from view. His friends, listening raptly to Greyfax, whirled to find their companion nowhere in sight. Bear, convinced they were ambushed, raised up to his dreadful height, claws unsheathed and fangs bared, turning in slow circles to face the invisible enemy.

Dwarf, having no weapon, clutched his dragon stone and called forth a spinning cloud of dust to hide their presence, while Greyfax simply walked to the edge of the Coda Pool and peered intently into the thorn thickets.

The small, sleek head of the little fellow broke through the roof of brush, and he gasped excitedly, "The pool isn't dry. There's water down below here that's good, and not like anything I've ever come across," and frowning, Otter went into a puzzled voice. "But then I've seen and been in or about almost all kinds of water there ever was, sea or lake or river, but this is the strangest sort." He broke off and plunged from view once more.

Bear, grumping and clearing his throat to cover his embarrassment, leaned far over the crumbling, unsteady wall, trying to see where Otter had gone.

"Be careful," warned Dwarf, too late, for the ancient structure gave way under Bear's great weight, and he plumped painfully down upon the sharp thorns below.

"Ooooow," wailed Bear, finding that every move he made to try to escape the cruel barbs only let others find new places to torment and sting through his thick fur, and suddenly amid the thrashing and flailing limbs, Bear tumbled straight down to the bottom of the thorn brakes, where a soft, damp, flower-smelling clearing lay, and Bear stared into the wide eyes of Otter, sitting beside him.

The bushes had swirled shut again above them, and a silence even deeper than the forest closed about the two friends, and for a moment neither of them spoke.

Far off, as if coming from a great distance, they heard Dwarf calling their names in a stricken, rising wail.

A Voice from the Past

"What in the name of Bruinthor," moaned Bear, rubbing his bruised backside, and rising slowly to find that the thorns made a high roof over his head, a dark green umbrella that cut out both direct light and sound, but a clear, dim white radiance glowed softly about the still walls, making moving shadows on the ancient carvings that still showed plainly through the rough moss that covered them.

Otter did not speak, but led his friend to the far edge of the pool, where, rimmed by rainbow-colored stones, a tiny pool glistened, no bigger than Bear's huge paw. The water, if water it was, mirrored the gold and red and blue rocks until they flickered across the roof of thorns above and circled the walls, blending color and silence into a stillness, until all time stopped. Within the depths of the center of the pool a flame began to spread across the rippling movement, first pale blue, then bright sunset orange, then a ruby color that made the eyes of the friends quickly shut, but the colors were still upon their minds and memories, and when they again looked on this shimmering, swirling blend of light, the fire had grown, and thin fingers of blazing white fire crept slowly out and drew Bear and Otter to the very edge of the pool.

They were terrified, but their gaze was drawn deeper into the fire within the crystal water, and a faintly outlined figure appeared within the wavering depths, and five fiery blue-white stars ringed the vision, then the fire faded away, flared, then disappeared to reveal a starry, moonless heaven, where golden flashes of light streamed to and fro from one star to another. The outlined figure came again into view, and it seemed that the cloak he wore was made of those heavens, and a face, or what might be called a face, began to form over the blinding surface of the pool.

Bear uttered the most ancient of words from somewhere deep within his memories and the memory of all ages, and Otter whistled a slow, soft, chirring sound that his mother before him had heard from her own, and on back until collective time had ceased, and all was within the sleep of the roots of the All, and nothing stirred across the depths of that breath.

"What seek ye, travelers of the Coda?" asked a voice. It asked Bear in his old tongue, and seemed to Otter to be a series of short whistles that slid easily down beyond the range of others' hearing.

When neither of the friends replied, a searing, sharp flash erupted through the lower depths of the pool, and both the friends were jarred to their senses.

Again came the question.

"What seek these travelers from beyond Calix Stay?"

Bear recovered his voice, though it was weak and very soft.

"O Highest of High, of the unnameable universe, we seek nothing save to serve your will."

Otter looked in amazement at Bear. His friend seemed the same, but his eyes were a deep, rich brown now, and Bear seemed not to notice that Otter had made any movement.

"Drink of this water, then, descendant of Borim Bruinthor," came the voice. "And you also, Olther, of the loyal line of Othlinden."

Without realizing that they had done so, Bear and Otter had touched their lips to the cool, bright water, and the figure cloaked by the heavens and the vision of the face vanished, and across the water came a dark cloud, reddish brown, followed by thousands of shrieking Worlughs and snarling Gorgolacs, their broad mouths tipped with dirty froth, all brandishing long, wicked stabbing spears and cold black fire-arms. All about them the bloodred flames leapt high and curled away into dense, suffocating orange-black smoke. The two companions reeled back to escape the onslaught of the horrible warriors, but soon they faded into a great distance, and a forest appeared, not like any forest they had ever seen. It had stunted, molding black trees that hung low to the ground, as if the sunlight and air had poisoned them. A smell of rot filled their minds, and within a deeper cover of the gnarled trees was another forest, older, yet greener, although the trunks were black and twisted. A building appeared, its once proud turrets fallen and the walls crumbling, and over the gate arch was the fading legend, *Garius Brosingamene, Fifth Watcher of Amarigin*. A shield below it bore the now almost indistinguishable figure of a sword standing upright, with a tall pillar behind it. There were figures then, in dark green that was almost black, and for a moment a withered face appeared, then vanished. Slowly a dark mist covered this, and a great wasteland spread before them, dotted with the dried corpses of trees, a waste so vast they could not see the end of it, and deep gullies and low barren hills made the landscape look parched and broken, and these visions, too, faded, until nothing remained but the low, desolate swamplands that stretched about them, and a stench of land long drowned filled the friends with loathing. A darkness enveloped the light, and there were many roaring sounds, like muted thunder, then a pale, golden day broke over what seemed to be a vast green lawn, bordered by stout, tall trees. And then there was nothing at all.

It was only when they became aware again of each other that they realized the pool had darkened and grown quiet. Bear looked about him, and saw only the moss-covered walls of the ancient pool and the under-roof of thorns above and Otter, lying flat, with his two tiny front paws barely touching the water of what was left of the Coda Pool.

Otter drew himself into a tight ball, brows furrowed for a moment, then shook himself violently, as if he had just come from a long swim.

"Whatever do you think that was, Bear? Did you see something, too?"

"What I saw has almost convinced me that we've all lost whatever little sense we possess, and I'm quite sure I can wait easily again in Cypher for this business to go away."

Bear scrambled quickly to his full height, and began pawing at the thorns.

"There must be a way out of here," he growled, bringing back a stung paw to put in his mouth.

"Oh bother, how did you get out before?"

"I climbed the steps," sniggered Otter, then quickly felt sorry, for his friend had pricked himself badly.

"There, Bear, it's this way. Come on, Greyfax and Dwarf are probably worried."

"To say that we're worried is another way of saying I should pummel you both," huffed Dwarf, appearing at the bottom of the hidden steps that led down unseen through the tangled growth. "Otter, I can always expect this from you, but you," Dwarf poked an accusing finger at Bear, "you have no excuse."

"But Dwarf," chirped Otter excitedly, "come and see. There are all sorts of fire and stars and voices and it all didn't make any sense and gave me bumps." Otter tried pulling Broco near the silent pool.

Greyfax appeared from the stairwell.

"What was that, Otter? What gave you bumps?"

"The pool. It turned all sorts of funny colors, and there was a voice, or sort of a voice, and lights and fires, and old castles and swamps, and man figures and everything, wasn't there, Bear?"

Bear grumped, cleared his throat a few times awkwardly, then stepped forward.

"Whatever it was, it wasn't meant for the likes of us, Otter. We've probably stumbled into a nest of wizards or some such, and it's none of our affair. Poking noses where they're not wanted only ends up with trouble, and the sooner we leave it alone, the better."

Paying no attention to Bear, Greyfax moved to the pool.

"So it's still here," he mused, smiling faintly. "I had no idea any of its spell still worked after all this time." He sat beside the water, thinking aloud. "Let's see, now when was it I was last here? Cybelle had not come, and," snapping his fingers almost gleefully he went on, "the feast of Fairenaus Fairingay's wedding. We had all gone to Havamal to the summer palace, and stopped here to show the lady Fairingay."

A light twinkled in the wizard's eyes, and as he turned, the pool threw forth a great sheet of startling blue flames, and two towering arms of blazing white reached above the small grotto, each bursting like crystal bubbles into parades of tiny dolphins, swimming over the air easily, and circling about the seated figure of the wizard.

Greyfax, for the first time ever in the three friends' hearing, burst forth into joyous laughter, and addressed the invisible figure in the pool in a language none had ever heard.

In reply, a great ivory-colored swan emerged from the pool, and the wind from its wings swirled into a silver dust that danced about the wizard's form, and the tiny dolphins took on the silvery wind and whirled faster about Greyfax, until at last all were gone, and in their place, a star-cloaked figure with silver-gray eyes and silver hair that hung long behind him smiled and spoke through a beard that reached almost to the floor.

"So you've come at last, have you? I only wish it were another wedding that brought you."

"If it were so, there would be only joy. I fear we come this way on a more desperate errand."

"Then it grows dim upon the Atlanton?"

"Day by day. We're on our way now to Starson, who is trapped upon the crown of Havamal."

The silver-maned figure frowned and turned toward the pool. After a time he spoke again, more softly.

"It is indeed the time, it seems, I have tarried here for ages, watching the darkness come. For a while the elves lived near the pool, then after the forest had grown, they, too, left, and only travelers to Cypher visited me, then no one for long years, until these two." He nodded at Bear and Otter. "But I had hoped the times had fared better for others, for I've many lives behind me, and not so much to do as wait."

Greyfax quickly told all that had happened, and where they were bound, and their mission.

The old man shook his head slowly. "It is indeed a dark hour. Melodias came as a young man for the wisdom of the pool." He looked around at the other seated figures. "What did you understand from your visions?"

Although he did not address them by name, Otter and Bear knew he spoke to them. Both blushed and lost their voices.

"Come, did you see something that will aid you?"

"I don't know, sir," stammered Otter. "It was all clear enough, but I don't know what it meant, or if it will help or not."

"Then it will help," decided the old man. "And now you, good spanner, may see what you might. It is the only assistance I can offer, for my power is only within the Coda Pool, and I cannot venture on with you, nor aid you except by what visions I might show." He motioned Dwarf closer to the pool, and turned back to Greyfax. "There is an old road that leads to Havamal," he said, "by ways only I am familiar with.

It might allow you to reach Melodias without the enemy's knowing."

"I had worried over that," said Greyfax thoughtfully, "and had feared I might be forced into revealing my presence too soon. Your road is a great assistance, and by it you have done us great service."

The old man bowed and returned to where Dwarf stood peering hesitantly into the pool.

"Oh, sir," pleaded Otter, "he's seen so much now, and has just recovered from terrible wounds, and the Dark Queen had him for a time and all, but please, sir, don't make him think of that."

Bear coughed and cleared his throat, and began gruffly. "Yes, sir, begging pardon, sir, he's seen much and it wouldn't do him any good seeing all that. That's well enough for you, sir, or Greyfax, and well, what I mean to say is, couldn't it be left alone, and Greyfax can hear all you have to say, and then we'll go on and follow him."

The old man smiled beneath the long silver-gray beard, and the grotto seemed to brighten.

"I have nothing to do with the Coda Pool, or what it chooses to show any who gaze upon its wisdom, but rest easy, for your friend will find nothing there to alarm him any more than what you saw."

"That alarmed me enough, sir," said Bear, a grim frown creeping over his features. "And whatever it was still doesn't tell me which way home is."

Chuckling, the old man turned to Dwarf. "Your friends, I see, are true. You're fortunate to have such companions, and I leave the decision up to you."

"I think I must see," said Dwarf, drawing himself up and leaning forward over the water.

"Our Dwarf is made of sterner stuff than you may think, Bear," said Greyfax. "I think he must look, for the success of what we must do will depend on how well we are prepared."

"It still makes no sense to me," complained Bear. "And I'd be as well off leaving alone what's got nothing to do with me."

"Cheer up, Bear, it's what we must do, so there's no way around it. And if we ever want to get back to a quiet fire and good bark tea, then the quicker we get on with it the better."

Bear stared at the pool a long moment before answering. "Now, it would have been different if the pool would have shown me a fresh barrel of my old bloom honey, or a hearth with a nice new log."

The old man smiled again at Bear, and at last said quietly, "I think if you'll look long enough, then that's exactly what you saw."

And that, looking again into the great depths of the Coda Pool, beyond all he had seen, is exactly what Bear saw, but very dim, and very far away, so that he wasn't sure later he had seen it at all, and Dwarf, when asked what he had seen, looked past his friends into an unfathomable distance, and remained disturbingly silent.

An Unseen Road

Addressing Greyfax, the old man moved slightly away from the others.

"Do you recall the Brilling Hall, and its rose fountain?"

"Of course. It was the feast hall of old, and the waters of the fountain were from the Four Pools."

"The road I shall show you runs to the very fountain itself, and with a drop of water from the pool here, it will open to you. It's been long since this pool flowed, so it may be in sad repair, but convenient enough to let you gain the Crown without detection." Lowering his voice, he added, "But what can you alone do, my dear Greyfax? If Starson is in such grave danger with an entire army, what can you hope to accomplish?"

Greyfax laughed grimly. "I, too, have my army," and he indicated the three sitting figures, seemingly small and helpless. "And for what I must do, numbers alone would be useless." The wizard shook his head slowly. "No, my friend, armies are not the tool demanded now, but stealth and quick wit may carry the day." He gazed for some moments at the three friends, quietly talking among themselves.

"And if you fail?" The old man now studied his long-absent friend carefully.

"We must not fail. One of the beasts has been abroad, and we came upon the foul body of an Ashgnazi, not far from this very spot."

The old man shook his head, eyes troubled, and deep folds creased his forehead. "The Ashgnazi," he almost whispered, and the word hurt his mouth to speak it. "Then she is moving in force."

"Something has provoked her to move quickly, something desperate. I feel that the defeat of her armies at Seven Hills weakened her hold over some, and she has thrown her most powerful horrors into the fray. I am afraid Doraki himself leads the attack on Melodias."

The old man's frail features seemed to drain, and he withdrew momentarily into himself. "Yes, I fear it is true. But if he has grown so powerful that even Starson cannot contain him, what hope have you?"

"This," said Greyfax gently, opening his cloak and taking out the Arkenchest.

A great brightness slowly lighted the pool area, and the old man drew himself up and sighed. "Then it is safe," he breathed, his silver-gray eyes shining with the power of the small glowing Chest.

"It, and the Secrets, too, and this is what I depend upon to turn the tide at the Crown. If we can but hearten the defenders there, and hold out long enough for Fairingay to lead an army from beyond the River, then the Crown shall hold."

"Is it not unwise to put the Chest in so grave a danger of capture? Could you not wield it from afar?"

"The situation demands desperate attention, and the enemy has gained great power from the strife that's been rampant across the world. No, to be effective, it must be where it can best give hope, and that lies at the Crown, with Melodias."

"Has the Council given approval to this plan of yours? It could turn into disaster for us all if the Chest fell to the enemy. Dorini has warred long and mercilessly for possession of it and the Secrets. I shudder to think of the fate of Atlanton Earth if she were to win it."

"If we do nothing to save Melodias, it shall only make her stronger, and then next would be Greymouse at Thirdwaite, then the very halls of Cypher. From there would be the end. Perhaps not quite so quickly, but inevitably it would come to pass."

Head drooping, the old man studied his ancient hands, then looked about him, the silver-gray eyes embracing the ruined walls of the once beautiful Coda Pool and the remnant of its once powerful waters.

His voice came a whisper, and filled with an almost forgotten memory of the dead past.

"Then go swiftly, brave Greyfax, and your small army. I shall show you the road, and pray you safety and success. I wish it were so written that I might be of greater service, but that is not to be. I am an old man whose life fled me when the pool was allowed to fall into ruin. Perhaps this shall be our last meeting." He looked steadily at Greyfax. "If it is to be."

"It shall not," broke in Greyfax, clasping the old man's

hands. And lowering his voice, he went on in the mother tongue of Windameir, "Deathless flame of being upon thy brow, and the brilliant wind of Windameir holds your heart in time, and the breath shall pause upon the stars and the Light not cease to shine."

"Until then," said the old man, his eyes alight. "Now come, I shall give you your road." His hand arched high above his head and as he uttered the ancient command, the hand aloft motioned slowly, and the Coda Pool opened wide, the depths of the water formed into shimmering, glistening ivory steps that led downward into a hazy, bright distance, and a great noise, like the snoring of oceans and mountains, drowned the four figures that entered upon the spiraling stairwell, and a great white flood of light sped them dizzily away downward, and ever downward until the four of them stood stunned by the silence of the tunnel they now found themselves in, the walls polished smooth by the flow of the ancient stream that once passed from the Coda Pool to the rose fountain in the great hall of the Crown of Havamal.

A Dark Tide Turns

By The Backway
to Havamal

After the passing of the brilliant white light, the narrow watercourse closed quickly into a thick curtain of black silence, and Otter bumped painfully into the smooth wall with a little stuttering chirp.

"What is it?" hissed Dwarf, groping blindly about.

"I bumped my nose," chittered Otter, his voice muffled by the two tiny paws that tried to hold the hurt.

"Shhh," warned Greyfax. "There is something here."

Freezing in the chilled dampness of the dark, the little company strained to hear or see anything amiss. Bear's hackles stiffened, and he cautiously tested the wind, but the dank, stale atmosphere spoke nothing but mold and disuse, something older even than the caves of his youth, when he had gone far underground exploring the roots of the very earth, and turning this way and that, he could discover nothing else.

Slowly, so slowly that at first it seemed nothing but a darker shadow of a shadow, an inky wash of gray crept into that stifled gloom, and they realized that a thin, dim flicker of light was coming from somewhere very far ahead in the tunnel.

Greyfax remained motionless for a time, then motioned the friends nearer to him. "It seems our secret road is not so secret any longer. There is a sentry station ahead there, and they aren't Melodias'."

"But how would they ever find this tunnel? They couldn't come this way through the Coda Pool." Dwarf's voice faltered at what he had meant to say next.

"Or through the fountain," finished Greyfax. "Unless the Crown has fallen."

An icy finger of fear slowly crept down Otter's back, making his fur tingle and drawing a faint cry from him. "Then we're trapped here," he said bleakly, looking up at Greyfax in hopes he would be corrected.

"It seems that, on the face of it, good Otter. And I fear to return to the Coda Pool would alert our ugly friends down there to our whereabouts. No, it seems we have but one road, and that is onward. If there are not many in the tunnel, perhaps we shall win the Crown after all." He smiled gravely at his three companions. "Bear, I don't think they would expect to run into such a nasty fellow as you down here. As soon as we've scouted nearer, and found their number, perhaps you could give them instructions as to how well your kind are adapted to underground living."

Otter whistled nervously. "I can go ahead and see how large their number is. I'm small, and the light is dim, and I can stay low against the walls."

"That is an excellent idea, my friend. But don't go too near, for those foul things have a remarkable sense of smell for flesh that's roastable."

Shuddering, Otter took a long breath to steady himself, then set off, blending with the gray darkness of the bottom of the wall where the light barely touched, and after a few feet, his friends could no longer distinguish him from the other grotesque shadows that flowed ominously about the cramped narrowness of the tunnel.

"Couldn't you use one of your spells, Greyfax?" whispered Dwarf, his eyes anxiously wide, staring futilely after the invisible Otter.

"That is exactly what I cannot do, Dwarf, for my presence will be of no use to Melodias if I reveal myself before we gain the Crown. If Doraki should discover our whereabouts, which he would surely do if I used my powers, then our journey would be wasted. Only in surprise shall we be of aid to Melodias, and if Doraki is unaware of my coming."

"How could he know if we're down here? I thought his power was only from the Dark Queen." Bear's voice was low, and hoarse with excitement.

"The power she wields is that which she received from the Lord of Windameir himself, ages and ages ago, which Lorini told you of. It is the power of the White Light, but Dorini has overreached herself, and now uses it for her own desires and designs. It springs from the same source of power as does Melodias', or that of any of the Circle, and any use can be made of it, even if for the black purposes of Dorini. And any of those who wield that power know if any other holder is working near them, so that if I removed those ugly fellows up ahead by spell, Doraki, as well as Melodias, would feel my presence. It would hearten Starson, but merely warn Doraki, and bring disaster down upon us all."

"Then what of dwarf spells? Is that also from the Light? Would they know if I used some of my old spells?"

"It is all the same, friend Broco. Yours is of a lower order, but I fear it would be felt as well." Greyfax reached down and touched the little man's shoulder. "Yet we still have a power that they can't detect, and that is the fearsome aspect of angered Bruinlen falling upon them out of the dark, and that fear will work for us, for these fellows will report back an army of Borim Bruinthor's attacking from the tombs of the earth, and by that time we shall be safely with Melodias."

"Too safely, if you ask me," grumbled Bear, "for once we're there, they'll only send more of those things to drive off whatever it was they thought was here, and then we'll be without a way out."

"Your reasoning is sound, Bear, except on one count. If the enemy above us is Ashgnazi, as I know now, they'll do anything but come back to a place they think defended by Borim Bruinthor, for in the last battles of the dragon beast, your distant ancestor destroyed all of that dreaded army but a few, and those that escaped with their lives have been made into Dorini's own palace guard. She has trained them especially in the use of the beasts, and terror is their main force." Greyfax paused, suddenly still, listening to some still unheard hint of sound. "I still think they will remember Borim Bruinthor quite vividly, though, and you, Bear, shall play that part."

Bear moved uneasily, but made no reply.

"And I think Otter is returned," said Greyfax, moving ahead a few paces and quietly calling the little animal's name.

Otter appeared before them as if he had materialized from the very wall itself.

"There are only four of them," whistled Otter hurriedly, "and I think they've been drinking some awful-smelling stuff that has put them to sleep. And there's what's left of a man they've eaten." The little fellow shivered as he spoke, and looked away.

Greyfax reached down and stroked Otter's quivering back. "Well done, Otter. Now come, we must arrange our plan to convince these brutes they have been fallen on in force by a mighty bear lord's army."

"We have no weapons. How shall we slay them?" asked Otter doubtfully.

"We don't want them slain, just convinced an army of thousands has taken the tunnel by force and is on its way to Melodias. Fear, friend Otter, is sometimes a more effective weapon than firearms, and if we fool our ugly friends here, they'll help us fool the rest above. And if they think secret reinforcements have reached Melodias, it may keep them from storming the Crown, and give us the precious time we so desperately need."

"I've found where they came from, too," said Otter, having forgotten about it in his momentary revulsion at the memory of the slain, half-eaten man. "They've dug tunnels all around up there, but one comes straight down from where the old wall has caved in. I guess they must have found it, and are trying to find where it leads."

"Then they must not know it is the back door to the Crown and that's as well." Greyfax looked away toward the pale torchlight. "For that's the door we shall use to our own advantage."

Greyfax hastily outlined his plan to his three companions, and they set off silently down the eerily lighted tunnel single file, with the frightened descendant of Borim Bruinthor warily leading the way.

The Ashgnazi

Adark, sour odor hung as thick as smoke as Bear neared the sentry post, the heavy sweat smell of foul Worlugh hide and decaying flesh, and heavier still, the smell of death, mixed with the oily flames that flickered incessantly in the putrid air of the confined tunnel.

Halting just outside the brighter circle of the torches, Bear quickly studied the four twisted figures lying sprawled about the cavern floor, hairy arms and stumpy legs askew, equipment littered about carelessly, and just within sight on the other side of the greasy, smoking fire, what appeared to be the torso of a man, thrown like a carcass next to a crude roasting pit. Low growls and snores came from the sleeping half-human beasts, and the sickening stench of burned flesh filled Bear with a sudden, chilling terror. One of the Worlughs turned a huge head, with thick black tongue lolling over broad, blood-smeared lips, and half-lidded, dull yellow eyes seemed to stare directly at Bear. Terrified, and angry at himself for it, and thinking he was discovered, Bear reared up to his full height, and quickly snatching up one of the discarded long-barbed stabbing spears, he let out a deafening roar that filled the tunnel with dreadful, howling echoes, teeth gleaming a deadly white in the torchlight, huge, gaunt frame filling the cavern from floor to roof and wall to wall, and lunging forward with alarming speed, he drove the sharp head of the spear completely through the thick body of the Ashgnazi warrior closest to the fire, and before the beast had time to awaken from his drunken stupor, his black soul had passed out through the gaping wound of his own wicked spear which had tasted the blood of a hundred men. The tunnel floor grew slippery from the oozing black oiliness that was his life. A great rumbling cry rang like the voices of a raging army, "Borim Bruinthor," echoing from the cold walls back a dozen times more, and the three remaining enemy soldiers started awake, yellow eyes wide behind the thick, coarse brows, to find they were set upon by the most dreaded warrior ever to move against their kind—the vile, merciless king that long ago had slain all but a ragged few of their armies upon the Dragon Wastes. Time and again they had heard that cruel tale from their commanders, two of whom had been at the battle and carried terrible scars to remind them of the viciousness of the bear king's fury. Rising out of their clouded nightmare minds came that same creature, wielding a blazing spear, intent upon devouring their entrails and leaving their cleaved heads to rot upon poles for the carrion birds to feast upon their eyes. Shrieking horribly, and scrambling drunkenly up to escape, they tripped across the corpse of the soldier of Melodias they had just feasted upon. In that agonizing, panicked second, the ghoulish king had savagely driven the barbed point of the spear through the tough, leather-collared throat of the Ashgnazi sergeant, spitting him like a hunk of meat and crushing him against the wall, snapping the head of the shaft, and leaving the lifeless body to collapse into a broken, blackened pool.

"Borim Bruinthor," bellowed the terrible voice, its din closing over the frantic Worlughs' ears like a dark, inescapable flood, and reeling, half crawling, half running, they fled that dreadful avenging giant, and sped up a low, crudely dug tunnel toward a broken opening that led into the safety of their camp.

Picking up one of the abandoned firearms, Bear fired twice up the hole toward the light, bellowing and crazed in his killing victory rage. Neither of the shots found its target, and he slowly calmed, watching the disappearing crouched shapes vanish through the tunnel mouth.

Otter danced about, spinning in quick, whirling motions, paws clenched, shouting as loud as his small voice would allow. "Borim Bruinthor, Borim Bruinthor."

And Dwarf, hat askew, darted back and forth, delivering horrible blows to the dark shadows, his eyes aflame with a deadly, cold light.

Greyfax broke this battle fever by walking swiftly to Bear and placing his hand on the animal's shoulder.

"Well done, Bear. They'll have it spread through all the camps by nightfall, and we shall be safely with Melodias by then."

Bear, breathing heavily, and calming, looked dazedly down at his two sprawling victims on the floor.

In an almost whisper, he spoke the ancient words of Beardom that were always spoken over a fallen foe, and wearily turned his back upon them.

Dwarf clutched Bear's huge paw, and looked up into his big friend's eyes.

"Someday we shall be quits with this, Bear, and go back to our own ways somewhere we can call home, in our old valley, or perhaps across Calix Stay again."

"I know, Dwarf, but it is sad to think on this, and any killing is a bad thing, even things as evil as these. I can never forget it, even if we ever get home."

"At least we won't have to think of it all the time there. But I know your feeling, Bear. It's against everything to take life. Even if it's as black as a Worlugh's." Otter shuddered at his own memories.

"Well, you can rest assured they wouldn't be thinking like that if the case were the other way about," Dwarf stated hotly, huffing himself until he stood upon tiptoe. "And as likely as not we'd be in their supper stew before anyone could say a word one way or another, and I suspect the only thing then would be to comment on the toughness of dwarf hide or otter roast."

A faint, faraway clamor reached vaguely into the tunnel the fleeing Worlughs had used to make their escape.

"Hmmmm, it sounds as if the arrival of Borim Bruinthor and his armies has reached the ears of our friends outside," Dwarf said thoughtfully. "I wonder if we should try to block up this passage?"

"They would only dig it out again. And anyway, I don't think even the bravest of them will want to come down that narrow tunnel knowing that Borim Bruinthor is here." Otter paced a little way into the low tunnel, and went on over his shoulder, "I wonder if I should go a little way farther on there, and see what they're up to?"

"No, leave it," Dwarf said hastily. "They might try just firing off their guns down it, even if they wouldn't come themselves."

A great volley of rifle fire finished Broco's sentence, sending the trio skittering to safety beyond the opening of the tunnel, but the winding low walls of the cavern stopped most of the bullets from reaching as far as the water-way, and only a few of the missiles spattered ineffectively into the smooth, hard rock behind them.

Greyfax, having remained silent as they talked, startled them when he spoke. "I think it would be wise to leave you and Otter here," he addressed Bear, "just to make a lot of noise so they won't become suspicious and return." He saw the apprehension cross Bear's glance, and went on. "Not that they're likely to, after the scare you threw into them. They've left all their firearms, and enough ammunition to last quite a long time, or at least long enough for me to have Melodias send down guards, then you two can rejoin us at the Crown. Dwarf and I will go on and find Melodias, and have you relieved in a short while."

"Shouldn't I stay, too, and help? I'm afraid I won't be of much use when you and Melodias meet, except maybe to be underfoot."

"No, you must come, Broco. Your place now is at my side."

Otter's hurt pride clearly revealed itself when he spoke. "Oh, you two go on. Bear and I can handle this all right."

"Your job is most important right now, Otter, for we need the time to reach Melodias. It wouldn't do any of us any good if we left the way open, and showed them right to the door."

"Well then, here we stay, but I'll feel better the sooner you find Melodias and send back someone to guard this cave. It's getting awfully damp, and I haven't had a bite to eat, and I'm starved."

"I should have known it," grumbled Dwarf. "Our danger must be real, for Bear's stomach is the best alarm for trouble I've ever come across."

"Then we'll be off, Dwarf. Come."

Greyfax patted the two animals quickly, and turned, his cloak flowing behind him, and strode hurriedly away into the gloom of the ancient tunnel, Dwarf puffing importantly on behind him. Just at the edge of the last light, Dwarf called over his shoulder, "Don't worry, there'll be someone back here soon." Then he too disappeared from sight and sound, the retreating footsteps muffled in the thick moss that lay like a rust-brown carpet over the floor of the tunnel.

"I shouldn't doubt it," complained Bear bitterly, hungry now, and still troubled by the dead Worlughs that lay beside the failing fire. "But I wonder if we'll still be here to meet them."

As if in answer, another long volley of shots broke the stillness, followed by the horrid war cries of the Ashgnazi. Bear sighed deeply, picked up his rifle, and fired a dozen shots down the darkening shaft to assure the enemy that Borim Bruinthor, dreaded warrior king, still held the tunnel against the forces of the Dark Queen.

Reinforcements Arrive

Burdened still with misgivings, and doubting the wisdom of leaving Bear and Otter to guard the tunnel alone, Broco yet waved over his shoulder jauntily as he followed the wizard's retreating form. Dwarf was of a delving heritage and he wasn't as uneasy as the others being underground. Although Bear was a sort of earth dweller, he wasn't interested in the sizes or types of tunnels, nor how they had been laid, nor the rock and stone work that had been put in. Dwarf thought in a passing superior manner that Bear would probably be perfectly happy to have something only halfway done as long as it had a large enough bed in it, and a door. But that thought quickly passed, for Bear was staying behind to keep the tunnel open, and Dwarf pummeled himself mentally for beginning to think such thoughts simply because he was traveling through a really first-rate dwarfish constructed work. At risk of losing sight of Greyfax, he stopped and carefully ran his hand lovingly over the smooth inlay and fitting work of the stone that made the wall. There was no doubt that this waterway was the handicraft of craftsmen, old masters, possibly even the dwarf-lords themselves, for they had been regular visitors to Cypher in those times, and the smoothly joined stonework was so fine even he couldn't detect the seams that must be there, and not having found such structures to wonder and marvel at since he reached Cypher, so long had the skills of those lords of old been forgotten, he now paused occasionally to tickle his fingertips with the artistry of the wall, and became so taken with it, he soon lost sight of the wizard, now far ahead, and failed to notice which way he had gone in the very faint light of the tunnel.

Dwarf, long used to living under the earth, possessed, as did all his kind, a second sight that depended not so much on light as on a sense of moving about unhampered in areas where only small amounts of light, or none at all, were available. He realized that Greyfax was somewhere ahead of him, and after testing his way in the manner of all dwarfish folk, he quickly chose the proper turning of the shaft, and hastily set off to catch up to his comrade.

He pondered as he walked the simple structural layout of the tunnel, then remembered it was only meant to be used as a waterway, decided that the crisscrossing evenness of it was more well suited to the purpose than the intricate upper- and lower-level patterns he had studied as a spanner, when the dwarflords had created great unfathomable labyrinths as their kingdoms, so complex and many-layered it had taken him years to see the beauty and underlying unity to them all, and he very much hoped someday to be able to study one firsthand.

He came to another of the great stone blocks that in times

of old had worked to even the flow of pressure from the pool to the Crown of Havamal, for the tunnel was indeed a series of locks developed to transport water uphill to the mountain from the pool, and each worked on a very simple system of pressure applied to a specific point on the stone, just as would have occurred when the water level built up the proper force, touching the masterfully conceived hinge trap that slid the huge stones swiftly and noiselessly back onto the counter-blocks, thereby releasing the water onto the next level.

He stood on tiptoe, and touched the stone at a point high up, near the roof, and the huge gate slid back noiselessly, faultlessly into its niche, and Dwarf marveled that they went on working effortlessly even after all the ages of disuse.

Dwarf stood back and watched as the solid stonework re-placed itself, for the absence of pressure relayed its message that the level of water (but of course there was none) had fallen and the lock must once more close to allow its process to repeat itself.

Broco marveled at its craftsmanship, and lamenting the passing of those who knew such secrets of earth and stone, pressed on, running his hand along the smoothness of the wall and regretting very much the destruction of Tubal Hall before he had ever seen the wonders that had been fashioned under-ground there.

"Dwarf," called Greyfax angrily, his voice hushed, but seem-ing louder in the confines of the tunnel.

Broco hurried on, and after withstanding the withering glare of the wizard, went on.

Ahead, not very much farther, was a dim oval of light, and the two sensed they had indeed reached the Crown, and would soon be upon the very steps to the rose fountain of the old summer palace.

Startled cries of surprise as they emerged in the center of a busy war camp announced their arrival as unheralded, and Greyfax sent word immediately to Melodias that help had at last reached the embattled hilltop fortress.

More than a few sneers and unbelieving looks convinced Dwarf as he waited for Greyfax to return from his meeting with Melodias that not much gladness showed in the faces of the exhausted men, and not much hope was aroused with the mere underground arrival of a thin gray figure of a man who seldom spoke and a dwarf in a dirty yellow-green hat and a riding cloak.

And what, he mused further, would they be able to make of a very large bear and a very small otter when the rest of the reinforcements arrived?

The Tunnel Becomes
a Tomb

Only a faint red glow still lighted the watercourse, and Bear and Otter, after looking about for any fuel to keep it alive, gave up hopelessly and watched as the narrow tunnel rapidly darkened. After a time, the only illumination they could see came from the distant rough oval of the cave mouth where the Worlughs waited. With a last, crackling hiss, the fire died completely away, and the cavern was plunged into a heavy, threatening gloom.

"It's going to be dark soon," exclaimed Otter nervously, straining to keep the pale opening visible. An endless line of imagined attackers crept stealthily upon them, ugly, curved Worlugh daggers drawn, yellow teeth bared in savage smiles.

"Do you hear anything?" asked Bear, turning his great head this way and that, testing the air, and shuffling forward toward the recently dug tunnel.

"Nothing, Bear." Otter, too, tried his nose, but the atmosphere of the confined place was heavy with the dead Ashgnazi and no other scent was evident, except the overpowering smell of danger, very strong, and very near.

"Wherever are the men Greyfax said he would send? Do you suppose he wasn't able to reach Melodias?" A long, foreboding chain of thoughts crossed Otter's mind, and try as he might to dispel them, the persistent idea that Dwarf and Greyfax lay dead somewhere in the dark tunnel would not leave him.

Nothing stirred in the dim shaft but the soft rush of their rapid breathing. The ring of distant light paled noticeably.

Imperceptible at first, then vaguely on the outside border of their awareness, came a sound, indistinguishable, yet consistent in its presence.

The two looked wildly around to locate the source of this noise, but the heavy gloom blanketed the tunnel in darkness, and they could barely make shadowy outlines of each other, no more than a paw's distance apart. The faint sound went on, as regular as a heartbeat, unhurried.

"Bear, that almost sounds like someone digging," said Otter in a tight whisper.

Bear's eyes widened in agreement, and they listened harder to try to find the direction from which this new danger came. In the dark, it seemed to come from all sides at once, and in desperation the two companions placed their heads close to the cool, damp walls.

"It's here," whispered Bear urgently, and Otter placed his ear near Bear's muzzle, listening intently.

A definite scraping could be heard, not distinctly, but not so far away as to threaten no danger.

"What can they be doing there?" asked Otter, confusion and fear making his voice tremble slightly.

Bear's great face drew up in a puzzled grimace. "That's from farther ahead somewhere," he said, indicating with his paw the direction in which Greyfax and Dwarf had gone.

With alarming speed, the troubling thoughts that had buzzed through his mind struck Otter anew.

"They shall cut us off, Bear. Help won't be able to reach us."

"Trapped," said Bear, the finality of his own voice startling him into dumb terror. "Trapped blind in this stinking shaft."

A flurry of rifle fire stuttered noisily at the distant opening, and a dozen or more whining ricochets whizzed angrily into their concealment. Snarling shouts and growls filled the chamber with echoes, and by the rapidly fading light, the two friends made out the grotesque outlines of an advancing cluster of enemy warriors crawling toward them through the rough-walled tunnel.

Bear roared viciously, and began firing his firearm into the shaft, and having exhausted the ammunition in it, reached for the freshly loaded one that Otter handed him. The noise of the gunfire echoed madly, drowning all other sound for a moment, then as quickly as it had begun, the attack ended, the only traces of it being three or four confused, unmoving heaps lying at the tunnel mouth.

"Trying to draw us here while they cut off our escape," growled Bear, anger and fear mixed in his voice.

"Then let's move farther up, Bear, beyond where they're digging now."

They noticed in great alarm that the sound of digging had gotten much louder, and they could hear muffled cursing coming through the wall at the point where they had listened.

"Get the rest of that gear, Otter. We must move quickly."
Bear stooped and snatched the rifles, and Otter struggled with
the heavy ammunition belts, and they ran clumsily on in the
dark tunnel in the direction the wizard and Dwarf had taken.
They had gone hardly more than a few dozen paces when
Bear collided noisily with something hard and damp, and Otter, trying to keep his balance with the heavily laden belts,
tumbled over Bear's fallen form. An unseen horror seized the
two, and scrambling blindly up, they rushed about in a fear-
crazed madness, stumbling and falling again and again, and
still the unseen cold hand cast them back, until Otter discovered that by going sideways instead of forward in the suffocating darkness, he could move unhindered. His hands felt
slowly about, and moving slightly back, came into contact
with the smooth surface of the old wall, then moved out into
emptiness.

"The tunnel splits here, Bear. It's a crossshaft."

A great crashing of rock being split and crumbling filled
the choked air, followed by guttural snarls.

"It leads off here, too," cried Bear, bewilderment and fear
making his voice rise. "We don't know which way leads to
Greyfax." Despair, cold and final, crept into his tone.

An explosion rocked the shaft, and a great splinter of stone
shattered a foot from Bear's head, and he leapt into the safety
of the corner where Otter crouched, and fired blindly back in
the direction of his attackers. A hoarse cry raised itself, followed by more shrieks and deafening explosions. The tunnel
erupted into a fiery blaze of rifle fire, and by that grim light,
Bear quickly looked about their hiding place and could dimly

make out the deeper hole of darkness that was the tunnel across the way.

A tremendous roar and blinding dirty orange flash exploded near them, knocking them both off their legs and spinning them backward against the wall.

"A hand bomb," cried Bear, ears ringing, and temporarily blinded by the flash. "They've got hand bombs." He put the muzzle of his rifle carefully around the corner and fired until he had emptied it.

Immediately, many return bursts answered, and the narrow shaft was again lighted with the angry orange trails of bullets as they smacked and buzzed into the wall of the cross-tunnel. More curses and shrieks swelled the din, and the two friends knew many Worlughs were now in the tunnel with them. Another hand bomb burst, and then another. The hoarse, guttural cries rang dully in the muffled, cramped space, and a harsh sound of heavily booted feet came toward them, accompanied by repeated rifle fire.

"Fly, Otter," cried Bear, picking up two firearms and the belts that weighted Otter's back. "They are too many." And wheeling, he fired another long burst down the tunnel at the onrushing shrieking Worlughs.

Otter darted wildly forward, his paws flung before him to avoid crashing headlong into another unseen wall, but there were none, and he heard Bear's running steps behind him, and the shouts and cries of the enemy soldiers as their relentless pursuit swept them onward to the turn in the shaft. Bomb bursts and rifle fire rolled through the tunnel in deafening chaos, and blazing red-orange streaks crossed and flashed above him. Over his shoulder, he saw Bear, running swiftly on all fours now, the rifles slung carelessly across his back.

Ahead, by the ugly red flashes, he saw with a choking cry another wall, smooth and hard, a dead end of the tunnel. In a final flash of despair, he knew they had taken the wrong turning, and that this way led only to this blocked passage, and in that same instant, knew they were lost.

His heart deadened with fear, Otter turned as Bear came stumbling up, his breath coming in jerking starts, and the two friends gazed for a moment into each other's eyes, then grimly clasped paws, and Bear handed the tiny fellow one of the rifles, which he had to place on the floor so that he could aim it, and filled with a calmness that neither of them understood, they prepared to meet the fiercely screaming Ashgnazi, now fallen into their bloodcurdling chant, sensing their prey hopelessly outnumbered and fatally trapped. Without speaking, each turned his thoughts to Cypher, and to their valley of long ago, and Dwarf and Greyfax, and Froghorn, and to the golden, beautiful sunshine their eyes would see no more. These thoughts saddened yet also heartened them, and a cold rage burned like a deadly fever in their eyes. Firing steadily into the onrushing merciless Ashgnazi warriors, Bear bellowed with a terrible fury the war cry of all his ancient kind, and Otter, bucked wildly about by the recoil of his blazing rifle, lifted his voice into the long, piercing whistle of defiance and death that King Othlinder had whistled before him. The narrow tunnel exploded into fiery, scarlet brightness, flying deadly darts, choking dust, and stinging smoke. Above the battle noise, high and clear, rang the defiant, ageless cries of the two companions.

Farther above, over the fallen ruins of the Crown of Havamal, a heavy rain began to fall like soot-gray ash over the exhausted defenders.

Out of the Crypt

Blinded by the thick, stinging smoke and flashing explosions, choking and battle-crazed, Otter reeled lurchingly with each recoil of the clumsy man weapon, his voice drowned now by the murderous Worlugh victory howls, magnified by the narrow walls that so fatally sealed them into their dank, confined crypt. He could no longer see Bear, nor hear him, but he felt his presence as they were backed cruelly against the solid stone block that barred their escape.

Another thundering blast flung Otter senseless against the cold face of their coffin wall, and was followed by a devouring, swelling roar that seemed to split the very bowels of the mountain, and great boulders of solid stone pitched and rocked in the depths that held the Crown upon its deep shoulders. Outside, in the gray shroud of ashen rain, huge carpets of earth sheared loose and slid free and unchecked down the slopes of Havamal, its monstrous, yawning jaws open to reveal its crushing, suffocating earthen belly. Tall trees snapped, and tons of smashing, madly spinning boulders danced about to deep, rumbling music, and the avalanche consumed all those moving upon the lower shelves of the mountain. The dark, dreary, rain-swept slope was filled with drowning shrieks and the harsh dying rattle of Ashgnazi soldiers. Below, in the vibrating tunnel of the ancient watercourse, an utter stillness fell, and a suffocating blackness thick with dust and broken stone settled with a shuddering sigh as the mountain quieted after its angry arousal.

Bear groped blindly about, trying to get his feet beneath him, calling in an agonized, pleading voice, "Otter, old fellow, call out, can you? I'm—I'm here." Scrambling madly about, he began to feel in the darkness for his friend. Only the hot, stuffy silence greeted his cries, and a rage so great took Bear he beat upon the stones that had split and fallen, and he roared out in a mighty voice that seemed to disturb the sleeping mountain once again. "By the fires that forged the sword of Borim Bruinthor, I'll eat the hearts of those who've slain my friend, and gorge myself with the black souls of those who've robbed me of him," and rearing up in the small tunnel until his great head touched the ceiling, his eyes burning with a terrible red fire, he roared out again. The trembling walls shivered and seemed to retreat from his horrible fury, and Bear began the dreaded dance that all enemies of his kind had looked upon in choking, numbing horror. Spinning around, great claws gleaming coldly and fangs flashing pale death, he worked himself into such a blazing fury he smote a ringing blow upon the hard face of the block wall that had been the end of his small friend, and fell back in amazement when with a noiseless motion it slid back smoothly into the tunnel side, revealing a spiraling stairwell that shone deep within the surface of its ivory-colored steps. It rose upward into a distance that Bear could not see an end of, but toward the top of which dim, shimmering lights could be made out, as if thousands of tiny rush lamps, or curtains of stars.

A cry escaped Bear as he stared at this unexpected avenue, and somewhere behind a tiny echo answered him.

"Bear?"

And small and weak though it was, Bear heard it, and flung his great head back and bellowed a long, triumphant call that seemed to trouble even the distant, flickering lights upon the stairwell far above.

"Ohhh, I wish you wouldn't, Bear. My head feels like it's been stepped on by a mountain."

Bear dropped to all fours and began feeling about for the tiny fellow, and finally, after searching a few moments, saw a small movement of earth sliding, and Otter's head came into view, ears wrinkling and nose twitching, followed by an explosion of sneezing.

Bear quickly hurried to his side, and began clapping the little fellow on the back and trying to dust him off, for his sleek coat was matted with small stones and a thick blanket of dirt.

"Phew, phooey," spat Otter, sticking his tongue out experimentally. "I think I've eaten my way through three courses of a worm's supper. Ugh, but it's hardly right for waterfolk." Otter gave a great shake to rid himself of the thick covering of dust.

"Here now, old fellow, let me look at you. No hurts?" Bear turned Otter about, feeling gently for a sign of wounds, and

Otter let out a squeal as the exploring paws ran down his flank.

"Is it bad?" asked Bear, bending closer to inspect the injured part.

"It's ticklish, you dolt. I'm perfectly all in a piece, if you don't count my ears, and they're still ringing like a drum. But what happened, Bear, did the bombs break the mountain?"

"I don't know, but there's stairs there, and they lead up from this snakes' tomb, and there's lights there, too."

Bear pointed to the spiraling stairway, and shuffled forward to squint up at the strange opening.

Otter cautiously peeked between Bear's huge hind legs.

"At least it's not full of those nasty fellows back there." He shivered violently, remembering the howling Worlughs, and their narrow escape. "Their bombs must have done it, don't you think?"

"Whatever it was, we got out. But we must go carefully. This could be another blind end, and I'm not anxious to run into more of them now. I lost my firearm somewhere about, and we'd be digging till this time tomorrow if we tried to find it under all that hill."

"Do you think Greyfax and Dwarf went this way? Maybe this is the way to Melodias."

"I don't know," mused Bear. "But wherever it leads, it takes us out of here. We'll have to try it, at any rate, for it's the only way open now." Bear crept out and placed a hind paw upon the bottom of the stairs, looking upward to try to detect its ending.

"It seems to run on forever," he said, craning his huge head until he was looking straight up.

"I hope they haven't found this out. I'm not anxious to meet any more of those ruffians." Otter's face fell into a dark scowl.

"It's not likely they've found this way, Otter. I don't smell anything here that would speak any presence at all." His nose lifted, Bear carefully tried the musty air.

Otter darted up a few of the stairs, sniffed at them carefully, and agreed.

"Nobody has been upon this way," he said thoughtfully. "But that means Greyfax and Dwarf weren't here either." Otter's hopes fell.

Bear moved carefully about, nose against the smooth steps, retraced his movement, tried all about the base, then up again, and at last sat heavily upon the bottom landing.

"These haven't been used for years and years, Otter. When Greyfax was talking before of the Crown, and the Coda Pool, this must have been some part of it when they still used the summer palace."

"And the keeper was so sad because no one had come to the Coda Pool for so long, until I found it." Otter paused, moving his paw thoughtfully over the cool surface of the step where he sat. "It all must have been so beautiful then, and the pool, how nice that was before. I've never seen water quite like it." He turned to Bear, who was frowning, deep in his own thoughts. "It all seems like a dream, Bear. I can't really remember what the keeper looked like, or if he really was there at all."

Bear started, looked wildly about for a moment, then as if he'd only just remembered where they were, jumped up and began climbing.

"He was there, all right, and no doubt about it, and we

must move on quickly. Wherever this leads, at least it's away from here, and those ugly lumps on the other side of that rock fall aren't likely to let a pile of earth stop them from having us in a roasting pit, and I suspect they're probably more at home out of the sunlight than we are." Bear began rapidly ascending the stair. "This way may not take us to Greyfax, but it must certainly lead us away from here, and if we can get a fresh breath of air, I won't be the worse for it." He snorted loudly. "And I would dearly love getting the foul stench of that murderer's nest out of my snoot with as little time wasted as possible."

Otter had to gallop to keep up with Bear's swift movement, and they had gone on for what seemed to the little fellow an hour before Bear paused again, raising a warning hand and testing the air once more.

"There's fresh air coming from somewhere. I can smell rain."

Otter had smelled it for some time, but said nothing and was more interested in inspecting the pale flowers of light that shone faintly through the wall of the staircase, for it was this mysterious source that gave off the flickering light that showed them the way. He had passed many on the long climb, but was too pressed to keep up with Bear to stop and look at them closer.

The wall itself was alive with these strange lights, and was of a blue so deep it appeared black at first glance, and the faint gleam of the lights glimmered from far within, so that the whole wall looked as if a curtain of night sky had been woven into the rock itself.

Otter was so engrossed in his discoveries he barely heard
Bear moving on.

"There's some sort of window," Bear whispered, halting in
midstride, beckoning Otter to come up. "And no, yes, there
are four windows."

Otter forgot his study of the amazing wall, and darted to
where Bear now stood motionless, staring about in silent wonder at the sight before him. The tiny animal drew in a sharp
breath and gazed about wide-eyed at the magnificent room
they had chanced upon.

A tall, circular chamber spread its domed roof away to a
height they could not detect an end to, and some brighter
lights than the others fell in soft, silver-edged shadows about
them, for the four windows Bear had seen were fashioned in
the shape of the four quarters of the moon, from Sycle Trine
to Full, each one facing inward from the points of a compass,
and these lights shone down onto the blue surface of a floor
so smooth it seemed that one walked upon the air itself instead
of solid stuff, and in the center of this, a five-pointed star
blazed in the silver light, alive in the movement of the deep
shadows, and a brighter shaft of dazzling fiery silver fire
burned within the star itself, and as they watched, stunned in
the amazement of the vision they saw, this star began to glow
more brightly, and a wind seemed to spring from the walls,
as if they had suddenly traveled to some far point of the universe, and with a roaring sound of swift water, the chamber
became like day, so bright was the finespun golden light, and
Bear and Otter were drawn by some unseen will into the very
circle of the blazing sunstar, and the room began to spin more
quickly still, and the starlights within the living wall multi-

plied, then diminished, and the passage of entire systems flashed and whirled about the trembling animals, until at last the swift rush of wind died away, and the room became stilled once more, and almost as if it had never happened at all the tall room was bathed in the same soft glow, and the moon-fashioned windows dimmed again into pale silver, and the breath of the soft glow of the walls became regular and steady, and seemed to pulse with their own steady heartbeats.

Bear glanced about him in a subdued way, and in a very quiet tone asked Otter for his paw, and reassured by the presence of each other, the two animals huddled in the center of the enchanted chamber, frightened but fearing no harm, for they sensed that they were in the heart of some secret hall of long ago, where the lady of Cypher must have held her court, or in the very place that powerful keepers of the Light carried on their mystical workings.

Gathering their courage, they crept out, gazing at the wonderful room, their eyes wide and reflecting the millions of tiny star lamps, paw in paw, hardly daring to breathe. As they neared the wall near the full moon, it soundlessly parted, slipping back upon itself, revealing a gloomy, rain-filled night, and in the near distance, they saw the broken wall of what once had been the southern wing of the broken Crown of Havamal. The silence was so profound, Bear and Otter thought at first they were looking upon another vision such as they had seen in the pool of the keeper of Coda, but the sudden flash and report of a rifle and hurried commands broke the stillness, and from the ruined walls, many rifles blazed into noisy answer, then fell silent once more.

"That must be where Greyfax and Dwarf are," whispered

Bear. "But how can we reach them? We can't go back the way we came, and I don't see how we can get out of here without a nasty fall."

"There must be some door, Bear, unless they were all bird kind that used this room."

"Wizards may have no use for doors and such, but bears and otters most certainly do, and I don't have a fancy for flying. It seems we've gotten away from one trap to land in another," Bear snorted. "And I don't expect to be so lucky this time."

Otter had scampered about the tall chamber as Bear spoke, feeling the walls and knocking to check the thickness. Every place seemed solid until his tiny paw sounded a thin note below the quarter trine window, and even before he could call to Bear of his discovery, a high, round-arched doorway had appeared in the unbroken face of the wall, and beyond it, Otter saw what once must have been a broad wall with a pathway on top, but which now lay jagged and tumbled, leading away toward where they had heard the rifle fire.

"Bear, quick, I've found a way." He turned to where a moment before the door had stood open upon the night outside, but all was as solid as before. Unbelieving, and hearing Bear's stern reproach, he again touched the wall, and as before the doorway appeared before him. He removed his paw, and after a few moments, the archway disappeared again.

"It is here, Bear. You have to touch the wall here, and it opens."

Bear came up behind Otter, and stood sullenly.

"A wizard has funny door handles then, if they wait upon an otter to open their way."

"Then you do it," said Otter, guiding Bear's hand to the wall. At his touch, the archway again mysteriously opened, then after a pause, vanished.

"See, Bear, it works for you, too."

Bear looked quizzically at his arm.

"By the sacred king, I've got a wizard's paw," he said in a pleased voice.

"Whatever sort of paw you've got, let's find Greyfax and Dwarf. I don't like the looks of this rain, and I'm afraid something is happening." He fell silent, and faintly at first, then louder, came the muffled thunder of many harsh voices raised in unison. He touched the wall again, and as before the archway appeared. A great rolling tide of voices and gunfire suddenly filled their ears.

"Hurry, we must reach the wall," Bear cried, and leaped forward through the doorway. Otter followed, and in a moment, as they stood trying to discover where they were, the wall closed behind them, and they could only dimly make out its faded, gray face, pocked and marked, and chipped in the dim light of a faint moon that broke momentarily through the wildly scudding clouds.

"Well, now we're for it," groaned Bear, facing in the direction of the battle below them.

The pale Sycle moon passed behind a darker mass of cloud, and just as they were creeping forward from the shadow of the tower, two gaunt black shapes landed heavily a few feet before them, and with a snarling hiss, loped away on short, gnarled legs.

Bear had not even raised a paw to keep Otter behind him when a volley of gunfire ahead of them broke out, then died suddenly, and a clear, strong voice reached them, in man tongue.

"Here, I think some of them have crawled over the old tower. More men here."

From farther down, a second voice answered. "There's none to spare. You'll have to hold with what you've got."

"Blast 'em to bloody blazes," returned the first voice. "Get on there and drag their stinking hides out of sight. We'll hold with the three of us."

After a few grunts, and the sound of heavy bodies being dragged over loose stones, the voices mumbled in a quieter tone.

"Blast, but these lugs weigh a lot," muttered a low voice.

"They're stuffed with our bunk mates, right enough, curse their black bones forever," answered another. "And they'll be having the lot of us if we don't get help soon."

"Quiet, you two," commanded the man obviously in charge of the small holding party. "They can hear you all the way to Fourthwaite."

After a few more muttered curses, the voices fell silent.

Bear whispered so quietly Otter had to place his ear next to the big fellow's mouth. "We'll have to take our man forms here, or they'll mistake us for Worlughs."

Otter, having forgotten the spell momentarily, answered frantically. "It's slipped my mind, Bear. I can't recall how to do it." He turned, and gazed terrified at a sitting man next to him. Chittering in a low whistle, he jumped back, falling over a large stone, and lay cringing on his back.

"Shhh," warned Bear, too late, for the distinct sound of bolts ramming home told him they had been heard.

Bear picked up the dazed animal in a huge hand, and stuffed the frightened fellow into his cloak.

"Shhh, I'll carry you. Just keep quiet."

Otter's racing mind finally managed to convey to his senses that it was Bear who held him, in his ungainly man form, and he ran over again what he had lost the thread of a moment before, but still the elusive spell escaped him.

Bear called out in a guarded voice, the slow common man tongue heavy and clumsy in his mouth.

"Friend, can you hear me?"

A dull metallic ring of a safety bolt thrown off assured Bear he had been heard.

"I'm seeking Greyfax Grimwald and Melodias Starson."

"Then step closer," came a cold, deadly voice.

"I'm called Bruinlen, and follow the Light. We've just come from Cypher, and have been parted from our companions." Bear advanced slowly, standing straight up.

The same cold voice checked him. "That's far enough. How many with you?"

Bear searched about, at a loss.

"Well, er, myself, rather," but the deadly voice spoke again.

"Step in, but mind don't move too lively."

Suddenly Bear felt the blunt fingers of two rifles painfully against his ribs.

"Now let's have a look at the fellow who travels so late, and in such odd places."

"Whatever else, at least he walks straight," suggested another man, who stood behind Bear.

"I came by way of the Coda Pool, and was upon the road to Melodias," explained Bear quickly, "and we had a fight of it, and Greyfax Grimwald and Dwarf came on to find help, but we were cut off in the tunnels and came through the tower there."

"Get him down to Melodias, but jump to it, we need your rifle here," ordered the cold voice.

"Aye," came the answer, and Bear was marched roughly away down a shallow road worn between the ruins of the old wall that led from the tower to the Crown, and at that moment Otter, tossed about harshly in the cloak of Bear, remembered his spell, and as he spoke it, the thick folds parted, and the stricken guard stared dumbly at the appearance of Otter, now standing before him beside the figure of what must be a powerful wizard indeed, and as they said, a companion of Greyfax Grimwald's.

"Come, friend," coaxed Bear in a companionable tone, "and show us the way to your camp. We mean no harm."

Their guard, unable to find his voice, nodded repeatedly and hurried on, looking over his shoulder every few steps, as if his eyes had surely played him false, and presently the three came into the besieged camp of Melodias Starson.

Wind and Fire

At a small fire near a broken turret stood a group of cloaked men, and one turned at their approach. Bear saw the face of Greyfax Grimwald brighten slightly, and it seemed for a moment to the two friends that he actually smiled, but it passed quickly, replaced by a tired frown.

"I thought maybe you'd find your way, but come. The enemy moves in force against us, and there's much yet to do." Greyfax turned to a figure close by. "Then it's settled, Melodias?"

Firelight played briefly across the face of the figure, revealing a strange likeness of Greyfax. The eyes were the same gray-blue, and troubled as they fell on the two companions. Melodias spoke gently.

"So you are the two who moved our mountain beneath us," he chuckled softly, almost to himself. "Then welcome and many thanks. It caused our friends below a deal of confusion, and gave us much needed time to plan our defense."

Melodias nodded to them, then addressed Greyfax once

more. "Your plan is foolhardy, old friend, but I fear our only hope. Let us not fail." He strode to the edge of the firelight and began speaking in hushed tones to one of his captains, who nodded wearily, saluted, and moved away.

Bear's attention was taken by what appeared to be a portion of thin-sliced potatoes sizzling on a small spit over the fire, and he failed to notice another figure, so short it almost looked to be a smaller shadow cast by the forms about the fire.

"Bear? Otter? Is that really you?" Dwarf's voice was full of wonder.

"Dwarf, if you love me, speak truly now. Is that a piece of food there on the fire, or have I grown pipe dreams in my poor starved, weakened state?"

"By the dwarflord's whiskers," huffed Broco. "You'll be the end of us yet, you lump of a rug, and even in that shape you appear to have a hollow leg." Dwarf stumped to the fire and brought plates of the hot potatoes for his friends.

"And if I weren't so glad to see you, I'd say well met, stomach, and think myself rid of a gangling pair of loafers that are grumbling about when there's important work afoot."

Dwarf glared ferociously at them a moment, then handed the steaming dishes to them, and went on in a softer tone. "But Greyfax has been worried sick, and tries not to let on. He was on his way just now with some of Melodias' men to see if they could find you in the tunnels."

Bear stopped in the middle of chewing and stared at Dwarf. "You mean he was coming himself?" he spluttered, mouth full.

"That's what he told Melodias, and he said there were some things left that even he and Melodias couldn't do."

"Now what could be done that they couldn't do?" broke in Otter. "I couldn't even remember the spell Froghorn taught us to get into this silly form."

Broco stood back, and looked closely at his two friends. "I'll admit you two do look a bit funny that way, but I guess it serves as well to go about like that here. I've been stared at more since we arrived than ever a dwarflord was, and I can't say I take it lightly." Dwarf huffed a bit. "And some lout kept wanting to buy my hat, but he changed his tune quick enough when Greyfax scolded him."

An angry burst of rifle fire drowned out their voices, and a flurry of hurried movement about the camp announced a new attack.

Greyfax appeared from the shadows beyond the fire, and motioned them quickly to him.

"Quickly now, we have little time. You three must keep close to me from here on, and do exactly as I say. No matter what I do, or what you think you see, you must keep close, even if I tell you to leave me. You must lock hands, and on no account touch me, and pay no heed to anything about you. When it's over, you shall know well enough."

"How shall we know that?" began Otter, but Greyfax had turned and hurried off, waving them to follow. They ran to catch up, and the wizard spoke quickly over his shoulder as they arrived beside him.

"Return to your own forms, you two, and hurry. There must be no spells lingering about you now."

And even as Bear and Otter repeated their rituals and returned to their natural forms, a faint ring of light began to grow around the wizard, and as they watched, his form slowly vanished, to be replaced by a shimmering halo of golden white light that blinded them, and hurriedly joining paw and hand, they ringed the spot where the wizard had been, and soon they were swallowed in a blinding sheet of golden fire, and spun wildly upward at such a rate they almost lost hold of each other, and a blue wind whistled over them with a terrifying blast, and from somewhere a mighty voice called out for Dwarf to give forth his Secret, and in a very different tone than Bear or Otter had ever heard, Broco called out in an odd way, then began to hum, softly first, then louder still, until the song was carried upon the very rushing wind and light and song were joined in a blazing, burning heat, still faster, and the sky cracked and opened, and the spinning cyclone of sound and light touched the lowering edge of the black cloud that hovered above Havamal, and from it leaped great icy green fingers of jagged lightning, flashing wickedly above sky and earth alike, and peals of thunder roared and walked across the troubled heavens until those below thought surely the end of all was upon them.

General Greymouse, miles away, felt, rather than heard, the tempestuous war storm that boiled and rolled over the Crown, and pacing uneasily about his camp at Thirdwaite, kept peering anxiously away in the direction of Melodias Starson's armies, bending his vision toward some sign of their fate, but the darkness rolled on unbroken, and his visions were all troubled with nothing but a malevolent dark cloud that erupted constantly in ugly tentacles of greenish lightning that hammered unceasingly into a tall mountain.

Froghorn, away beyond Calix Stay, was suddenly troubled with a startlingly clear vision of Greyfax locked in deadly combat with a towering gray-black mist-shrouded malignant form, and coming out of his trance-like state, he hurried off to seek Urien Typhon and his newly gathered army to begin their move.

Without doubt, he was sure it had been a call for help from Greyfax from the embattled Crown, and a more desperate need, Froghorn knew, his friend had never known before, through all the dangers they had passed, and knew also that no moment was to be lost if he were to be in time to aid Greyfax in his last desperate hour as he struggled with no other than Doraki himself, Dorini's malicious, powerful underlord.

Across the Meadows of the Sun, not far from where the three friends had dwelled of old, a great war horn now blew, full and long, and the rattle of a great elfin army gathering shattered the peaceful air, as in the first beginnings of an age-less, unbroken lifetime.

The black plague of war fires had crept at last like grim iron smoke even to the very havens across Calix Stay, and as Faragon Fairingay led the great elfin hosts of Urien Typhon across the boiling waters, the River rose higher still in a deadly flaming white mist, and touched all those there with a terrible silver mantle that gleamed like dagger blades in the waning dusk of Atlanton Earth.

Star of Windameir

Agrim stillness settled upon the Crown, and the frail trine moon cast a sliver of ghostly light over the mountain slope, and the gray rain that had soaked the earth into a black quagmire now wavered, then ceased, and a cold damp wind sprang up from the north, blowing away the scattered battle fires, and all fell into deeper shadows.

Both armies remained restlessly quiet, undecided to strike, and all eyes were upon the strange glow that whirled in circular motions at the very peak of Havamal.

When the three friends had come to their senses after the numbing, brilliant cyclone of light, they looked about them dumbly for a moment, trying to discover their present predicament, and their hold upon each other tightened impulsively when they saw before them in their circle of hands a great, bloodred stone that hummed in a toneless fashion and upon which sat the deep pearl-colored vision of the Arkenchest, giving off the faintest breath of life, pulsing brighter, then dimming, as if resting. Greyfax was nowhere in sight.

Directly over Dwarf's head, a yellowish green mist began to grow, and a vaporous, cruelly smiling face appeared in the foul-smelling air, and Broco, upon seeing it, gave a long, high wail, and his hands almost tore loose from Bear and Otter's grasp.

The two animals, petrified by this malignant, wicked presence, clung tighter to Dwarf, and stood shivering, repeating the wizard's name, and wondering why they had been so treacherously deserted.

"So we meet again, Master Dwarf," sneered a bone-chilling, icy breath from the dark haze. "I have long sought you over Atlanton Earth to entreat you to return to our most generous hospitality. It seems you left in rather a hurry the last visit you so kindly paid us." A shrieking gale of frosted, snow-blown wind froze the animals' hearts within them, and a cold hand clutched Dwarf, reopening the terror of the memory of his capture, and before him spread the vast frozen palace again, and his mind filled with the numbness of death.

Broco's eyes met the black holes that were sunken in the yellowish face, and a great desire to sleep crept heavily into his limbs, and he tried to withdraw his hands from his friends.

"No. Dwarf, don't let go," came Otter's small, trembling voice, and he could barely speak, so heavy was the flying frozen snow that swirled about them, and the chilling wind tried to crush his breath, but the tiny animal grasped Broco's hand harder, and held tightly on.

"We have not forgotten you, my small friend," boomed the ghastly voice, "nor has Cakgor had the delicacy of bear flesh since he devoured that feeble, wretched offspring of Borim Bruinthor upon the fields near Grimm Crossing." A shivering splinter of ugly laughter rattled like bones breaking, and the wind howled and shrieked about the three helpless figures. From far away, a greater sound arose, of trees groaning at their roots, and seas lashed in battering fury, and a thousand shrieking wings tore the very air from lungs and heart alike.

"Now Cakgor shall have his revenge upon you. Harken his arrival." The toneless, creaking voice rose into a horrible burst of nameless sounds in a tongue so vile it hurt the ears of the three shuddering comrades, and they watched transfixed as a whirling, oozing greenish cloud tipped with yellow wings came rushing toward them, and the mist-shrouded figure began to grow clearer, and they felt the dreadful stare knife through them, and once more came a peal of fiendish laughter, like frozen leaves rattling against an icy gale.

The spectral mist shape began to grow and move forward, and two gaunt black claws came forth, long, curved talons bared in a deathly pale yellow-glowing light, and unable to move or cry out, the friends watched helplessly as those grisly fists reached between them for the Arkenchest, unprotected and lost, lying openly upon the bloodred stone.

As the foul claws touched the chest, the stone turned a deeper, burning red, and with a flashing blast of white-hot light that turned the blackness into dazzling day, an orb of golden, sparkling stars spun high up into the air, whirling faster until they appeared as a circle drawn upon the sky, and crashing with a suddenness from the Arkenchest, a blazing sword of silver cleaved the misshapen claws from the body of the mist form, and the terrible voice of Greyfax Grimwald rang out like doom over the Crown of Havamal.

"Thy heart in darkness, fallen sun
　　cries out with many deeds undone.
But blazing star of Windameir
　　commands thy shriveled soul appear.
And touching yet this Chest of Light
I say thee now
　　　Thy life take flight."

And a blistering sheet of flames consumed the mountain and sky, and with a deafening shriek, the dark mist shape burst into a burning, roaring pyre of twisting gray smoke, and the very air became like molten liquid fire, and the fur of the animals was singed, and Dwarf's hat smoldered dangerously on his head, and the Worlughs and Gorgolacs below who were near the pickets of Melodias Starson stumbled madly, jostling each other and falling, their yellow dirty eyes now no more than smoking, empty sockets.

Cakgor, crazed with defeat and rage, raised his deadly, howling voice, and in a single bite devoured with his cruel, dripping, icy jaws a dozen of the stunned defenders, and reeling away savagely, fled the unbearable blazing light, carrying with him the black disembodied soul that was Doraki, and at last all grew still, and the dazzling light and fires diminished, then dimmed altogether, and once more only the pale trine moon showed over the peak of the dark mountain, and Bear and Otter at last lifted their heads from the earth where they'd fallen, and saw the silent, motionless figure of the wizard half covering the shuddering, sobbing Dwarf.

Below, the sound of rifle fire began again, but farther away now, and much diminished. Melodias Starson formed his

straggling, exhausted forces together, and set out to counterattack the dispirited but still stubborn Ashgnazi Worlughs and
the Gorgolac forces of Doraki.

Soon the only figures left at the Crown of Havamal were
the two animals, the unmoving wizard, and the unconscious
Dwarf, who yet struggled deep inside himself with the icy,
terrifying hand that tried to touch his racing heart.

The Arkenchest Lost

"Here, Otter, quickly," snapped Bear, picking up the cold hand of the wizard and stroking it. "Fetch some water, will you, or a cloak. His hands are like ice."

Otter ran frantically about, whistling and chittering in his effort to be three places at once. He half started back to the small fire in the now empty camp, then whirled to return to where Bear sat beside Greyfax and Dwarf.

"What shall we do, Bear? I don't know where the water is," Otter cried bitterly, looking about hopelessly.

"Then get a cloak, but hurry. I can't feel him breathing," he moaned, leaning close to the wizard's chest.

Otter raced away to where the big fire had been, and searched about for anything that might be used to warm Greyfax, but found nothing. In the hurried counterattack, everything that had been useful had been taken, and only a few sprawling bodies of the slain soldiers of Melodias lay about the broken walls, and Otter could not bring himself to touch them, even for their cloaks. He looked wildly around, and he glimpsed the tall shadow of the tower away behind him, and an idea suddenly struck him. He raced back to Bear.

"Let's take them to the tower, Bear. Maybe being there will help him. It's safe there at least."

Without replying, Bear looked down into the haggard features of the wizard. After a moment he rose, lifting Greyfax as gently as he could, and moved away toward the path that led to the base of the dark tower.

"Stay with Dwarf until I'm back," he said, and disappeared from Otter's sight.

Dwarf lay jerking and moaning, and Otter saw a sheen of cold sweat running down the little man's brow, and his fists clenched convulsively to his chest, as if trying to remove a barbed dagger from his heart. His eyes were wide and glazed, and his mouth formed jumbled words that Otter could not make out.

The little animal lay down beside Dwarf, and tried to shield his friend from the damp wind, and patted his arm with his tiny paws, and spoke reassuringly in Broco's ear, although he felt far from reassured himself.

"Here, here, old fellow, mind you don't pull your cloak open like that, you'll get no end of the sniffles. Bear will be back soon, and we'll have you safe and sound in a cozy place in no time." Otter froze at the sound of a rock clacking, and he strained to catch sight or smell of any intruder, but no other noise followed, and he went back to soothing his senseless friend.

Another sharp sound brought Otter to his feet, a rough stone in his tiny paw.

"Otter," called Bear quietly.

"Here, Bear. You frightened me."

"Let's get Dwarf there. I can't find the way to open the wall, but at least there's part of an old shed of some sort we can shelter in."

Bear picked up the groaning Dwarf, and set off in a shambling trot, followed closely by Otter, who kept glancing uneasily behind him.

They reached the spot where they had left the tower, and there next to it was a half-fallen rock shed overgrown with thick brush. Bear forced aside the hanging limbs and entered a protected place in one corner, and placed Dwarf beside the still figure of Greyfax.

"We'll look about for those dead Worlughs, Otter, for their weapons must still be about somewhere."

Otter, unable to shake his uneasiness, agreed, and they retraced their steps to where they thought the Worlughs had been ambushed, and cast about in the rough stones and thick brush until Bear called out triumphantly.

"I've found one here. And here's the other. They threw their rifles in here with them."

The rotten stench almost gagged Otter, but he crept toward Bear's voice and took the firearm he was handed, dragging it along by the barrel behind him.

"Now we're armed," said Bear, "in case any of those fellows are left about."

"I keep thinking we're not alone here, Bear. Before you came back, I thought I heard something, a footstep, or someone kicking a loose stone."

"It must have been the wind, old fellow. We've had a nasty time of it tonight, and I'm all wound up too, but there can't be anyone left about here. Listen. You can hear Melodias' attack carrying off down there somewhere." Bear indicated with a nod away toward the eastern slope of Havamal.

"I suppose you're right. I hope so. But let's try the tower again. I'd feel safer if we could get back inside there."

"Then let's go, and I'll stand watch over Greyfax and Dwarf. You seem to be more clever about door knobs tonight than I do."

They quickly regained the shed, and Otter went out once more to try to find the opening to the tower.

The cold wind had died down somewhat, and as he stepped near the wall that soared up high above him, another sound caused him to catch his breath and stand motionless. Nothing more than a bush blown by the wind, he thought, trying to convince himself that that surely must be it, and he quickly began running his paws over the rough outer wall of stone before him.

Otter worked his way back and forth across the entire face of the wall without success, and had finally begun to despair when his paw touched a thin ledge a few feet above his head. Hardly daring to breathe, he explored it carefully, and felt a carved surface of some sort that seemed to be fashioned in the shape of a quill or feather. He tried moving it this way and that, but it held firmly in place, and resisted all his efforts, until at last he gave up, and sorely disappointed, moved on. A few feet farther around, another small crevice marked the surface of the wall, and this one held what seemed to be a small key. Otter's heart leapt to his throat, and he violently twisted the carved stone, and jumped up joyfully as a great opening in the dim shape of a tall tree appeared in the wall.

It closed again immediately, but Otter raced back to the rough shelter where Bear kept guard over Greyfax and Dwarf, and heedless of the great clamor he made running, breathlessly broke in upon the startled Bear, who had leveled the barrel of the Worlugh firearm dangerously toward the door, and upon seeing the noisy threat only a clumsy-footed Otter, scolded him severely. "I've almost blown your ears off, you heavy-toed water rat. You'd waken the sleep of a deaf log clumping about like that."

Otter ignored Bear's rebuke, and chittered excitedly. "I've found it, Bear, I've a way inside. There was an old stone key hidden along the lower wall, and it opens a big door." Otter drew breath to go on, but Bear cut him short.

"Then I'll take Greyfax now, but we'll have to leave Dwarf here for the time. Show me this secret place you've found." Bear gently lifted the wizard and went out, Otter close behind.

At the base of the tower, Otter went on before Bear, guiding himself in animal fashion exactly back to where he'd found the stone key sunken into its small recess in the moss-grown wall. He struggled with the key a moment, and stood back as the noiseless doorway appeared, making a deep darkness in the black shadow of night.

Bear hurried forward into the tall opening, placed the wizard carefully down just inside, and motioned Otter to wait while he went to fetch the feverish, delirious Dwarf.

No sooner than Bear's footsteps had been cut off by the soundless closing of the wall, a faint rush of light began to spread in the chamber, and Otter, fearing the worst, darted to Greyfax's side, ears laid back and tiny fangs bared. The raised hackles along his back tingled with fear and anger at once, and he cursed himself soundly for not having inspected the room more closely before Bear's leaving.

A soft chuckle filled the room, a laugh worn with exhaustion, but full of warmth, and the faint light glowed bright, and Melodias Starson stepped from behind a large ivory carven pillar that raised its head dizzily away into the upper darkness.

"As usual, my good Grimwald has chosen his companions wisely. He was most concerned when he feared you had fallen into graver danger than he thought in the old waterway, and of course, he told me Dwarf had long carried one of the Five that he had entrusted to Broco's father ages ago."

"Oh, sir," sputtered Otter, relief washing over him, "what's happened to him? All sorts of lights and noises were going on until I lost my senses, and when it was over, Greyfax was like this. Can you help him?" Otter gazed with growing fear at the unmoving wizard, and it seemed to him all life had fled the gray-cloaked form lying beside him.

"He has had a great battle, my friend, an encounter with the underlord of the Dark Queen, and it has weakened him greatly. But I think we shall soon find him quite his old self again."

"Was that all the lights and noise, sir? And there was a red stone, and a chest, and I seem to remember a great voice, and Dwarf singing, but then a wind came, and that's all I remember until I woke up."

"That was it, my friend. It left the hill ablaze for quite a time. My army is chasing the remnants of the enemy away toward Fourth-waite. Yet I fear their exhaustion is too great to rid us of that dark horde completely." Melodias threw back the hood of his stained cloak with a weary sweep of his hand.

"Now let me have a look at Master Grimwald here."

Melodias knelt beside Greyfax, his eyes suddenly misty and sad.

"Even in this sleep you do not rest, old friend? Do I see you before the Sacred Flame? Such a long journey to make, but how taxed your strength to face the Darkness alone. Or not quite alone."

Melodias held one of Greyfax's cold hands in his own.

At that moment, Bear appeared in the opening, and stood taking in the unexpected presence of the other wizard. Dwarf writhed in torment in his friend's great arms.

"Bring him here, good Bruinlen. Let me see if I can aid the brave fellow." Melodias bade Bear place Dwarf down beside Greyfax, and laid a soothing hand to the little man's forehead.

Dwarf's eyes rolled back, and a great trembling overcame him, and in a harsh fear-choked voice gasped, "The Arkenchest, the Arkenchest," and struggled feebly to his feet.

Bear caught his swaying body and eased him down again, a sudden leaden fear settling upon his heart.

Melodias paled, then looked away. Speaking with his back to them, he asked, "Have you the Chest with you?"

The unbroken silence confirmed his worst fear, that the Arkenchest was gone.

"But we must have left it where we were, Bear. I didn't even think, with Greyfax and Dwarf hurt." Otter wrung his paws, and looked desperately at Melodias.

"It wasn't your fault, Otter. In all that confusion it would be easy enough to misplace yourself. But quickly, we must find it."

Melodias was at the wall in a second, and without making any outward sign or motion, it slid open before the wizard.

"Otter, you stay here with them," he said, nodding toward the two figures on the floor, and to Bear, he beckoned with a short movement of his hand.

Before Otter could protest or move, he was left alone in the sudden darkness of the tall chamber.

A Desperate Errand

Melodias drew Bear beside him. "Now, where was it you last saw the Chest?"

Bear, casting about with his nose, quickly discovered the way he and Otter had come.

"This way, sir. It's not far."

Bear shuffled away on all fours, keeping his muzzle close to the ground. After a few minutes, he raised his great head in puzzlement.

"This is where we circled Greyfax right enough, but there's fresh man scent here now."

A cone of light at the end of the wizard's arm illuminated the ground, then as quickly as it had come, was gone.

"And whoever left that man scent has the Arkenchest. We must be quick, Bear. Whoever he is, he can't have much of a start."

"But if it's a man, he surely must be one of your own, sir. It's not a Worlugh, nor a Gorgolac."

"There's vile things that grow in even the fairest gardens,

my friend, and regretfully there are those yet in my armies that border upon evil ways. I've had my eye upon such men, who joined me from the far north, near the Roaring Sea. They've long been nearest Dorini's sway, and they seem to be most easily led into wickedness." Melodias started away in a downward direction, toward where far away now, and very faintly, the sound of battle went on. "Now range ahead, stout Bear, and see if your sturdy legs can catch us up our thief."

And Bear, in his silent swiftness, flew forth into the night in pursuit of the fleeing man who now held the Arkenchest, and great muzzle near the earth, sought unerringly the fresh spoor that rapidly grew stronger, until at the very bottom of the hill, he could hear the crashing feet of the man, who ran now, knowing he was found out.

A volley of rifle fire rang out, and a shriek of pain torn from dying lungs followed it, and harsh, guttural voices dully reached Bear's ears. He drew up where he had checked his forward rush, and listened, his heart pounding in his throat.

"Here's us a nice roast, and us was thinking to has no fresh meat tonight."

"He's a fat one, ain't he. Give me a gnaw on his leg there. I's hungry enough to bolt two of 'em." Great noisy smacking and chewing reached Bear, sickened and frightened in his concealment.

After a time, a heavy, drooling voice snarled.

"Tie him to your lazy back, Rag, we's got to get away from this cursed hill, or us will be hunted like dogs by daylight. We can roast what's left of him over a safe fire as soon as us is far from here." More growls and oaths, then the sound of heavy-shod feet noisily running reached Bear.

He turned, and was upon the point of returning to the wizard when Melodias appeared beside him.

"I heard, Bear. Ashgnazi stragglers that my men have missed." Melodias drove a fist into the palm of his hand. "What dark fortune smiles on us tonight, even in brilliant victory." He stood looking away after the retreating Worlugh ambushers, and fell into a profound silence that Bear dared not interrupt.

Reaching a decision, Melodias placed a hand on Bear's shoulder.

"We must hurry and bring Otter here. Then you two must follow to see where they make for. I shall tend to Dwarf and Greyfax, and send help after you as soon as it is daylight. I don't think there is any place for them to get through our lines without detection, but if they have a chance to hide, it might take days to hunt them out."

Melodias handed Bear a small stone, of a deep bluish green.

"You may mark your way with this, for it leaves a bright reflection even in the dark, and I'll warn my men to look for it."

Bear took the sparkling stone, then looked at the wizard in embarrassment.

"I've got no pockets in my fur, sir. And, pardon my asking, but isn't there some way you could get the Chest back? I mean, it seems like you could do something magical, put some sort of spell on them?"

Melodias took the stone back with a small laugh.

"No, my friend, there's no spell that I or any other of the

Circle can work against this moment. To draw attention un-
necessarily now would be inviting disaster, and we are all
weakened by this battle. So you must go, in your own forms,
for any magic at all will warn our thief someone is following.
Just make as broad a trail as possible, so that my men may
follow."

"Then I shall make stone cairns along our way, stacked
high enough to see," explained Bear, "or sticks to point our
direction."

"Good. Then let's be on our way now, for we have not
much time before dayfall."

They hurried back to the tower, and found Otter sitting
morosely between Greyfax and Dwarf, a tiny paw on each of
his friend's arms. He jumped up at their entry.

"I thought something must have happened," he scolded.
"Did you find the Chest?"

"We found it gone," said Melodias, "stolen by one of my
own, then taken by a band of Worlugh stragglers. They have
it now, but don't know it, or I hope not. You and Bear must
follow them, and keep them within sight until I can send some
of my men to take them."

Otter looked at Bear drearily.

"They've not gone far, Otter. I don't think they'll dare to
go about in daylight, and it's almost dawn now," Bear en-
couraged. "Then we can get a bite, and a nap, too."

"I could use both easily," agreed Otter. "But I don't look
forward to earning them by following those nasty fellows
about in the dark." He looked back at Greyfax and Dwarf.
"Will they be all right here, sir? I thought it was the same
room at first, but it's different than where we were. The other

had all sorts of moons and star lamps in it, and this one is so dark."

"You were in the solarium then," said Melodias. "Not many, except those of the Council, have ever set foot inside that chamber. In better times of old, the Elders could go there to meditate, and look upon the fields of Windameir. It was also a window across Atlanton Earth."

"Then what is this room, sir?" asked Bear, hoping to delay their departure for a while, until the sun should rise.

"This was the chamber of the Spirits," said Melodias, kneeling over Greyfax solemnly. "But now you must go, before they leave their tracks cold. I'll tend to these two here, and have help sent as soon as I can find the men."

"Let's go, Bear. If I don't move soon, I shall fall asleep on my nose."

"Should we take arms, sir?" asked Bear, shuddering at the thought of meeting with the ugly Worlughs in the dark.

"You shouldn't go so close as to need them, Bruinlen. Don't alert them, or they might possibly be driven to escape. If they think they're safe, they most likely will hide out for a day or two in hopes of more loot or meat. No, I think carrying weapons would only slow you."

With no further cause to delay, the two animals reluctantly bade Melodias goodbye, and cast worried gazes upon the silent forms upon the floor.

"They shall be as good as well by the time you see them next," assured the wizard, taking from his cloak a small, sculptured vial that he opened and placed between Greyfax and Dwarf, and the air seemed to sweeten, and the weariness that had borne heavily upon the two animals seemed to

lighten, and they turned to their errand with hearts eased and
hopes returning.

At the bottom of the hill they found the place where the
man had been ambushed, and after searching about on a
chance the Arkenchest might have been dropped, Bear and
Otter set off grimly, following the broad, smelly swath of a
trail the Worlughs left behind them, and very soon they found
themselves a great distance away from Havamal and the
Crown, among low shrubs and broken gullies on the lower
ground.

All along the way they had come were piles of stone, or
sticks marking their trail, and it led off toward Thirdwaite,
many miles to the east, where General Greymouse waited
with his armies.

As deformed as the Worlughs were, they traveled very
swiftly when need arose, and by daylight, the old summer
palace was no more than a tiny dot upon the peak of the
distant mountain.

The Light Begins To Dim

Once More By Horseback

Gradually the sweet-smelling incense from Melodias Starson's vial brought Dwarf to a barely perceptible awareness of his surroundings, and he sat stiffly up, his arms clasped closely to his body, and shivering violently.

Melodias sat upon the floor by Greyfax's side, and so still and withdrawn were they, Dwarf thought them both asleep, until Melodias looked up at him at length, and a weary smile crept about his drawn mouth.

"Well, my friend, so you have wakened?" He brought forth another small flask from his cloak, and handed it to Dwarf, who took it with trembling hands.

"Drink up, it will warm the chill you feel. From all I've heard, it's not the first time you've felt that icy breath, and indeed, that you escaped from the very Palace of Ice."

"That's not so much to recommend me," stammered Dwarf. "But what's happened to Greyfax? Does he sleep?"

"Not sleep exactly," explained Melodias, "but something

very like it. He has used up much of his strength, and now must restore himself."

Feeling somewhat better, Dwarf looked wildly around him.

"And Bear and Otter? Are they safe?"

"Quite safe, and upon an errand at the moment. They brought you here."

"What of the battle?" asked Dwarf, realizing for the first time Melodias was not with his armies.

"It goes well. We have won back Havamal and Hel, and my men are pursuing what is left of the enemy toward Fourth-waite. The Light has held for the moment."

"Then reinforcements arrived from General Greymouse? Or from some other quarter?"

"Only Greyfax, and you, and the two animals. And the presence of the Chest has carried the day."

Broco shook his head in disbelief.

"Yet we've still many ends to make before we rest. The Arkenchest has been captured by a band of straggling Ash-gnazi, although I doubt they know it. It is to mark the trail of those marauders that Bear and Otter have gone."

"Alone?" quizzed Dwarf.

"I've instructed them only to follow carefully, my good fellow. They shall wait on my men to capture the Chest back."

"Will you go also?"

"I must stay with Greyfax for the time. I shall send you to bear the Chest back here to me."

Dwarf rose on unsteady legs.

"Then I must find my hat, and a weapon." He looked about in a puzzled manner. "But where are we now?"

"Come, I'll show you the door," said Melodias, and spoke

a low command, upon which the tall, slender shape of a blooming tree opened in the wall. Outside, the first hint of sunrise turned the now scattered clouds a faint reddish pink, and a fair wind came with the light, and the Crown was silent and empty.

Hurrying out, Dwarf quickly found his hat, somewhat rumpled and dirty, but otherwise unharmed, and after another hasty search, armed himself with a stout cudgel of strong green wood.

A weak, watery light began to grow, and Dwarf looked about the land below, hoping to see Bear and Otter returning, but the sparse scene remained motionless, and no living thing stirred in any direction.

"I hope the silly asses have sense enough to find their way here again," mumbled Broco aloud, trying to quiet his fears that his friends were in grave danger. "They wouldn't be much more than mincemeat if they ran into that gruesome beast again." Dwarf trembled over his body remembering their narrow escape, and he had to sit down to steady his legs.

"But there's nothing for it. We must win back the Chest before it's discovered. What foul fortune has filled our lives since we crossed Calix Stay. Maybe better that I should have come alone, for all the grief and injuries I have caused those two." Dwarf's eyes clouded, and a single tear slid down his cheek onto the hand that held his chin.

"Oh gribbit, what gibberish am I spouting," he bravely huffed. "Sitting here like a ninny when I should be on my way to aid them. Come, Dwarf, bottle-headed lame-brain, let's find Melodias and be off where we may do some good,

instead of sunning ourselves like a worthless sack of saw-
dust."

He walked briskly back to the tower, a spring in his step,
and soon was pounding on the outer wall to be allowed once
more inside.

Broco thought he heard the barely audible low whinny of
a horse somewhere close by, and fell back speechless when
the tree-shaped archway appeared, filled by the presence of
Froghorn Fairingay astride the noble Pe'lon.

"Froghorn," gasped Dwarf in astonishment. "I thought you
were across the River."

Froghorn dismounted, laughing in his easy way. "I'm forever amazed by meeting you in the most untoward places, old
friend, since I first kept my watch on you in your old valley.
But all as well, for Melodias has told me Bear and Otter are
on the trail of some Worlugh band that has captured the Chest,
and he has no men at the moment who are rested enough to
give chase, so you shall ride behind me, and we'll soon put
things aright."

Dwarf balked at the thought of going horseback again, and
the old bruises and aches reminded him of his unhorsemanlike
ways.

"If it's all the same, sir," said Dwarf testily, "I shall go on
my own two feet. Stirrups weren't made to the tastes of dwarfish folk."

Froghorn laughed, and clapped a hand on Pe'lon's saddle.
"You've ridden once on my good steed, but you knew it not,
and not a bump or jolt did he give you, so gentle his step.
You'll find him quite apart from other mounts in that respect."

Pe'lon nudged Froghorn playfully, chastising his master for his speech.

"And we must make all speed, for time is short, and our friends will be weary and hungry."

Froghorn swung smoothly into the soft saddle, and held out a hand to aid Dwarf up, and after a clumsy scramble, and many dwarf oaths, Broco sat unsteadily behind the young wizard.

Melodias placed a hand on Froghorn's tall riding boot, and pointed out the direction which the two animals had taken.

"They were to leave markers to follow, so I doubt not you'll find the way easily enough. I shall remain here for the time with Grimwald, and regroup my army when they return."

"I've left Urien Typhon with his elves at Fourthwaite, ready to strike those who may escape your men, or to go to the aid of Greymouse, should the need arise. Tyron the Green is poised beyond Calix Stay, and I have his oath he'll come if need be. Barring any ill chance, we should be with you again sometime tonight." Froghorn spoke a low word to Pe'lon, and the mighty horse leapt forward.

Dwarf, clinging on behind with eyes tightly closed and hands clenched in Froghorn's cloak, hardly noticed the move, and not thinking them gone, called out in a fear-tightened voice, "If I must go on this beast, then let's be on with it, otherwise I'll get down and walk."

Feeling the tumbling laughter shaking Froghorn's sides, Broco opened his eyes and was on the point of huffing when he saw nothing about him but the sliding, careening sky and flashes of light that made his heart come to his throat, and he redoubled his grip upon the wizard and shut his eyes quickly to avoid a fainting feeling that welled inside him.

"We shall be there soon, Master Dwarf, and you can go about as you seem to wish quick enough. Now loose your hug a bit, or I shall collapse. Pe'lon won't drop you."

Dwarf, paying no attention, hung grimly on, and the flashing light and wind rustled swiftly about the speeding, great horse, until after what seemed to Broco long hours, Froghorn spoke over his shoulder.

"They're there below. You may ease your dwarf vise now. If you hug a Worlugh as you do me, no wonder the foul fellows loathe all your kind."

Without a sound or sudden motion, Pe'lon gently slowed, and came to a halt a few feet from the terrified animals, cowering in a low thicket of stunted trees.

The Pace Quickens

After pulling his hat squarely down over his brow, Broco commenced the job of getting down from his high seat. Froghorn offered a guiding hand, which the little man refused, but after dangling with his short legs kicking, and feeling Pe'lon becoming nervous at having pointed boots so close to his flank, he had to give in and be handed down by the wizard.

"That's a mighty, powerful beast you have, sir, but built for those with knees that reach up a bit higher than mine," Dwarf grumbled, straightening his hat and rearranging his cloak, paying no attention to the stunned animals, who gaped wide-eyed at the unexpected arrival.

"And you two," puffed Broco, "lie napping when you're sent to track the Chest, and I guess you'd be sleeping until noon if there weren't someone about to bounce your heads occasionally."

An angry buzzing sound cracked across the thicket, and Pe'lon reared high in the air, his great mane flying behind him. Froghorn turned him, and leapt a low hedge at a run, disappearing from sight. The report of the rifle echoed dully over the small clearing where the three crouched down behind a loose pile of stones.

"They're just on the other side of the thicket, Dwarf. They must have heard you," whispered Bear.

"Well, no matter," returned Dwarf. "Froghorn will deal with them soon enough."

Confused shouts and curses rang out from the Worlughs' direction, and shots hurriedly fired, then a silence crept over the enemy camp.

"You can come along now," called Froghorn. "But hurry, we must make a search."

Dwarf led the way, and the three friends entered the clearing where the seven Worlughs were sprawled as they had fallen, slain by the terrible strokes of Froghorn's elfin blade and Pe'lon's deadly hooves.

"That was quick work," said Otter, hesitating as he looked at the fierce, murderous faces, dumb with hatred, and fangs bared.

"They're having a quick nap," answered Froghorn, searching about the ground for the slain soldier of Melodias and finding him at length, horribly mutilated and headless, half buried by firewood in a crudely dug pit.

"They must have found it," he went on grimly, giving up the grisly task of searching the remains of the torn body. He went next to one of the fallen, misshapen warriors, and ran his hand over the area of the short tunic that held the pockets. He quickly searched about, then went to the next, and on until all the slain Worlughs had been felt, and patted, and gone over thoroughly, to no avail, for the Chest was not among them.

The four then scoured the ground about the area, but that too proved futile, until Otter, at some distance from the others, cried out in a sharp voice.

"Look here. There's tracks that lead off from here, and they're not too old. Three of them have gotten away."

There in the hard earth were the prints of heavy boots, two sets of different sizes, very broad and flat, and a third that showed its owner to have one foot larger than the other, and in the smaller print, a distinct mark, like that of a broken tusk, showed clearly in a dozen or more places. From the length between prints, they decided the Worlughs had been running, and the trail headed off in the direction of the Cross.

"Then one of these fine fellows has it," said Dwarf, following the trail with his eyes, his hand shading them from the sun. "And from the looks of it, they know we're on to them. They won't be going slow now until they're sure they're safely beyond our reach."

Froghorn had taken down a small cloth bag from Pe'lon's saddle, and handed it to Bear.

"Here's food enough for a week's journey, and a flask of water from beyond Calix Stay. That will keep you until I return. I must search on ahead now, and warn Greymouse to be alert for enemy stragglers trying to reach the Dragur Wood by way of Thirdwaite."

"What about us?" questioned Bear, feeling very uneasy.

"Take their arms, and follow on by foot, as quickly as you may. Armed, I don't doubt the three of you are more than a match for some frightened Worlughs. And they are heading toward Greymouse, which is where you may as well make for now."

Froghorn raised a hand, and speaking in the tongue of Windameir, called out a sacred sign of the Fifth Circle.

"To Greymouse?" chittered Otter, ill humor coming into his voice. "Aren't we returning to Melodias?"

"Not yet, my friend. You must still use those wonderful noses a bit longer, in case I don't happen across our jolly friends who've escaped us. And you can follow on until you reach Thirdwaite, and rejoin me there."

"That's leagues and leagues, and we've only food for seven days," complained Bear uncertainly.

"It's five days' marching to Thirdwaite, three, if you keep up with those Worlughs. They won't be crawling, since they've been discovered. And in any event they'll likely be caught up by our armies before they go too far. But it's important that you don't let some unforeseen catastrophe befall them without being there to recover the Chest. So if I don't find them first, it's urgent you be there to search them."

Otter sat down wearily.

"I guess I must have walked off a layer or two of my paws before this, but it seems I shall have to wear them down some more before long."

"Come, old softfoot, you can ride awhile with me," soothed Bear. "I guess your kind tire less quickly in water of some sort."

"Now if *that* were the case, I should be carrying your big hide after a while." Otter cheered visibly at the thought of riding on Bear's broad back.

"You might just as well come up, too," said Bear, looking

at Dwarf. "The two of you won't break me, and it'll be easier not having to wait upon short legs, however sturdy they might prove to be."

"Harrumph, I dare say I'd rather go about on short limbs than have an empty head," shot Dwarf, slightly huffed.

"Enough, enough," laughed the wizard. "While we debate the merits of different anatomies, the Chest is stolen farther from us. Let us use whatever means we possess to recapture it, then we can argue these points over a safe fire, with time enough to enjoy its subtle trappings."

Froghorn gently touched Pe'lon's mane, and the great horse reared, then vanished, so sudden was the swiftness of his flight.

Surprised at the disappearance of Froghorn, Dwarf turned sullenly to Bear.

"I've come to think these fellows have no manners in their partings," he said sulkily. "Every time I find something in question, they seem to be losing their hats getting away."

"I think he was just worried, Dwarf, with the Chest gone, and all. He has much upon his mind of late," Otter gazed away toward the high noon sun.

"I've much upon mine, too," snapped Dwarf testily. "And that's including more than my hat."

Broco followed the direction of the Worlughs' retreat with his glance. "How in the name of High Dwarfdom are we ever going to catch those louts, and what shall we do when we've done it?" Dwarf left the question dangling, unanswered in the growing heat of the spiritless countryside.

Bear tested a savage expression on Otter, his great jaws

wide and menacing. "Eekk, but that should frighten the wits out of them, I'll wager."

"Oh, Bear, you silly ass, they're Worlughs, and I don't doubt but that they would look on that as a smile, from what they're used to." Otter trembled at the thought of what the Worlughs must look like to each other.

Broco stamped his foot loudly. "Here you go, you two, thinking about more nonsense. Whatever they're used to or not, they can move more quickly than three trees rooted in the shade, and that's exactly where we'll be this time tomorrow, our legs grown to these rocks, if we don't make a start. Now, let's pick up these weapons and get on with it." Dwarf hastily slung a firearm on his back, then smashed the remaining guns with a rock.

"Now, here, Bear, give me a hand up."

Effortlessly, the big animal lowered himself and took Dwarf and Otter upon his strong back, and started off at a galloping trot that soon had Broco hanging wildly onto his neck, and Otter clinging desperately to the seat of the little man's pants.

And Froghorn, racing away farther and farther into a cloudless sky, cursed himself soundly, and urged Pe'lon on until all space and time were but a blur, and the young Master crossed over into the fields of the Meadows of the Sun, where, as Urien Typhon had told him in the unbroken waves of his thoughts, Tyron the Green was preparing to move his armies across Calix Stay, to attack the Darkness without word from the Circle.

And to Froghorn's dismay, Tyron had raised the tender topic of the Secret that he held, and let it be known that as long as he held it, no hand of the Circle could move against him, unless he willingly surrendered it. Which, as Urien Typhon assured the young Master, he had no intention of doing.

So Froghorn had left the three friends to pursue the Chest while he went on to see what must be done with this new danger which threatened the very heart of the Circle.

Donark

Loping along at a fierce pace, the three Worlugh warriors began to see signs of others, also fleeing, discarded rifles or battle helms, dark, stained tunics and stabbing spears, and soon they were in a crowd of a hundred or more Gorgolacs, who were all that remained of Donark's vicious army. At the van of this straggling mob galloped Donark himself, the low, cruel brow glaring fitfully toward the western sun, cold eyes glowing with hatred for the day and the light that gave their presence away to the pursuers who so ruthlessly stalked their tracks.

A scout came up breathless beside him, and told him of the three Worlughs who ran at the very tail of the confused formation. The intense distrust of the Worlughs broke forth in a fiery announcement that they should be slain and left, for it was to the Worlugh chieftain that Donark laid their defeat, for it had been Thiazi whose lines had broken, allowing the detestable man soldiers to flank him and drive him from the heights of Havamal. So near victory, yet now so forever lost.

It had been the first battle of combined units fighting side by side, and turned out as Donark had feared. Worlughs were an inferior, ugly lot, and even the best of the Ashgnazi only barely equal to one of his own worst warriors.

"When we take our rest break, slay them," ordered Donark, the thick, hissing sound of their tongue bitten off sharply. The grinning Gorgolac sergeant fell back to pass the order down.

At last, the gray dusk began to settle, the Gorgolac leader signaled a halt, and soon heavy breathing was all that could be discerned of the presence of the Gorgolac survivors.

The grizzled form of the sergeant slid next to Donark. "They is suspicious of us," he laughed grimly. "Won't sleep without leaving one of them as watch."

Donark removed the black battle helm with its blood-colored plume and began to pour an ugly, foul-smelling liquid into it.

"Treat them nice, give them meat. They'll have to sleep sometime."

"Ugly, foul things, them sorts. I doesn't know why they sent them anyhows. Black hearts and yellow gizzards they is."

Donark lifted the helmet to his wide, curling lips and drank noisily, slurping down the smoky liquid fire of the harsh drink, and wiping his slack mouth, gurgled deep in his throat. "No firearms. I think someone is close behind us."

"They is thickheaded. I don't knows about cracking their skulls, but we has got sharp blades to stick their filthy hides with." The sergeant pulled out a long, curved dull yellow knife from his belt, and ran a stubby finger down its blade. "It's better to stick those foul man beasts with this heart-finder. The hone is lost if it ain't drinking blood. I is going to tickle their ribs with this afore this night's out." Clucking harshly to himself, the Gorgolac left.

Donark stood and looked away in the direction they had come. There was no movement to be seen, but he knew they were followed closely. He half thought of sending out an ambush to surprise whoever it was, then decided against it. Whatever happened, he had a hundred chosen men beside him, the best of his command, and they would soon be safe enough in the Dragur Wood. They would wait there for the reinforcements coming up from the swamps. If they persisted in following into the dark woods, they'd find a nasty surprise, he thought savagely, and provide a stew for the hungry soldiers.

A sharp scuffle jerked him from his pleasant line of thought. Grunts and low snarls broke over the concealed encampment, and he hurried to the clump of dark thicket where the three Worlughs had crawled to rest.

Two shots in rapid succession exploded through the gathering darkness, followed by a howl of outrage and pain, and a mortally wounded Gorgolac crashed toward him out of the stunted trees, thick bluish blood pouring from his chest and twisted lips.

Donark unslung his blunt firearm and hurried forward. Another shriek raised itself to a long, harsh, rattling sound, and as he rushed into the concealment of the trees, he saw that two of the Worlughs had leapt back to back, holding at bay a dozen of his soldiers. No one moved as he stalked up to the sergeant, who held the dripping blade of his wicked, curved knife threateningly before him.

Recognizing Donark, one of the Worlughs whined in a harsh whisper.

"We's done no harm to these here, and they's cut out Mard's heart. We's done no harm." Seeing the hard glint in Donark's eyes, the Worlugh's plea ran roughly down, and seeing no hope of rescue, they both dropped to their knees and began firing wildly at their attackers.

Sharp explosions rippled back and forth, then paused for a moment, then faded into a powder-singed silence. The Worlughs and three Gorgolacs lay dead in a heap. Donark walked to his slain sergeant, kicked him brutally over onto his back, and spat into the wide, glazed yellow eyes.

"Stupid fool. You've killed yourself and three of my warriors. May you rot in darkness," he snarled, then whirled to the trembling Gorgolacs who ringed him. "Strip them of their gear," he barked, then knelt beside the Worlughs and methodically went over their bodies.

As he searched the second one, his rough, scaly hands felt what appeared to be a small tinderbox, and drew it from the bloodsmeared tunic.

"Ha. A pretty trinket for a lout like that to have. I wonder which of his officers he killed to have that?"

The small box seemed to grow hot in his hand, as if it still was warmed by the body heat of the Worlugh.

"What Worlugh trick is this?" he growled, and pried at the fine catch. As he prised the top open, a great roll of thunder deafened him, and a white sheet of flames blinded him, and he stumbled backward screaming.

"A bomb," shrieked one of the dazed Gorgolacs, and picking the box up where Donark had let it fall, he flung it away into the thickets. The hand that had touched it hung shriveled and withered at his side, and the writhing soldier moaned and howled with pain. In the noise and confusion, the remainder of the Gorgolac party fled into the darkness, thinking they were ambushed, and soon the night was torn by shouts and rifle fire as the frenzied soldiers ran in circles, killing their friends in the chaos, until at last those who had escaped were far away, running hard, back in the way they had just come, or toward the barrenness that led off toward Seven Hills.

Donark sat stunned, trying to calm his blurred thoughts. Was it indeed an ambush? All about him lay his maimed or dying warriors, and listening to the silence once more creep forward, he waited impatiently for someone to report their situation. When no one came after a long length of time, he assumed the worst, and limped out cautiously to see if his own escape were possible.

After a long while, eyes and ears strained into the surrounding darkness, he picked up his weapon, and a gourd of the fiery liquid, and set off limping hurriedly, away in the direction of the Dragur Wood, his only hope of safety now.

With every painful step, he cursed vilely, and swore vengeance on the traitorous cowards who had so treacherously defeated him.

Trag

"What is it?" whispered Broco, looking up to Otter, who was perched on Bear's shoulders, peering out in the direction of the enemy camp.

"There's a lot of rifle fire," reported Otter.

"I can hear that," snapped Dwarf. "Can you see what's happening?"

"Nothing but a lot of shooting," answered the little animal. "It's too dark to see who's attacking them."

"It must be some of Melodias' men," said Bear.

"Whoever it is, they must have bombs. There was a big flash and explosion just before it all started."

Otter lost his balance from leaning too far over Bear's head. "Hold still, can't you?" he chittered at Bear.

"I can't see," growled the big animal, coming down off the rock he had tried to climb onto to allow himself a clearer view.

"Just hold still a minute, and I can see what's happening."

Over Bear's protests, Otter clutched the big animal's ears to steady himself.

"Could it be Froghorn?" asked Dwarf. "Some of those flashes have the look of a wizard's fireworks about them."

"I don't think so. Or maybe. It's too dark and too far to see very well. Maybe if we could get closer."

Otter's voice was drowned out by a horrible, rattling cry and a burst of firearms not far from their concealment, and the running sound of heavily booted feet came directly at them. Terrified, they froze for a moment, and the next instant, a huge Gorgolac warrior crashed through the surrounding thicket, eyes rolled back in blind terror, firearm held before him. The hairy hide of the Gorgolac's leg brushed against Otter, and the tiny animal had to dart quickly aside to avoid being crushed by the thick-soled boot.

Recovering himself, the ugly enemy warrior snapped a shot at Broco, spinning the little man's hat off. Bear was directly in the line of fire and Otter, teeth flashing, leapt to their assailant and buried his small fangs to the hilt in the foul-tasting thick hide, and clung desperately on, wrenched this way and that, until at last he fell senseless to the ground, clubbed by the hard butt of the firearm, but Bear had moved so quickly during the brief struggle that he was now in paw's reach of the swart, frenzied Gorgolac, and a great arm slashed wickedly out, striking a bone-jarring blow to the low, thick brow of the enemy's oval head. Stunned, the Gorgolac dropped the firearm, but instinctively drew out the curved, jagged stabbing knife, backing away slowly from Bear's reach. The wicked blade hissed dangerously through the air as the enemy warrior cut great swaths before him.

Dwarf dodged, and dashed for the dropped rifle, but a swift movement of a stout leg kicked him breathlessly backward.

Feeling himself no longer threatened, the Gorgolac began to grin, a cruel grimace that drew the thick lips back to reveal the yellow, crooked fangs, and he uttered a sharp, rushing echo of laughter.

Bear, confronted with an adversary of almost his own size, reared up once more, and began his savage battle dance, spinning around quickly, drawing back his great head and roaring the dreadful battle cry, claws gleaming fiercely in the dim light, like barbed daggers reflecting battle fires.

Round and round they circled, waiting for the advantage, making feints, retreating, darting in, then quickly backing away. A red, murderous light blazed in Bear's eyes, and reflected dull yellow in the huge Gorgolac's.

Otter awakened, and took in the grim scene. Dwarf lay witless at the clearing's edge, a few paces from the firearm the Gorgolac had dropped.

Otter darted between the two circling enemies and retrieved the cold, smooth man weapon. Spinning around, and repeating the ritual, he stood upright, in the form of a tall, gray-brown-haired man, and leveling the weapon at the Gorgolac, shouted out in hesitating man tongue the command to halt.

A cold, hesitant voice answered him.

"So it's more fancy tricks, are it? I's seen souls turned insides out with these kinds of black magic, but I's never thought it would be the end of Trag." The Gorgolac edged nearer the thick bushes that bordered the clearing.

"Shoot," snapped Bear, "before he escapes us."

"Trag thunk he had a sport, with no one else to chip in.

You is all dirty, treacherous things, you is. You fights only with the heaviest numbers."

"Give us your knife, and we'll think of mercy," said Otter, his new body clumsy and awkward-feeling.

"When you throw down my rifle. That's when Trag will give up his own protection. I's never seen no harm in taking care of myself none. Now takes that box them Lughs had. See, no harm to themselfs they thinks. But out and out, it proves how they was turning us to the enemy all the while. I was lucky to gets out of that, I was. So's you can't says to Trag throw down the only thing what is going to keep old Trag alive." The Gorgolac advanced meekly toward the man figure of Otter.

"What spoke you of a box? And stand away there." Otter pointed the firearm menacingly.

"A pretty toy, old Trag's toy, you's got. Makes nasty holes. Be careful where you points it."

"I have no pains at ridding someone of the likes of you. Now what box? Had the Worlughs found it? And who attacked your camp?" Otter scowled harshly down the short barrel of the firearm, waving it back and forth near the Gorgolac's crusted, foul-smelling tunic.

"Then you wants it back? Trag can find it for his friends. Trag knows where it hides."

Bear repeated the words that Froghorn had taught him so long ago, and emerged in the gloom as a tall man.

"Gets away from me. Old Trag weren't giving nothing away. Trag didn't knows it was nothing important." The Gorgolac cowered, falling back at Bear's transition.

Sensing that the Gorgolac was terrified that this new development was more of Doraki's magic. Bear spoke in an ice-hard voice.

"Where is the box?" he bluffed.

It was threatening enough to make even Otter tremble at it.

Trag simply pointed away in the direction of the earlier sounds of fighting, unable to utter a word.

"Show us," demanded the stern, cold voice of Bear's man form.

"Aye, Trag shows his friend. Trag knows, Trag knows." The Gorgolac's voice became oily, sickeningly sweet.

"Here, Bear," said Otter, handing over the firearm.

"I'll see to Dwarf."

"Let's go, and no tricks from you. And drop that fancy sticker while you're at it."

The Gorgolac reluctantly let his knife fall, looking innocently at Bear.

"Trag weren't going to hurts no friend of his, and there you is pointing that boomer at his own self."

"Never mind. Show me the box. Otter, carry Dwarf along here. We'll see what's happened ahead." Bear marched the enemy warrior briskly off ahead of him, and Otter, in his man form, stooped and took the senseless dwarf in his unfamiliar arms, and finding he could carry the little man easily, strode off after the two marching before him.

A Hidden Fear Vanished

Aheavy smell of gunpowder and a low ground haze hung over the concealed thicket where the Gorgolac camp had been.

Many slain Gorgolacs lay sprawled about, as if a great number had fallen on them and thrown them to rout, and Otter tripped many times coming upon a corpse in the dark, for the night had grown darker, and no stars shone out from the skies, and the moon would not be out for many hours.

Bear marched ahead with the much tamed enemy soldier, and Otter, looking about fearfully, hurried along to keep Bear in sight.

"Us was here," whined Trag in a pleading tone. "Us was here when them Worlughs tricked us with them dirty ways they has." He stepped aside dutifully to offer Bear to go before him.

"Get on there. No funny moves, mind you, and stay where I can see you." Bear nudged the Gorgolac rudely with the rifle barrel.

"I wants no minding of my ways. I are only a low Gorgolac soldier, good and true. I aren't one of them filthy Worlugh beasts. They is the ones what will use you rough." His tone was one of wounded pride.

Inside the low thicket, the darkness was complete, and dim shapes lay shadowed and threatening, and Bear instinctively placed the firearm right against the prisoner's back.

As his eyes grew accustomed to this deeper blackness, Bear made out the shadows of slain warriors, many of them, and the remnants of a fierce, savage struggle lay scattered about.

Stooping slowly, the Gorgolac made to sit down. "I's weary now. A little rest will mend me," he whined.

Bear was too busy searching the gloom for any sign of the Chest to notice the rifle the Gorgolac was slowly inching toward him with his foot.

Otter's warning was a moment too late, and a loud explosion rocked the clearing, and a great gust of fiery wind whirred through Bear's cloak, scorching his ribs. He flung himself down, and trying to work the rifle in his hands, jammed it. Another shot deafened him, and he vaguely made out the low, crouching form of the Gorgolac bolting by Otter, who stood helplessly, his arms full of the still dazed Dwarf.

Scrambling to his feet, Bear ran to the place in the bushes through which the prisoner had escaped.

"Blast it," he growled. "Now we've got to keep watch that he doesn't return."

"It's just as well he's gone, Bear. I wouldn't want his company all the way back to Havamal," Otter said in a comforting tone.

"Yes, that's fine, but at least we would have known where

he was. Now he may be laying for us out there somewhere."
Bear sat down, full of remorse, and angry at his unwatchful-
ness.

"What shall we do with Dwarf?" asked Otter, placing the
little man down at his feet.

"It's certain we can't have a fire. We'll just have to keep
turns watching until daylight, then we'll search for the Chest."
Bear sighed wearily. "But now I'm getting out of this dis-
guise, and shall stay up while you try to get some rest."

The two friends returned to their natural forms, and Otter
curled up next to Dwarf and tried to go to sleep, but his
anxious thoughts kept him awake until at last, Bear gently
touched his shoulder to see if he were awake, and finding him
still up, took his own turn at rest.

The night was filled with hushed, ominous sounds, and the
trine moon showed her face briefly over the lower horizon,
and a few stars shone weakly from their distant perches.
Twice Otter thought he heard someone stealthily moving
about in the bushes near them, but the sounds seemed to disappear when he turned to listen more closely. Finally his eyes
grew weary, and too tired to be frightened by the wind rus-
tling some unseen leaf or branch, he dozed fitfully. When he
awakened with a start, the first watery gray light of dawn crept
into the thicket, and he rubbed the sleep from his eyes, looking quickly about him. Bear slept peacefully at his side, and
Broco was adjusting his cloak more closely around him to
ward off the chill of the early morning air.

"If I had been of the mind to, I could have carried both of
you lummoxes off in the night. Harrumph, some sentries you
two make."

"Oh, Dwarf, why didn't you wake me? You should have been sleeping."

"I had a long enough nap at the toe of that nasty fellow that surprised us last night. Besides, I couldn't sleep with a head like I had, and my poor ribs feel as if I'd been thumped by a dragon."

Bear roused himself when he heard his friend's voice. "Well, Master Broco, you seem none too worse in spite of a nasty kick."

"Not half as bad as you will from mine if you don't hand us something to fill up our stomachs. It seems to be growing used to always being empty enough to be played like a drum."

"Oho, do I see a dwarf coming round to my own sort of thought about food?"

"Well, that's a relief. Whenever you're hungry, we'd best mind our defenses, for something foul is afoot. I shall have my breakfast in safety." Broco opened the cloth sack Bear handed him, and drew out three small, tough-looking patties of a dull tan color.

"Wizard vittles indeed. I shouldn't wonder they're always bolting their food, if this is the fare they have." Dwarf frowned, then bit off a mouthful and began to chew. To his delight, the taste of dwarf cake of old filled him with restful memories, and a burden seemed to lift from his weary spirit.

"It's good," giggled Otter, savoring the flavor of fresh river plums.

"Almost like my old clover honey," agreed Bear, and they all three washed it down with the water in the gray carved flask from the sack. Amazingly, the small portions filled them up, and the water seemed to wash them clean of fatigue.

Refreshed, they held a hurried council.

"Let's search this camp for the Chest first," suggested Otter. "Then if it's not here, we'll have to keep on, I guess."

"Keep on to where? Whoever ambushed these fellows might have found the Chest," scowled Dwarf. "But first, the search. On that count, you're right, Otter. Perhaps we can find a clue as to what happened here last night."

The three friends spread out and began going over the ruins of the battle camp, and carefully, hesitantly, went through the pockets and packs of the slain warriors. At midday, they still had come up with no explanation as to who had set upon the Gorgolacs, or the strange presence of the three Worlughs, or where, if any had escaped, they made for.

Toward the later part of the afternoon, Bear stumbled over an object half hidden in the dense underbrush, and upon kicking at it petulantly, noticed that it reflected back the golden rays of sunlight that penetrated into that gloom. He stooped to peer at it more closely, and fell back with a cry.

"It's here. The Chest, quickly, it's here." Wild hope surged suddenly up in Bear's heart, and the hidden fear lurking there vanished without a trace.

Dwarf and Otter scrambled madly to where he stood, and looked in silent thanksgiving at the small thing Bear held, now fouled and dull from the Worlughs and Gorgolacs who had held it, but even as they watched, it began to glow faintly silver, then white, and its pulse returned, until at last it was once more the burnished pearl-silver color they remembered.

"Here, Dwarf, you keep it," said Bear in an awed tone.

"Melodias bade me carry it to him, so I shall bear it. Yet it's more burden than the heaviest stone. I shall be glad to pass it back to someone who is used to it." Broco reverently put it inside the folds of his cloak.

"And now we should make our start back to Havamal, and Melodias. The sooner I hand it to him, the better I'll feel. I don't like going about this country with it."

"Then come up again, you two, and I shall cover some ground in a hurry. It's always easier when returning to food and friends." Bear helped the two upon his broad back, and began a rapid trot back in the way they had come. Their errand done, and the Chest safely again in the hands of the Light, Dwarf and Otter hardly minded the jostle and bumps of their steed, and even looked about occasionally to enjoy the sunburned scenery. So at ease, and relieved they were, they failed to notice a shadow following along their wake, moving quickly, and always at a distance, and always in the concealment of the stunted trees and gnarled underbrush.

When they at last stopped to make their supper and find a cozy place to sleep, no one thought it necessary to keep a watch, and after eating and talking quietly for a while, one by one they dropped off to rest, and the unsleeping, watchful shadow crept closer still as the night wore on.

The Flame Of Cypher
Burns Low

Ill Omens

"The Light of Windemeir be with you," said Froghorn, dismounting from Pe'lon's high saddle. "Well met, Greymouse."

"The Light," spoke Greymouse delightedly, holding out both hands to his young friend. "Much has happened since Seven Hills, and I had no hopes of seeing you so soon among us. But come in, come in, I was ready to take some supper."

"I'll look to Pe'lon first, sir. We've traveled far this day, and fortune rode not with us. I have sad tidings, I fear. The Chest has been taken by a band of Worlugh stragglers from the Battle of Havamal. And Tyron the Green is upon the point of wielding the Secret he holds. He is at this moment ready to move across Calix Stay. I rode to warn you to be on the lookout for any of the Worlughs who might be trying to enter the Dragur Wood through your pickets, and to be on your guard should Tyron choose to cross here to begin his attack."

Greymouse seemed to sway visibly, his lined, weary face paling.

"Bitter news is this. Without the Chest, our hopes are lost. And Tyron, too? It is indeed ill tidings you bear, young friend."

"Not so bitter as that, sir. I have reason to believe the Worlughs know not what they carry. And as for Tyron, that shall be mended."

"Still the Chest is outside the Circle, and that is grave enough. But if it should be discovered . . ." The older wizard did not complete his depressing thought.

"There is no need to carry it to those lengths. If we watch everywhere carefully, we shall retake it before it might be carried beyond our reach."

Froghorn took from his saddle a silken bag, and from it began to feed Pe'lon.

"Then I shall post pickets along the wood as far as the Cross, and send out ambush parties to make for Seven Hills. And we shall keep our eyes out for signs of Tyron or his army." Greymouse excused himself, and hurried away to gather his captains.

Froghorn finished feeding the great steed, and stood musing to himself, when a timid hand touched his riding cloak.

"Excuse, sir, but might you be Froghorn Fairingay?" A tall, thin man stood before him, hat in hand.

"I'm called that sometimes, yes. What is it you seek, friend?"

To his great surprise, the man clutched his hand and began to pump it up and down rapidly, tears starting to his eyes.

"I knew it was true, I knew it. Oh, sir, thanks is all I can give, but you don't know how glad I is to shake your hand, for all you has done for Ned Thinvoice and his friends." Tears welled up in the man's eyes as he finished speaking, and Froghorn looked long and steadily at him, the depths of his own clear gray eyes slowly moving back in time, and he at length recognized the man, and the place as the Battle of Seven Hills. He reached out his hand and touched Ned gently on his shoulder.

"And what of your friend Cranfallow? My men carried him also."

"Old Cranny is of a piece, sir. Hide as tough as any Worlugh, and twice as stubborn, old Cranny is. I was coming down to pick up some mess for us when I seed you, sir, and heard the general address you so friendly like, and your horse is such as no ordinary man would own. I remembered it all at Seven Hills, and when I woke up at that field hospital it all seemed like a dream, sort of, but then I knowed deep down it must have been so."

The young wizard smiled briefly. "You have served long and true, Ned Thinvoice, you and your comrades. And I have a friend who will be glad to hear of you again."

"Might he be a dwarf, sir? Odd sort of fellow with spells in his hat and such?"

"The same as you speak of. He asked after you often while he was being healed of his wounds."

Ned Thinvoice laughed, and slapped his knee with his hand.

"I knowed it were true. And all them orderlies telling me I was wound sick and full of fever."

"I have reason to believe you may see your old friend soon, Ned. They are upon the trail of a straggling band of raiders, not too many days' distance from here."

"Then he are still at all this?" Ned moved a hand in a wide arc to indicate the sprawling battle camp.

"Along with the rest of us, friend," Froghorn answered, turning on his heel as he heard Greymouse returning. Thinvoice snapped a smart salute and moved backward, preparing to depart.

"Wait a minute there," said Froghorn, motioning for him to come forth. "Mithramuse, this is one of the brave fellows who fought beside our Dwarf so gallantly upon Seven Hills. You have good men if they are all like him."

"Sergeant Thinvoice has always proved himself loyal, and a steady hand," said Greymouse, smiling quickly, "and his comrades have proved the same. I'm sending them out in charge of an ambush party to make for the Cross, to see if they might chance across our quarry. Gather your squadron and return here, Sergeant."

"Sir," answered Thinvoice, hurrying away.

"Now come inside where we may talk before they return." Greymouse moved under the tent flap, leading Froghorn into a cavernous structure, furnished simply with a table and chairs, and in a far corner, a simple iron cot. Upon a large field desk a map was laid, studded here and there with bright-colored pins.

"There are many movements in Dragur Wood these past weeks, and I fear it is the building up to try to take Thirdwaite. And I've seen large raiding parties gathering in the swamps of Grimm now for more than a month." Greymouse shook his head slowly as he pointed out the danger areas. "And I've only enough men to hold Thirdwaite. I can't spare anyone to clear the wood, or to risk so long a march as the swamps of Grimm."

Froghorn frowned as he studied the menacing pins on the map.

"Melodias has cleared Fourthwaite for the time," he said at last, "and the Gorgolacs and Worlughs have been thrown to rout. I know they will be moving back to the wood, or Grimm, hoping to find friends waiting there. They are all only one or two, but counted up, they could swell the ranks of those in Dragur, so it is important you cut off their escape. I've left an elfin host under Urien Typhon at Seven Hills, but I would rather hold those in reserve for the moment, for I fear the threat there is great. This is a time when we could dearly use the aid of Tyron's elves, but I don't know. This might be the one time he might yet remain loyal, or it might not. I shall have to see when I meet him. Yet the threat here is great."

"It is great all across our borders, my dear friend. It's only a matter of discovering where they shall thrust first." Greymouse placed a hand under his chin, looking glumly at the map spread before him. "And now we risk the loss of the Chest," he sighed, bowing his head.

"We've not lost it yet, old fellow. If we strike quickly, all is not lost." Froghorn clasped the older wizard by the shoulders. "And I think you could use a quick visit to Lorini in Cypher. You could use a rest, and she is anxious for your news."

Greymouse rubbed a hand across his eyes, nodding. "Yes, a rest would be most welcome. But I fear I'm needed more here."

"I'll stay here until you return. After we set the pickets and send out the patrols, there will be nothing more to do than wait."

Greymouse looked long into his young friend's eyes. "What shall I say of the Chest, then? And of the disturbing news of Tyron?"

Without blinking, Froghorn answered quickly. "Don't mention them unless asked. And we should have recovered the Chest by then, and have our renegade elf at bay, at any rate. And the lady is troubled enough as it is without this dire news."

"Then I shall wait until these things are taken care of before I go. I couldn't be the bearer of such ill tidings. And you should be seeing to your errand across Calix Stay, rather than minding my shop here."

Their gazes met and held a moment.

"Then I shall set out the way I've come, in chance I may come across our friends and the Chest. Till then." Froghorn raised his hand in the ancient manner of Windameir, and went out to where Pe'lon waited.

"We must make all speed, old friend. We have the Chest to find, and an ambitious elf to quell. It is a chore that I should just as well leave to others, but I fear we must bear it."

Pe'lon nudged his master gently, and threw back his mane.

"Then on, my steed, on. We shall range far tonight, over Dragur Wood, and back from the Cross to Seven Hills, and on across the River, to find our rogue elf."

Pe'lon waited impatiently as Froghorn mounted. As he readied himself for the swift plunge into speed, the young wizard spied Ned Thinvoice leading a group of men to the headquarters of General Greymouse.

"If you find our Dwarf before I, take him the message I shall see him soon. And keep a sharp watch that no enemy slips by you unaware."

Froghorn raised his hand in farewell and Ned returned it eagerly, then turned to Flewingam and Cranfallow.

"You see, Cranny. It wasn't just gourd dreams or fever what done it. I talked with him myself, mug to mug, as it was, and he knowed my name without me saying it, and all about Broco, and he knowed your name right out of his hat, without me saying nothing at all."

Flewingam looked long after the disappearing rider had faded into a faint blur of speed and silence.

"I wonder if he knows of my two companions, or where they might be?"

"I'd wager he knows a fat lot more than you or me," broke in Cranfallow, staring at the spot where the vanished horseman had been.

"But come along here, step lively. We has got to get our orders and set out. It must be something big if Froghorn Fairingay comes all this way to see the general."

"It must be another push," added Cranfallow gloomily. "We has sat here with our boots catching dust without nothing at all happening for too long. I knowed it was too bloody good to last."

They fell to silence and saluted as Greymouse, weary and pale, came out of his tent to brief them. He quickly filled them in on their mission, and that all slain Worlughs were to be searched for a small chest, which if found was to be brought to him immediately.

After the squadron set out, he returned to his tent and sat

heavily down at his desk, sighing and staring at the vast map spread before him.

"So much to do, and so little time," he said aloud, and turned inward upon himself to see what he might in the direction of Melodias Starson's camp. His thought touched upon vast, spiritless country, the Fallow Hills with stunted shrub trees, and endless crisscrossing washes from floods long since dried, and was upon the point of resting when he brushed a shade of darkening silence, a crackling, upsetting something that he had almost dismissed. Bending closer, his will sought what had troubled his seeing thought, and searched ruthlessly through the cloud form that concealed its heart. Vaguely, he had the impression of the Chest's faint pulsing presence, and knew that it was in friendly hands, but something evil threatened it. He tried to search the minds of those who held it, unsuccessfully at first, then he realized it was sleep that was darkening the mind beings. He switched to the threatening force, and a savage hate filled him with horrible visions of the Gorgolac's black mind. He knew he must wake the sleepers, and repeating a litany of verses from the far reaches of space and time, he sent out a tall, plumed warrior from the plane of Maldan, the destroyed world Lorini had conquered, to warn whoever held the Chest of their danger.

Far away, Dwarf awoke screaming from a deep sleep, where he had dreamed of a wraith that rode a thundering black stallion of smoke, and the shrouded figure of the ghostly rider lifted high up in the air a fiercely gleaming sword that a pale golden fire seemed to drip from.

"What is it, Dwarf?" cried Bear, leaping up drowsily.

"I'm sorry," apologized Broco. "I've had a dream that frightened me, is all." He shuddered with a sudden chill that seemed to linger at the back of his scalp.

Otter yawned, and went to Dwarf's side.

"I'm not sleepy anymore, anyway. We may as well have an early breakfast of it. It can't be more than an hour or two until dawn now."

"An excellent idea, Otter," agreed Bear, rummaging about for the sack of stores, smacking his lips loudly. "These cakes of Froghorn's are almost like good clover honey. If I didn't know better, I would swear he made them from a barrel I'd put up in our old valley."

"I was of a mind they were dwarf cakes," offered Broco, "but then I guess that's what makes them seem so good. Wizards have a great deal of knowledge of baking, whatever else they may know."

"Sprouts," said Otter stubbornly. "Good sprouts from Cheerweir, or I've never tasted any."

"Whatever, my mouth is busy talking, and it's time to make use of my chompers. Hand us that, old fellow, and let's save our gossip for after." Dwarf moved closer to Bear, and took the offered cake.

After a few mouthfuls, Otter pricked up his ears, and the paw that was raised with its morsel halted midway. "Shh. Listen," he whispered.

Bear and Dwarf froze where they sat, and all strained to hear the barely audible scuffling that came from somewhere off in the dense brush.

"Do you think it could be our nasty friend following us?" asked Otter.

"I would think not. His only safety lies toward Dragur. Surely he wouldn't come back alone." Dwarf stood, staring out into the darkness.

"Maybe he brought some friends with him," suggested Bear.

"If that's the case, we must make haste. We're bound to run into some of Melodias' men today." Dwarf began hastily packing the leavings of their meal into the bag. "I don't fancy carrying the Chest about out here alone, and the sooner I've handed it over to Melodias or Greyfax, the better I'll feel."

"Maybe we'll be returning to Cypher," Otter chittered hopefully. "I mean since we've got the Chest back, and Greyfax and Melodias, and they'll want to make sure the Chest is safe now."

The thought of returning to Lorini's halls heartened the companions, and they set out almost gaily, Bear carrying his two smaller friends upon his great back, and as the sun slowly filled the horizon with a faint window of light through the low, dark bank of clouds, they saw before them the distant peak of Havamal, glowing dimly in the distance like a small, dark pearl. If any of them had chanced to look behind them, or had their thoughts not been wrapped in the soothing splendor of Lorini's realms, they would have seen the dull yellow eyes burning their hatred at the three friends, following along silently in their wake.

An ugly rim of thought burned dimly in Trag's feverish mind, and his hands clutched at the savage vengeance he would wreak upon the misshapen beasts that had tricked him, and robbed him of the Worlughs' treasure. From the talk he had overheard, the treasure must be very powerful, and with

it he might raise himself to take over even Donark's general-
ship, and spurring himself on with that thought, he crept
silently along behind, awaiting the darkness when he could
slay the ugly things, and escape back to the Dragur Wood,
far away now behind him.

And Froghorn, ranging far to the south toward Seven Hills,
and his mind occupied with Tyron the Green and his army,
saw nothing of his friends' danger.

A Frozen Wind begins
to Blow

Darkness hung cruelly in the Ice Palace as Dorini
ministered to the defeated Doraki. His black soul
hovered upon her breath, touched at the edges by faint, flickering green flames, and the Dark Queen's mind seethed with
a revenge so terrible it would topple all Atlanton Earth into
unending, frozen night.

A plan had been slowly formulating in her cruel dreams,
but she would need the aid of her underlord, and first he must
be given new strength. A bitter mirth stung her heart, and she
threw back her beautiful head, and long peals of hollow
laughter rang through the chilled stone halls. Fireslayer
howled in time far below, and Cakgor gnawed at the heavy
chains that bound him, rattling his yellow fangs like death
strokes at the throat of a hated enemy.

In the coldness of her fortress, she had held many elves
and men, and dwarfs, and animal kind, and even the hated
Greyfax Grimwald for a time. But he had spurned her, and

joined with the rest to overthrow her scheme of controlling these lower worlds forever.

Her piercing gaze fell upon the still form of Doraki.

"Yes, my sleeping one, we shall have our hour, you and I. The high and mighty Lord of Windameir himself has willed that no one shall have the power to overthrow me here, where I command. And I but improve upon his Law."

Dorini rose from her dull-gleaming greenish throne and paced restlessly.

"We shall have all the fools paying homage to us before all is played out. And my useless weakling of a sister will find herself cast down from her ill-gotten kingdoms. It was I, Dorini, that was willed to rule these lower worlds, and I who should have held my court in Cypher, at the side of Trianion Starseeker."

She slashed her hand viciously into the air.

"But all that shall be. And I shall have the power as soon as I have taken that brat of Starseeker's and my sister's. With her, I shall open the war upon the Light in earnest."

Doraki, deep, sightless sockets burning with dull yellow and red flames, began to groan, and Dorini went to stand beside his bier.

Dirty greenish fires blazed from her mind into his, and she placed a cold hand to his unfeeling heart.

With a convulsive shudder, his body was wracked with fire and icy blasts, and he sat bolt upright.

"Rise, my love, our time grows near. We have plans to plan, and matters to see to. I shall be making a trip to Cypher soon, if that accursed pack of hounds of the Circle are but elsewhere."

She laughed, harsh and guttural.

This time she could not fail, and she began to cast her thoughts away toward Cypher and her hated sister.

The fools could not refuse her her victory with the schemes she envisioned as she slowly nursed Doraki back to strength.

An Unheralded Return

Darkness was falling once more before the three friends halted to rest. Havamal and Hel rose before them, only an hour's march farther. A heavy silence seemed to settle as the sun retired, and shadowy forms flickered and soundlessly moved in the shrub trees and gorse bushes where they sat, peering about them.

"I haven's heard so much as a rifle shot all day," complained Dwarf, removing his hat and staring at it, as if it would explain the stillness.

"Surely some of Melodias' men are left hereabout. Perhaps we should go on to the tower to find Greyfax." Otter looked away toward the Crown wistfully. "At least we'd have a roof, and maybe a warm meal for a change."

Bear looked longingly toward the tower of Havamal, then announced, "It's empty there. I can't see a single movement there now. No campfires, no sentries. Even the wind is quiet."

The three friends studied the stillness before them in growing concern.

"You don't think anything happened, do you, Dwarf?" Otter scampered forward a few feet, then put both his forepaws to his muzzle.

"It's unnatural enough, but I don't know what to make of it. There's a funny smell to the air, something that doesn't set right with all the other scents." Bear glowered, and raised his great muzzle to test the evening's dark cloak.

"I think I know what you're talking of," said Dwarf, his brows drawn down in a sharp arch above his eyes. "There's something not right, nor wrong, but I can't nose out anything really amiss."

A great gray dark cloud covered the mountaintops, blotting out the thin, high stars.

"Let's go on, then," said Otter, his voice high and strained. "My nose can't detect anything other than emptiness, but it would feel better to be among friends, with a wall between us and the night."

Nodding hasty agreement, Bear carried the two upon his back again, and set off at a quick loping gait toward the frowning brow of the lowest foothills that ringed the two tall peaks.

The Light and the Dark

Cypher's towers trembled, and a long, low, rushing wind swept the warm gardens with a trace of never-before-felt frost, and the elves set up a high, wailing warning that hung about the frail golden light like tombs of pale silver smoke blown at the sun, and a chill of lifeless, empty years covered the fair realm of Lorini in a sudden, tomblike shudder.

"What is it, Mother?" cried Cybelle, rushing into her mother's study.

"Hush, child, hush and listen." Lorini stood trembling at her desk, her hand half upraised as if to fend off an unseen blow. She turned an ashen face to her daughter, and spoke hurriedly. "Whatever happens, keep your thoughts in the Light. And on no account look into the face of whom you are about to meet."

The tall chamber grew colder, and an icy breath hung like a shroud over the sunlit windows. In an instant, the rainbow fountains in the sleeping wing were a leaden gray, and a cold hand touched the hearts of all those who dwelt within Cypher's realms. As Cybelle watched, horrified, a vague, hazy form began to take shape before her mother's table, slithering wraithlike toward form, then slipping back again.

"It is forbidden that either of us should even use our names to each other, sister, but welcome to my halls. It is a long journey from your dwelling." Lorini stood erect, her head high, proud eyes dancing in their cool blue-gray depths. A golden ring of light glowed brightly about her, and as the wraith form advanced, it touched the halo, and fell back with a bitter, hissing sound.

"My own greetings to you, my foolish one. I have come to seek a truce of you, to discuss a surrender." Dorini's voice was without substance, as if she spoke from a great, frozen distance.

"Are you then prepared for exile?" asked Lorini, hardly daring to let her hopes rise.

"Not I, but you, pale sister. I offer you exile, and in return for that promise of safety, I shall have Cypher." Dorini's harsh voice crackled and broke with mirthless, cold laughter.

"You have wasted your energy in coming here," replied Lorini, "and placed yourself in grave danger. If I choose, I may imprison you here, or send you back into the Light."

"Do it, Mother," cried Cybelle, her voice breaking with the effort to remain calm.

"You cannot, my weak kindred, and well I know your thoughts. It cannot be you who returns my being into darkness. Light, you say." She laughed malignantly. "Light only for you. It means I shall be returned into the lost part of the

Lord of Windameir's cold memories. And I shall have to give up my kingdoms."

"Would that not be better then than the unhappiness you bear and bring others?"

"To cease existing would not bring me peace, nor you. It is I who follow the Law. And I have chosen my time for visiting wisely, for I know none of your lackeys are about to interfere. Only they could trap me in that cruel Light to banish me forever. I have seen to it that they shall be busy elsewhere for the time." Dorini's harsh, chilling laughter wavered before her like frozen crystals of dead, gray light.

"Then we have no more to say to each other. There will be no surrender or truce until you've been returned to the Fire." Lorini's tone grew hard.

Cybelle looked closely at the wraith shape, and could make out the exact mirrored reflection of her own mother in the vaporous features, yet harder, and ill-defined, as if uncompleted.

"Won't you do as Mother asks, and give up your struggle? Surely you know it is useless to go on. We could end the misery now for all of us."

"My seeds are too deeply sown across this world now," snarled Dorini, "and only my victory will accomplish anything. I follow the Law, as it was given in the beginning. I am in charge of holding those souls captive which are on these lower planes. There is no place for sniveling magicians and soft rulers there. The only way is iron power to keep those fools under control. If you want an end to all the chaos, then surrender yourself, and it shall cease."

"You know it would not, sister, not until the last darkness

swallowed Atlanton Earth as it did Maldan and Origin. That is not peace, nor is it the Law."

Dorini's form grew stronger, until Cybelle could see the deep, swirling glitter of her hard green-black eyes. They seemed as endless as a harsh, cold heaven with frozen stars, but the blackness was so deep and terrifying, she found herself gazing on, trying to locate the bottom of the pitiless stare. She trembled, and pulled away, feeling as if she had looked into an abyss without end.

"Don't meet her eyes," cried Lorini to her daughter, for Cybelle had begun swaying to and fro, trying to escape from the inescapable thought of the mind of Dorini, who pulled at her mercilessly.

"Mother, Mother," cried Cybelle, "I can't look away." And in another moment, she fell to the floor at her mother's feet in a deep trance.

Lorini's eyes flashed, and a pillar of white, towering fire flared up brilliantly in the room, devouring the shadow form of Dorini. She knelt beside her daughter, and felt a cold, smooth hand. Cybelle's eyes fluttered twice, then closed, and she fell into a dark nightmare of sleep, and she felt her being traveling over a great space of blackness, without star or moon, and she cried out in agony as the bitter, icy fingers of Dorini's mind grasped her heart. Soon a greenish light grew, looming still larger, and larger still, until Cybelle knew it was the walls of the Dark Palace, in the very depths of Dorini's kingdom. She struggled, calling out to her mother and Froghorn, all to no avail.

And Lorini, kneeling beside the silent form of her daughter, knew her dark sister's mind, and that Cybelle had been taken to where she dare not go.

Tears poured down her fair face, slipping from her cheeks onto the upturned sleeping features of her stolen daughter, and a wild, bitter despair so profound and deep came over her she wailed aloud, a great sobbing wracking her shoulders until she trembled uncontrollably.

A tall, golden-helmeted elf broke in at hearing his mistress' cries, and seeing at once what had happened, sent out couriers to find Greyfax and Melodias, and one to seek out Froghorn and the host of Urion Typhon who waited at Seven Hills.

Outside, the bright sunlight of Cypher was cloaked with thin gray clouds that drifted slowly in from the North Realm gate, dimming the day until even the bright towers of Lorini's halls stood dull and lifeless in the darkening gloom.

At Thirdwaite, a great horde of Gorgolacs assailed General Greymouse, their numbers coming up from the Dragur Wood where they'd waited to strike, and Faragon Fairingay marshaled his elfin host to stem that onrushing tide.

Unknown Designs

"I don't like the looks of this at all, Cranny," said Flewingam, as they walked along spread out through the gnarled, stunted trees.

"We can't see everything, and there's a lot of country for someone to disappear in."

"If you is human folk, maybe. If you stinks like them others, you don't needs no eyes to find 'em." Ned Thinvoice proved his point by lifting his nose high in the air and snorting twice.

"There are the smell of them there, right enough," said Cranfallow, looking carefully about at the ground.

"You needs to go quicker, I says, or we'll never get nowheres near the Cross before this time next year. Shake a leg there, can't you, and let's move on." Ned started off in a slow dog-trot, shuffling up the dry, powdery dust with his boots.

"I think Ned's right," replied Flewingam. "We'll depend on speed and surprise, rather than careful tracking."

"Everybody seems in an awful sorts of hurry to catch up

with trouble, but then if that's it, then Cranny ain't the one to be the slow shoe."

At a signal from Ned, the line of soldiers moved forward at a more rapid shuffle.

Ned returned to Flewingam's side, and strode along silently for a time, then addressed his friend in a quiet voice. "You know, I keeps getting the feeling that we is somehow on the trail of more than Gorgolacs and Lughs here."

"I feel it too, Ned. And from what you told me about your talk with Froghorn Fairingay, I wouldn't be surprised if we don't run into our old friends again soon."

Ned shifted his firearm to his other hand, and spat over his shoulder. "Not that I is any too sure that would be a great thing. Dwarf witches and such is a funny lot, and as likable and all as he was, there was sure enough a bag of troubles when we was together."

Flewingam laughed. "There's a lot of truth to what you say, Ned. But I would like to see my friends again."

"I always used to say I'd turns out to be no account if I went for a sodjer's life, and I was right as rain. I ain't never seen an end of trouble since I's been toting a gun, but then I gots to where I can see it coming and gets out of its way, if I has a chance. If we gets tied up with them friends of ours now, I knows we is just asking for another bout of bad luck."

"A fine one you are, Ned. You talked to a different tune in the rest camp."

"Then there wasn't no danger. Now it's all around us as thick as old Cranny's sour molasses beer."

"Well, we'll see what we'll see. As for me, I'll be glad to see Otter and Bear again."

Cranfallow jogged alongside.

"You two is busy jawing so, you couldn't spot a trail as broad as my backside. We's come across some old tracks leading off toward Fourthwaite. I doesn't know why any of them would be in a hurry to gets back down thataways, but that's where they seems to point."

Ned raised a hand, and motioned off in a new direction, and the company put on new speed.

"These fellows wasn't losing no time," panted Cranfallow, looking down at the wide-spaced marks of a dozen or more running, heavy boots.

"But why would they be going back this way?" questioned Flewingam. "If they were escaping from a battle, wouldn't they be going toward safety?"

"They probably was all turned to in the fuss," offered Cranfallow.

"Or more likely, they is just trying to gets out of our way," added Thinvoice.

Flewingam nodded, but was convinced there was some sense of purpose to the trail, for it bore on in a straight line toward Fourthwaite, and there were no discarded firearms, or other equipment, as is usual in an unorderly retreat, or worse, in a general rout. This trail left a single thought in his mind, that whoever these enemy troops were, they were marching in a known direction, and with a purpose, however dark it might be.

A Narrow Escape

Broco stared with startled concern at the empty face of
the tower upon the Crown.

"Are you sure it's gone?" Dwarf asked, watching Otter
carefully searching the outer wall for the small chink that
would allow them entrance.

"I can't find it, Dwarf. It was here before, but there's nothing I can find now. It's all smooth."

Otter chittered nervously, and whistled a low, trilling note
to himself.

"Oh, Otter, you ass, you've probably overlooked it somehow," snapped Bear churlishly, and brushed the small animal
aside. "It was here before, as big as daylight. You must have
gone past it in your haste."

"I didn't, Bear. I've been over it all twice, and run my paws
over every stone, from the ground to as high as I can reach,
and it's all gone."

A growing uneasiness edged Otter's voice.

"This is where we were to bring the Chest to Melodias."

said Dwarf, fingering the heavy presence inside his cloak. "Melodias told me to bring it back here if we found it."

"Then where are they?" chirped Otter in a high-pitched chitter. "Call out, Bear. Maybe they've been attacked, and had to hide the entrance to the tower."

"I can't do that," stammered Bear. I've never called their names aloud anywhere, and I'd feel a fool to do it now." He looked furtively about him. "Besides, you never know who's listening."

A chill ran down Broco's spine, and he began to feel as if they were being watched. "Then I'll do it," he said, taking off his hat and twirling it on his fingers once. "I'll use the old tongue of my kindred, so if anyone overhears, he won't be able to make beans out of it."

"Then we'll stand watch, Dwarf. You try to call Melodias or Greyfax, and we'll make sure there's no one about." Otter drew himself up to his full height, which came to Bear's knee.

"Go ahead, Dwarf. We'll keep an eye out, in case," added Bear, glancing about and testing the early evening air.

Broco stepped up to the wall, called forth the names of his three eldest teachers, and knocked three times upon the wall. A small ray of silver light glimmered about his hand as he touched the cold stones, but the silence was as heavy as before. He tried twice more, but the stillness remained unbroken, and only the gray slab wall stood as quietly in front of him as a tomb, and no answering voices called back to him from within the dark tower.

He tried one last time, and flung his hat angrily down.

"They've left us," he huffed. "There's no one inside now, and we don't have any place to go, and no one to guide us back through the forests. A fine lot of dwarf cake this has turned out to be." Dwarf stamped heavily upon his hat, giving it a wrenching twist with his foot.

"They must be here, Dwarf. They wouldn't have gone without the Chest," Otter soothed, moving closer to Broco.

"Can't we call Froghorn back?" suggested Bear. "I mean, isn't there some way we could call him now?"

"I've never known a wizard to answer anyone, if it didn't suit him," pouted Dwarf. "Especially if he's off doing whatever it is that interests him."

"But they were all so upset about the Chest," said Otter. "Surely they wouldn't have gone unless it were something important."

Dwarf sat wearily down on a rock outcropping, and wiped his hand across his brow.

"Then what am I to do with the Chest? We've no place to go, and we can't return to Cypher without a guide. Oh grumpty fie, why did I ever leave my old home to go out among a pack of magicians that are forever disappearing when you most need them?"

"There must be something to explain it, Dwarf. They wouldn't have left us alone if something hadn't happened." Otter knit his whiskers up until his nose tickled.

"Then if something happened, why did they leave me with the Chest? It's already tired me out carrying it this far. So what do I do now? Sit down here to wait until they think it proper to come back and take it off my hands?" Broco's voice was on the verge of hysteria.

"If we wait until morning, I'm sure someone will be back," comforted Bear. "After all, Melodias had an army to look after, and if Greyfax wasn't feeling well, he probably went back to Cypher. There's an explanation to it all."

"So we just wait quietly while they're off at their chores, do we? When who knows how many of the other side knows we've got it, and here we are, waiting about on a dark night, ill-fed, and ill-armed, without any safe place to go?" Dwarf broke off his sentence, and stood upright at an unseen movement in the direction of the deserted battle camp. "There's someone there," hissed Broco through clenched teeth. "I've sensed them for the entire day, but I'm sure we've been followed."

"Then it must be Melodias' men," chimed Bear. "And about time, too, I say. Let's call them over, and find out where the camp has been moved to."

"Shush, Bear," warned Otter. "They're not of Mankind there. I think Dwarf is right. I've felt it, too, at times today, and I'd wager it's our ugly friend who escaped us when we found the Chest, or some of his cronies."

"You mean the Gorgolac?" asked Bear, his great hackles beginning to rise.

"You didn't have time to watch, carrying us like you were, but I kept feeling we were being followed. I thought at first it might have been Froghorn making sure we reached here safely, but now I know it's no one who wishes us any good." Otter spoke in a rushing whisper, trying to see away in the darkness.

"Then what shall we do?" asked Bear, lowering himself silently down to all fours.

"We can make for the Forest of Cypher, and hide until Melodias or Froghorn or Greyfax finds us," said Dwarf. "If we could find the Coda Pool again, we could stay there."

Otter thought hard for a moment.

"That's probably our safest concealment. If we could get in touch with the keeper, he could tell Lorini where we were."

"Then let's don't sit here all night gabbing," grumbled Bear. "Let's try to see if we can find the pool before it gets any later."

Broco looked once more at the tower, now only a gray finger pointing skyward.

"I hate to leave here, but I guess you're right. If something's happened to take them away, there's no telling how long we'd wait for their return."

A loud snapping, like a faint rifle report, broke the stillness of the Crown, followed by a distinct, heavy boot step.

"Now, let's go," whispered Dwarf urgently. "We'll make for the Coda Pool."

Bear started to lower himself to enable Otter and Dwarf to crawl onto his back, but the night was suddenly broken with guttural cries, and shots, seeming to come from everywhere.

"Trag gets the big meat, Trag has him. Nasty thing tried to hurts Trag."

More volleys of shots, and a dozen Gorgolac warriors sprang from the darkness at the three companions.

Dwarf's hat flew to his hand, and a deafening rumble erupted about them, and Broco's high-pitched voice called out twice, "Brion Brandagore, Brion Brandagore," and a glimmering pale blade swept from the sky downward in a great swooshing arc.

"This way," shouted Bear, delivering a terrible blow to a stunned Gorgolac, who crumpled at the knees and fell flat onto his broad, fierce face, neck broken. Bear snatched the fallen warrior's weapon, and dragging Otter and Dwarf along behind him, disappeared into the sharp bushes, followed by wild rifle shots and harsh curses. Staggering on for what seemed hours, the three at last stopped to catch their breath and listen to see if they were being pursued.

Only a thick black silence hung behind them, and not a breath of wind stirred.

In their wild flight, Bear had not looked to see in which direction he fled, but chose the thinnest defense, and ran. The tower was behind them somewhere but the blackness was too dense to enable them to see anything more than a paw's length from them, and Bear groaned aloud.

"I don't know where we are."

"We must still be on Havamal," chittered Otter. "If we can wait until daybreak, we can see where we've gotten to, and then go on to the Coda Pool."

"But we can also be seen once it gets light," corrected Dwarf. "We'd best go on awhile yet."

Heavy, running footsteps and loud curses decided the three companions.

"Get up, you two. Take the firearm, Dwarf. I can run more quickly and quietly than you two. We'll put a little distance between those louts, then rest until daylight. Melodias or someone should be about by then."

Otter handed Broco the heavy Gorgolac firearm after the little fellow was seated, then climbed up behind.

"We're on, Bear," he whispered, and swiftly and silently, the big animal made his way into the darkness.

In their haste and fear, Bear did not notice that his flight led downward, and as the hours wore on, he galloped on quietly, his great pads almost silent on the rough ground.

After a time they stopped to rest, and Otter fell into an exhausted sleep, while Bear kept watch and Broco peered about him, trying to pierce the starless night for a glimmer of something familiar that would tell him where they were.

At first light, as the gray watery morning began to grow, Broco saw Havamal and Hel far behind, and his heart sank as he realized they had fled back the way they had come but a few hours before.

The Forest of Cypher was far away now, and a Gorgolac raiding party between.

He let his friends sleep on, rather than wake them with his disheartening news, and sat stiffly with the enemy firearm across his lap.

When the frail sun finally rose, he dozed for a moment, head down on his dust-stained cloak, and he dreamed, or dreamed he dreamed, of Greyfax, standing before a great tower, touched by the sun itself at its highest point, and its base went below even the deepest dwarf dwellings ever delved, and in his dreaming mind, Greyfax touched him, and those clear gray eyes seemed deeply troubled. Broco reached out for the wizard's hand, but there was nothing there but shadows, yet the eyes still looked at him, and at last Greyfax spoke.

"You must cross Calix Stay with the Chest, my friend. Do not try to reach Cypher now."

Broco answered in a voice he hardly recognized as his own. "But how? We're days and days away from the River here."

"Faircrossing," said Greyfax, "Faircrossing of Old."

Dwarf was about to ask where that might be, but something kept nudging his side, and before he could talk further with the wizard, the gray-whiskered face of Otter appeared before him.

"Dwarf, come on, old fellow. You've dozed off."

Broco pushed the tiny animal roughly away.

"Now you've done it, you blasted water rat. I was talking to Greyfax, and you've spoiled it all."

Dwarf huffed into a sullen silence, trying to recapture the wizard's words.

"I was trying to tell you, Dwarf, that he came while you were asleep, or at least, I think he came. He said we must make for a place called Faircrossing, but I don't know of any place like that. Do you?"

Broco straightened himself, and looked long at his small friend. "Did you say Faircrossing?"

"That's all I could make of it. But maybe Bear would know."

Otter turned to find Bear snoring loudly beside him.

"But if Greyfax had really come, he wouldn't have just left us, would he? I mean he would have done something, or taken us with him." Otter wrinkled his whiskers into a perplexed, worried frown.

"Unless he came to you while you were asleep, Otter. I just heard Greyfax speak, as clearly as you or I now. And he spoke the same words. Faircrossing of Old. Those were his exact words."

"Bear, wake up, come on, it's broad noon now, wake up."

Otter chittered about the big animal until a great paw swatted at him, and grumble-yawning, Bear sat up.

"Whatever has happened to you two? I'm having pleasant dreams about a big breakfast, and I'm denied even that." He groaned and rubbed his stomach. "Such a table I haven't seen since Cypher, too."

Dwarf rolled onto his side with a moan. "I knew it, I knew it. He's had dreams about eating. Now I know we're in trouble."

"Did you dream about Faircrossing, Bear? Or Froghorn, or Greyfax, or Melodias?"

Bear studied Otter with upraised eyebrows. "Wizard stew? Faircrossing sauce? I don't think I've ever thought of that, old fellow. Not a tasty dish, I wouldn't imagine."

Broco whined in a loud, cutting voice. "By the great beard of Tubal, I'll see my end yet because of you."

Bear looked at Otter, then to Dwarf. "What did I say?"

"It's what you didn't say that matters. I should have known it. Give him a nap, and all he wakes up with is an appetite." Broco looked wearily around. "But help yourself, Master Bruinlen. I rather think scrub tree bark is most excellent fare for rising travelers."

"Well, I'm hungry too, Dwarf, and there's a bit of food left in Froghorn's sack. Whatever we're to do, or wherever it is we're supposed to go, we can't starve ourselves to death here waiting for breakfast. Let's eat, then we'll see what's to be done."

Dwarf swelled in a mighty huff, but said nothing, and stomped off to the edge of the clearing while Otter broke one of the wizard's cakes into three portions.

"I remember now," cried Dwarf, startling Bear into swallowing his cake whole, and setting him off on a wild, choking cough. Otter leapt up, hackles rising, upsetting the small gray sack and dropping Dwarf's share in the dirt with a plopping sound.

"I just remembered from my old maps. There was a Faircrossing not too far from here, but it's not called that now, not since the Dragon Wars. It's up somewhere beyond the old Mellow Wood."

"Unless you plan on eating old charts for breakfast, you'd best keep your voice down," scolded Otter. "Now I've dropped your share, and it's going to be a mess."

"It doesn't matter," said Broco absentmindedly. "I've remembered it now. Faircrossing is the ancient name for it, before the Dragon Wars."

"Fine lot of help that is," growled Bear, recovering somewhat from his choking fit. "Why don't we just ask someone, that's all."

Dwarf retrieved the wizard cake and began chewing listlessly. "If I could only remember the rest of the map, or where it was I'd seen it." Slowly a light of recognition crossed Broco's face.

"The swamps of Grimm. Fairlake in the ancient tongues, beyond the Dragon Wastes now Grimm Crossing," he said decisively. "Fairlake, and Faircrossing, beyond the Mellow Wood. I was reading all about it that day you came to fetch me down to supper in Cypher, Otter. A big volume, with no end of maps of Atlanton Earth, and the Circle embossed upon the front of it."

Dwarf's fingers turned over the fine, imaginary pages of the beautifully bound book.

"Don't you remember, Otter?" asked Broco, his eyes returning from the distance of that far day.

Otter and Bear had fallen silent.

"You mean the Dragur Wood, Dwarf? That Froghorn was talking of?"

"Yes, that's what they call it now, I think."

Otter's eyes fell, and he slumped down beside Bear's huge hindpaws. "That must have been what we saw in the pool, Bear."

"Those awful woods, with the old ruins, and the trees all black."

Dwarf's dreamy look disappeared. "But that's even beyond Greymouse at Thirdwaite," he said in a faint voice.

"Eek, and a long march, even if we had the food," echoed Bear.

Before Dwarf could reply, a long volley of rifle fire shattered the gray stillness of the morning, and a gaunt Gorgolac warrior, dressed in black cape and battle helm, crashed out of the thickets only a few yards behind them. Dwarf fired two clumsy shots that spun the huge swart warrior around in his tracks, and scrambling to his feet, shouted in a high, wailing note, "Fly, fly, to Graymouse." Otter grabbed the small, almost empty sack of food, and swarmed onto Bear's already running back. Dwarf swung up awkwardly, and the three friends dashed for safety in the next line of trees, heads down and holding grimly on.

A great whooping cry went up behind them, followed by more shouts and a savage scream.

Crashing blindly ahead, not daring to look up long enough to see where they were headed, Bear pounded wildly on, away from the sounds of their pursuers. More shots rang out on both sides of them, and throwing silence to the wind, Bear increased his speed, knocking aside small bushes and undergrowth, and Otter and Dwarf had to renew their grips on his loose hide to keep from being thrown from his madly pitching back.

Dwarf cast one fleeting glance over his shoulder, and saw a grim, loping figure racing toward them, and in the brief glance, he recognized the Gorgolac prisoner that had escaped, leading a band of enemy soldiers.

"Fly, Bear," he shrieked, but the rushing wind of Bear's flight drowned out his words, and a low tree branch almost swept him away, but he clung frantically on, fighting aside his fright, and Otter, beside him, clutched him by the arm to keep from losing his balance and tumbling off into the vicious grasp of their attackers.

Bear increased his pace still more, and by midday, the three were headed away toward the Cross, the last road before the Dragur Wood, and Greymouse's last pickets to fall beneath the unstemmed tide of Gorgolacs that swept out of the dark woods of the Dragur. Even as Bear raced on, the attack was renewed upon Thirdwaite and the failing defenses that guarded Cypher's East Realm gate.

Elders of Windameir

Melodias sat near Greyfax in the dim tower, watching the healing vial sweeten the room with its soothing presence.

"You stay gone long, my friend," said Melodias aloud. "Your trial was indeed a severe one, and but for the Arkenchest, I fear even you would have been lost. A great risk, old friend, and great danger still, if you should meet with any of the Darkness now."

Melodias withdrew into himself, and faint shafts of light spun in the room, glowing about the form of Greyfax, then spilling over onto himself. The light grew fainter, then farther away, and as Melodias spoke the last of the ancient words, brilliant flashes of stars passed, as he followed the long journey of Greyfax back into the secret fields of Windameir.

A dark shadow flickered past as he sped on, and in that brief recognition, he knew powers of the Darkness were about, and he hurried on to find Greyfax. The wraithlike blackness that he had encountered he knew to be none other

than the Dark Queen herself, so powerful was the pull upon
him, and he wondered as he traveled on, to what dark ren-
dezvous she was going.

Then the lights whirled rapidly away, and time and distance
parted, and all things held their breath as Melodias drew near
the most ancient of all universes. A brilliant white star
touched him briefly as he reached the plane of the Starkeeper,
and as quickly dimmed, and before he could prepare himself
further, he sat at the end of a long table, where Greyfax was
deep in thought, across from Cephus Starkeeper, who raised
an eyebrow at Melodias' appearance.

"It is you, then. Well, I've kept council here with dear
Grimwald for a time, but I thought not you would be here so
soon upon his heels."

The old man bowed his mane of silver-gray hair, and
looked deeply into the clear glass before him.

"Hail, and well met, sir. It is not upon a journey of my
own necessity, but one of guarding Grimwald's passage. I
have come across many comings and goings on my way here,
and it seems I have chosen right, for I have felt the presence
of the Dark Queen, on her way to somewhere I cannot fathom.
Her armies were in rout before this, yet I doubt she has gone
to a field of battle."

"Not a field of combat, my own Starson, but to Cypher.
She has taken the lady Cybelle, I fear, as hostage."

Melodias paled, and drew quick breath. A film covered his
eyes, and he looked away as he spoke.

"And how is that, Master?"

"Because Lorini is powerless against her, and there were
none there with her. Lorini cannot strike at Dorini without

destroying herself. Cybelle looked long into those death sockets, and her mind was numbed with the Darkness."

Cephus Starkeeper gazed at Greyfax.

"And Grimwald has read the Book, and it was there written."

"Isn't there something to be done?" asked Melodias, striding up the length of the chamber, then back, hands locked tightly behind his back.

"Grimwald has seen. He can tell you."

Greyfax Grimwald raised his head, and spoke for the first time. "Cypher will fall before Cybelle is returned. It is all there to see, if you wish."

His eyes were ringed with dark hollows, and his mouth drawn down with the effort of the words.

"Cypher? It's not possible. Are we to bargain away the best of all that's left to vouchsafe the lady's safety?"

Melodias drove a fist into his open palm.

"It is not a barter, my friend. We will not deal Cypher her death blow in return for Cybelle. It is written it shall fall before the lady is returned, no more."

"Then we must return at once," said Melodias, sweeping back his cloak.

"It is done, my dear fellow. There is nothing left to prevent it. Even as we speak, it has occurred."

Cephus Starkeeper faced out upon the twinkling windows of the worlds of Windameir.

"I have already sent word to Dwarf, who carried the Chest. He must make his way across the River now, as best he can. There is nothing in our power left to be done at the moment."

Melodias stared at Greyfax, frozen in mid-stride. "Dwarf is in possession of the Chest, then?"

"For the moment, yes."

Greyfax met Melodias' grave look.

"But if we move to take the Chest now, she will be watching. We are not strong enough to hold Cypher, with Cybelle taken, and it would be too much of a temptation to trade the five for her safe return. I could not deny Lorini that, nor, I think, could you."

Melodias groaned, and turned to the Starkeeper. "And what say you, sir?"

"I've been here since the first breath drawn, and still I can't say one way or the other. All things are as they were, or are, or shall be. No one of us can change what is written in the Book. It is his Law."

Melodias glanced angrily at the ancient man. "Unsound advice, sir, from you. Can't you hint a little closer as to what should be done?"

"If it were so, then all would be solved long since, my impetuous young friend. You sound as if you'd been speaking with our fair heir of Fairingay."

"Does he know the lady has been taken?" asked Melodias.

"Not as yet. He's a fool in some ways, and I dare say he'd storm the Dark Place without further bother if he thought Cybelle were held there."

"Then isn't she?"

"Only her spirit. Her mortal being lies in Cypher, robbed. Dorini hopes to gain from the holding of the daughter what she missed having long ago. Trianion Starseeker wed Lorini, and Trianion Starseeker was what Dorini had wanted for her own. She is now having her revenge on Lorini."

Greyfax listened as Cephus Starkeeper finished, then rose and walked to the casement that opened upon the heavens.

"Enough, Melodias. We must keep Faragon from learning of this until it is time for us to move. What's done is done, and we have long roads between us if anything is to be saved, or the dark tide turned. You must return to your armies, and I, I must seek the roads beyond the River. It is a hard fate to know we depend all upon a dwarf and his companions."

"We have depended upon less, in time gone by."

"And what if he does not make the River?"

Greyfax looked steadily into his old friend's eyes. "Then if the Chest is taken, we will have lost the three lower realms to Dorini, my dearest friend, as simple as that."

Melodias gazed long into Greyfax's eyes, then turned to the Starkeeper. "What would Erophin say to this?"

"He would have no more to say than what is already in the Book."

"Is this so, sir?"

The old man looked away into the boundless sky and stars in answer, and did not speak.

In Cypher, an unknown winter began to settle in a gray cloud over the sunlight, and no sounds of laughter rang from the great halls or gardens. The rainbow fountains ceased to speak, their waters a muddy brown. Elves and men began drifting away, some to havens beyond the River, Calix Stay, others to the armies that stood at Fourthwaite and Thirdwaite, at the very realms' edge of the once golden Cypher.

* * *

Dwarf, peering back toward Havamal in the early morning light, turned to Bear and Otter.

"Does it seem darker back there, or is it my eyesight gone sore on me?"

The two animals stared away into the distance Broco pointed out.

A cold wind seemed to chill their bones, and before they could answer, Dwarf felt an icy finger upon his heart, and cried out in a weak voice.

"What is it, Dwarf?" chittered Otter, holding the little man's cold hand.

"I seemed to hear her laughter just then. And her finger tried to touch me."

"Well, it's all right, old fellow. We shall just get on with it, the sooner the better. Once we cross the River, I'm sure Froghorn or Greyfax will find us and tell us what to do."

Otter patted Broco reassuringly, although he felt none too sure of himself. Then he brightened as he thought of crossing Calix Stay again and seeing his old river, perhaps.

"Come aboard, you two. We've got a long day's walk ahead of us. We may as well make the best speed we can."

Bear rose, trying to ignore his troubled stomach, hoping it was the cause of the uneasiness that rested on his spirit.

As they climbed onto Bear's broad back, Broco looked back once more, his eyes distant and anxious.

"I hope all is well in Cypher," he muttered aside to Otter.

"What could possibly be wrong in Cypher, Dwarf?" chittered Otter, great surprise in his voice.

"Oh, nothing, I suppose. I'm sure it's just the weight of the Chest. It's not meant to be lugged about by the likes of me."

The three friends set out at a rapid jogging pace, leaving their troubled questions unanswered, and at day's end, Havamal and the Forest of Cypher were far behind, now only a faint blur in the rust-colored sunlight that set over the wide reaches of Atlanton Earth, and they were still far from Calix Stay, away beyond the Dragur Wood and the swamps of Grimm. It would be a long journey, and they had made a slow beginning.

An ominous darkness fell suddenly, the wind rose threateningly, and a night as still and cold as death itself was upon them.

A Silent Wood

The Forest of the Dragur

"This isn't going to get us anywhere," groaned Dwarf, stooping to pick up his hat, which had been knocked off by the wind.

"We have to get through the woods, Dwarf, or we can't find Faircrossing," complained Otter, his coat a sooty black from the fine-powdered dust that rose like ash as they walked. "We should keep on the road until we reach the Cross. We'll never find our way through any other way."

Dwarf sat down in a faint huff.

"Besides, the only way I remember seeing on the map was the old road that leads from Thirdwaite, and the road from the Cross. We'll just get more lost if we continue this way."

Otter sat down beside Dwarf as he finished speaking.

"We've been lost, to my way of thinking, ever since we left Cypher," mumbled Bear, sitting down in a dejected slump. "And now we're expected to get through this dismal mess of a wood to find a place no one even knows for sure is still there."

Bear snorted into silence.

"I know it's a bit of a bother, Bear. But we couldn't wait at Havamal to find Melodias or Greyfax, not with those horrible things after us. And we have to protect the Chest, no matter what."

Dwarf gave Bear a reassuring pat.

"How much of that food is left, Bear?" asked Otter.

The big animal took out the small sack Froghorn had given them, and looked through it gingerly.

"Only crumbs now," he groaned.

"Then first of all we'll have to find food," suggested Otter, peering around their desolate surroundings. "If there was water, we might find berries or herbs," he said doubtfully.

"I wouldn't want anything that grew in these dark woods," grumped Broco, looking out sullenly from beneath the brim of his hat.

"We'll have to eat whatever comes along. And something to drink would sit well too, for that matter."

"Bear's right, Dwarf. I guess we'll have to make do with whatever we find."

Otter tried knocking the dark ash from his coat.

"Ugh, this stuff makes you all sneezy."

As he finished speaking, he went into a coughing fit that left him gasping.

Broco studied the silent wood before him, then stood.

"I guess we'll have to go back to the road, and travel as far as the Cross, then. I don't like it, but it seems the only choice we have."

"At least we'll be able to go more quickly," offered Bear, anxious to have this unpleasant task over as soon as possible.

"And more visible to anyone that's interested. Unless we travel by night."

Dwarf had gotten to his feet and walked a few paces in the direction they had come. Suddenly he stiffened.

Bear and Otter both heard it at the same time.

From the direction of the road came the heavy tread of feet and the harsh chanting of Worlugh warriors.

Broco scrambled down beside a fallen tree, peering away into the thickets that bordered the road.

"Where are they going, Dwarf?" whispered Otter, as he crawled up beside his friend.

"I don't like the looks of it," hissed Broco. "They don't appear to be stragglers trying to get to safety. And they're heading back toward Thirdwaite."

"You mean they're fresh troops?" asked Bear, staring wide-eyed at the marching lines of enemy soldiers.

"Fresh, and numerous. Look at that line."

The three companions counted more than five hundred ugly Worlugh soldiers in the first formation alone, and the road was thick with the misshapen forms.

"Now what are we to do?" asked Bear, a sour twist in his voice.

"We'll have to wait until they're by," answered Dwarf, ignoring his friend's bitterness.

"We may be here come snow time, at this rate."

Bear pointed away toward the horizon, and the line of black-clad troops seemed to flow on unbroken.

"We'll stay here until dark, then if they're still on the road, we'll have to risk traveling through the wood."

Dwarf looked hastily over his shoulder.

"I don't care for the choice, but it's that, or march with those rude fellows."

Without realizing what he was doing, he placed a protective hand over the Chest inside his cloak.

"But however we do it, we must reach Calix Stay. It's our only hope now."

"We need a hiding place until dark," chittered Otter softly. "I'd feel better if we were farther from those smelly beasts."

"Then we'll go on a bit before we rest," said Dwarf. "With their sense of smell being what it is, a little distance may make us safe from seeing the inside of one of those stewpots."

"That's one more piece of scenery I could do without," growled Bear, wrinkling his nose in disapproval of everything in general.

Carefully, and undetected by the enemy hordes on the road, the comrades crept away into the heavier growth of stunted trees, and kept on until they did not fear being heard. When they were out of earshot, they pressed on at a rapid pace, and had gone far into the wood before they halted for a rest.

As they sat, Otter picked up a small stone to play with, and had rolled it up and down his chest twice before he noticed it was not an ordinary rock. He put it very close to his muzzle and studied it intently, screwing up his whiskers and making small whistling noises.

"Look at this, Bear. There's writing on this stone."

Bear snorted, then opened a weary eye to squint at the small thing Otter pushed toward him.

"So there is," he agreed, then shut his eye again.

"Let me see that, Otter."

Otter handed Dwarf the stone.

Broco held the small object to the sun, and carefully turned it this way and that, trying to decipher the odd runes carved minutely on the smooth gray face.

"It's a map of some sort," he said at length, "But I can't make out the names. It looks to be some sort of fortress or walled city."

Otter, growing tired of his toy, had begun pawing about in the ashen dust. Almost where he had found the first, he discovered another small stone, much like the one Dwarf held.

"Look at this," chirped Otter. "It's another one."

Broco took the other stone and held it to the first one.

"I believe it's a piece of a mosaic stone," mused Dwarf. "Are there any more of these there? I can't make sense of so small a part."

Otter dug and pawed the earth where he had found the stones. His small hands felt something large and cold beneath a layer of the fine black earth.

"Now whatever could this be?" he asked, puzzled.

He drew forth what appeared at first to be an old, rusted jar of some odd fashion.

"It's a helmet," said Bear.

"Why, it is," agreed Otter, pleased with his discovery. "And look at this."

He pointed out a dim outline of a tall pillar that was emblazoned on the visor of the ancient headpiece.

"Doesn't this look like what we saw in the Coda Pool, Bear? And see. That could be a sword there in front of it."

Bear was too busy digging to pay attention to Otter. His

huge paws had uncovered what looked to be part of a human skeleton.

"And here's the poor fellow that wore it," said Bear, his hackles slightly raised. "And there's another one here, too."

Dwarf and Otter went to stand at Bear's side.

"I wonder what war these fellows died from?"

Otter felt cautiously about the shallow black grave.

"Look, here's more."

Broco shoved back the sooty earth, revealing more bones.

"Maybe this was a battlefield," suggested Otter, feeling uneasy among so many unmarked graves.

"It must have been," concluded Dwarf, pushing the dirt back over his grisly discovery.

"Then those stones must have belonged to them, Dwarf. Maybe they were a battle map, or something like that."

"Yet I don't see any ruins of a fort or a city here," said Broco, looking about. "I don't think it had anything to do with these parts."

Bear handed Dwarf another small stone.

"There's more here, under this fellow."

Bear brushed the earth gently from the grim white bones.

"He must have carried them on him."

Dwarf hastily placed the stones in a rough fashion on the ground, and fitted them carefully together as Bear handed them to him.

After a few moments, he cried out in an excited voice.

"It is a map. Of these very woods."

Bear and Otter jostled each other to peer over Broco's shoulder at the dim patterns the stones made.

"See, look at this."

Broco pointed at a faint outline of a road that wound through figures of trees, and ended in what he thought to be a fort.

"And here. See where it looks like wiggly lines? That's an old form of High Man tongue. It says something, something, I can't make it out, then Garius, or Gareth, Brosingamene, something, Watcher of something Earth. And there it is. Or was. A settlement in these woods."

"Do you think it might still be here, Dwarf?"

"I don't know, Otter. These woods have changed greatly since the Dragon Wars. Most of the men who must have lived hereabout have surely all perished, or moved on."

"But there could have been some that stayed, couldn't there?"

"Possibly. But these are dangerous parts now."

Broco placed more pieces on the ground before him, arranging some, then adding more.

"This may be the road we're on," he said at last. "If we could be sure, it might lead us through to the other side, or farther. I think beyond us, on the far side, was what used to be Fairlake. And there somewhere is the crossing."

"Then we should try to follow along this road, if it is one. We can't go back to the other path. And we might wander around lost for days if we don't have some way to take us through."

"I think Otter is right on that count, Dwarf. And if we don't find food and water soon, no road is going to be of any help to us."

Broco studied his dim stone map, then nodded his head.

"It seems to carry on toward the direction we should follow

if we are to reach the crossing at Fairlake. There may be a stream nearby, if I make out this chart right."

Otter leaned over Dwarf's shoulder and chittered.

"Why, that may not be a road at all, Dwarf. It has too many squiggles in it. It looks more like a creek, or a river."

Dwarf smacked his hand on his knee.

"Of course. A river. I didn't recall any other roads through here. Not man-made roads, anyway. But a waterway, of course. They used a river to travel."

"It may have been a river once, Dwarf, but where is it now?"

Bear looked a gloomy question at Broco.

"Let's search ahead, Bear. It may be here close by," cried Otter, the thought of water easing his fear and hunger.

He raced ahead of his friends, nose high, sniffing for the familiar sweet smell of his favorite element.

"Don't get out of sight," called Bear gruffly.

"And don't be so noisy," grumped Dwarf. "We may not be alone here."

Otter slowed, remembering the graves, and recalling their danger, went on in a quieter trot.

Another hundred steps brought him to a sudden halt on the edge of a rocky, dry river channel, overgrown with thick black weeds and prickly gorse bushes that choked the stream bed from side to side.

His heart fell, but his disappointment didn't keep him from plunging down to see if any water at all still flowed through the thick brush below. At the very bottom, he found a thin trickle of brackish, slimy black water, almost oozing through the gnarled roots of the gorse.

He sighed, giving up thoughts of a swim.

"At least it's enough to drink," he said aloud, then scampered back up the bank to tell his friends of his small discovery.

Fire and Destruction

Adry, harsh wind had sprung up from the north, making the brittle limbs of the stunted trees rattle like bones. The black dust swirled over the parched ground until visibility was gone, and the three friends huddled miserably in the river channel, waiting for the storm to blow over. A droning sound moaned through the branches, setting the animals' hackles on end, and Dwarf's hair stood out on the back of his neck.

"I wonder how long this wind will last?" complained Otter, shuddering violently.

"Not for long, I hope. We can't travel in this sort of weather. I can barely see the tip of my nose."

Dwarf put out a hand before him, and strained to see it. There was nothing but the whirling black dust.

A renewed gust blew Dwarf's hat from his head, and he scrambled to retrieve it. A low thorn brake caught and held it, and Broco, groping almost blindly, flailed wildly about, trying to catch it before it might escape again.

The sudden sound of metal ringing against metal came clearly over the howling of the wind.

Broco froze where he stood, staring desperately toward the noise, but the wind confused his senses, and it seemed to surround him. Otter's voice chimed somewhere behind him, and Dwarf flew into a silent rage at his little friend's clumsy habit of noisy chatter, and there was no way he could warn him with a signal. Dwarf knew his friends were only a few feet away, but all he could make out was the dull brownish line of the thorn bushes, and beyond that, nothing.

The metal clink came again, and the distinct sound of a rifle bolt slamming home told Dwarf that Otter had been heard.

The silence that followed the cocking of the weapon was foreboding and deadly.

Broco crept as quickly away as he could, trying not to step on anything that might give him away. He reached the two animals just as Otter was drawing breath to speak again.

Dwarf's fierce look silenced the small gray creature.

Broco pointed back toward the thorn brake, and went through the motion of firing a gun. Bear's eyes grew wide, and he slowly began raising his own weapon, but Dwarf halted him with a violent shake of his head. He motioned for them to follow him, and set out stealthily down the river channel, away from the danger that threatened them.

The wind increased, and tiny particles of the hard black earth stung their eyes, blinding them, but they held their arms out to protect their faces, and pushed on, stumbling and bumping against the sharp thorns of the scrub trees, and Dwarf, unable to see, fell headlong into a deep channel, scraping himself badly, and before he could recover his senses, down came Bear and Otter on top of him.

Bear, thinking they had fallen into ambush, wheeled crazily up, and slashed savagely out with deadly claws, barely missing Otter in his rage and fear, and the little animal, confused and terrified, bit viciously at the nearest thing to him, which, as it happened, was Broco's cloak, flapping wildly in the wind.

After a few maddening seconds, Dwarf spluttered and kicked Otter roughly away.

"Stop it, you louts. You've almost crushed me, and now I'm in danger of being bitten to death by a ragged water dog."

Broco coughed, and cleared his throat of the black earth he had swallowed under the crushing weight of Bear.

"Dwarf?" chirped Otter apologetically.

"Who else were you expecting? I dare say you'd have had a tasty morsel of smushed dwarf if my cloak hadn't gotten in your way."

"Oh, Dwarf, I thought they had caught us."

Otter hurriedly helped Broco up, and began clumsily trying to dust him off.

A whistling whirr buzzed dangerously near the little man's head.

"Bear," cried Otter, "it's us."

With a wheezing grunt, Bear's huge head loomed out of the curtain of darkness.

"So it is," he agreed, looking about in confusion.

"Were we attacked?"

"I fell down a bank, and two lumbering stumblefeet fell right down on top of me."

Dwarf huffed, and began feeling himself to make sure nothing was broken or misplaced. He gingerly took the Chest from his cloak to inspect it.

A pale, gray-white light brightened the watercourse, and the black wall of blowing dirt seemed to lift.

"Well, the Chest is safe," mumbled Dwarf, after closely studying the small object in his hands.

"We can see with that, Dwarf," said Otter, frowning away into the brighter area the Chest had lightened.

Dwarf replaced the Chest in his cloak, and as before, they could see nothing but the black cloud of dust settling down over them.

Bear started to ask Broco to bring the Chest out again, when from the brush on their right, a sharp, shrill cry rang out above the wail of the wind, and the wall of darkness that surrounded them seemed to explode in flashes of rifle fire and bursting bombs.

Suddenly their shelter was afire from a hand bomb, and almost instantly the flames were fanned by the wind into an inferno that seemed to threaten them from all sides.

Away over the angry roar of the fire, they could hear hideous shrieks and harsh voices cursing, and the horrible smell of roasting flesh was heavy in the stifling air.

As Dwarf called out to flee, a blazing figure broke through the thick wall of brush, a ball of fire enveloping the writhing form, and a long, high-pitched shriek came from somewhere in its throat. A second later, the burned black Worlugh lay in a smoking, still heap at Bear's feet.

"This way," cried Otter, finding a hole through the almost solid sheet of fire.

Bear and Dwarf leapt quickly behind the tiny animal, and the three companions crashed unheedingly through the watercourse, trying to find a way that led to higher ground, and away from the blazing inferno behind them.

The wind seemed to change course, and just as Otter vaulted up the bank that would take them out of the river bed, the fire hissed and flared all along the edge of the channel, and they were forced to run on in the deep waterway. Otter splashed wearily on, followed by Bear and Dwarf, until he came to a sharp turn that seemed to be blocked up completely with thick thorns and water scrub.

"Quickly, we must go up now," shouted Otter, scrambling madly up the steep embankment.

As he reached the top, he saw the wildfire shooting out long fingers toward where he stood, and trees and small bushes burst into fire as the blazing red hand touched them.

"Hurry, you two," he urged in a tight voice, and as he turned to find an escape path, two large figures loomed out of the black curtain, and running blindly, fled past him without breaking stride. He recognized them as Worlughs by the bent, misshapen bodies and the heavy tread of their running forms.

Before he could caution Bear and Dwarf, another figure fled by.

As the panting friends came up to his side, Otter realized the last shadow he had seen was that of a man.

"This way, but watch out. There are Worlughs all about. And I just saw a man."

"A man?" shot Bear and Broco in unison.

"And running fast," exclaimed Otter excitedly.

Broco remembered vividly his encounter with the Urinine warriors at Seven Hills.

"Was he with the Worlughs?" questioned Dwarf.

"He was just running," said Otter. "And there's another one now."

Otter pointed an excited paw at a fast-moving form that skirted their hiding place and leapt away in the direction the other fleeing figures had gone.

"That seems to lead away from the fire, at any rate," said Bear, growing uneasy with the roaring flames that closed them in.

Before they could decide further, a dozen or more crashing, cursing shadows hurtled up the embankment not far from where they stood, and streaked by them, running hard.

The smell of the Worlughs startled them into flight, and they sprang along behind the enemy soldiers without any thought but of escaping the consuming flames.

Otter grabbed hold of Bear's broad back and clung stubbornly on, in order that he wouldn't get lost from his friends. He heard Dwarf chugging doggedly along behind.

After a brief time, firing broke out again, now to their right, then to their left, then seemingly behind them.

Bear repeated his spell, and emerged through the swirling dust and smoke in his man form.

"Quickly, Otter. We shall make better time this way. And we may have need of our weapons, from the sound of this fight."

Otter muttered his spell, and suddenly stood beside Bear,

his unfamiliar body awkward-feeling and clumsy.

"Now, Dwarf, which way?" asked Bear.

"The way we're going, I suppose. I can't recall where the river is, so we'll have to do what we can, at least until we get away from the Worlughs."

"But what about the men? They must surely be from Melodias." Otter spoke anxiously, trying to hear where the gunfire was coming from that had erupted as they spoke.

"Possibly, but we can't risk meeting up with anyone until we're sure how they stand. And now, I think our best way is to keep on toward our road undiscovered."

Bear started to agree with Dwarf, but was cut short by a volley of rifle fire that came from so close by they could hear the grunts and curses of the soldiers.

A dazed and badly wounded man staggered from the undergrowth, and fell in a groaning heap near Otter.

"By the great Othlinden, it's one of our side," gasped Otter, staring at the crest the man wore on his badly dented and blood-covered helmet.

As he knelt to aid the man, two Worlughs crashed heavily into sight, great yellow eyes wide, teeth bared to rip the flesh of their prey.

Bear snapped off a dozen quick rounds, and the Worlughs fell where they stood, their black lives oozing away like dark mud.

Otter held up the wounded man's head and put Bear's water flask to his lips.

"What army are you, friend?" asked Otter, trying not to let the injured man drink too quickly.

"He has the insignia of Greymouse," said Bear.

The man coughed, choked, and tried to speak.

"Here, take it easy, friend. You're among comrades now," Otter soothed.

"They caught us unaware," the man stammered. "All gone but the four of us."

He lapsed into another coughing spell that seemed to tear his body apart. Before he could speak again, Otter laid him gently back.

"He's gone," said Otter grimly.

"Let's cover him. At least we'll save him from those foul things, if there are any more of them about."

Dwarf began gathering stones and dead limbs from the thorn brush and piling it over the still figure of the slain man.

"I wonder if they killed his comrades, too? He said there were three others."

Otter worked as he spoke, gently laying the rocks over the man's chest.

"Not so lucky, probably. I imagine those beasts are as hungry as we are."

Broco hastily laid the last stones over the man's pale face.

The firing had slackened, and the wind seemed calmer.

"We'll have to go more carefully from now on. The storm seems to be about done."

"But the fire isn't," Bear said, nodding toward the crackling snap of the fire and the tall pillars of smoke that rode the wind like coiled black snakes.

"Then we'd best move on. But those Worlughs are all around us, so let's be quieter, if we can. We'll have to find our way back to the stream bed. And that's probably exactly what they're doing."

Broco slung his firearm across his back, and tightened his cloak about him.

"I think it's back this way, Dwarf," said Otter, pointing toward a dark line of low trees that ran away in a line toward the denser wall of the forest behind.

"Then let's see if we can find it."

The three companions set warily off, glancing about frequently, moving quickly toward the dying sun that broke through the dust storm as the wind began to diminish, and the fire behind them devoured itself and sank into a pale yellow-orange halo that seemed to hang like a low cloud over the Dragur Wood.

Greymouse and Fairingay

Wandering lost in the Dragur Wood, the three companions could not see the hordes of Gargolacs and Worlughs that marched to the attack launched upon General Greymouse at Thirdwaite. The long lines of the enemy they had seen upon the road were but a small portion of the great armies that ringed off the Dragur Wood and enclosed Thirdwaite in a black death grip.

General Greymouse watched warily as line on line of dark-clad troops took up assault positions all about the three hills that guarded the road into the Forest of Cypher and the very East Realm gate of Lorini's halls.

A gaunt captain stood beside the older man, his glance anxious.

"I don't like the lay of this, sir," he said, his face careworn and thoughtful.

"Nor do I, my good Norlin. It seems we are to be the object of much attention, by the looks of it."

Greymouse studied the horizon. Far away, barely perceptible, he saw what looked to be ugly black smoke boiling up on the wind over the Dragur Wood.

"This wind seems to bear more ill will than many I've seen. Look there, Norlin. Does that look like smoke to you?"

"I'd seen it earlier, sir. There was a lot of wind and dust there earlier, but the smoke started not long ago. A fire in the forest, I would think."

"But who is in that wood, and what mischief can they be up to?" Greymouse shook his head. "We've not had word all day from our pickets at the Cross, nor any of the others along the road. I'm afraid they've been lost, or taken to the wood to escape."

"That could explain the smoke, sir. Perhaps it's some of our pickets signaling."

"They would hardly give away their position to do that. It may be some battle, some struggle to escape. It does not sit well."

The older man searched the wood, but the black earth that hung on the wind and the billowing tower of smoke filled his visions, and he only caught confused glimpses of dark forms swimming dimly in the murky depths. For a brief moment, he thought he had detected some light, some presence that lifted his worn hopes, but it faded beneath the gloom, and he lost it. His mind roamed back and forth above the Grimm wastes, but only occasional glimpses of enemy troops filled his mind, and he once more sought whatever he had touched with that brief moment. It seemed to come again, more clearly, and a sudden flicker of understanding flooded his mind. He wondered how he had mistaken it. It was the light of the Arkenchest, cloaked and very still, but it yet was in the hands of the Circle. The frightening news Faragon Fairingay had disclosed to him began to ease from his mind, and he thought perhaps at this moment the youngest son of his old friend had the Chest safe, and was upon his way with it at the very moment.

But his eyes turned once more to the crawling hordes below him, and he knew it would not be wise to return the Chest here, not with the dangerous battle that was looming.

"You'd best see to the disposition of the troops, Norlin. It seems we're in for a time of it."

The young captain saluted and strode away to the headquarters tent.

Greymouse sat heavily upon his camp stool, and began plans for his defense of Thirdwaite. His mind ranged across the enemy armies, seeking clues to their intentions, but only a savage hatred burned in those dark souls, and nothing but murder and destruction met his wandering thoughts. There were Ashgnazi among these troops, and the elite of the Gorgolacs, the Ugil warriors, filled a long flank on his right side, lower down on the second hill of Thirdwaite. And he found men among the gathering hordes, tall dark men from below the borders of the Grimm wastes, who had fallen in with the Darkness after the high kings of Fairlake had gone, their kingdoms destroyed.

Yet he found no presence of Dorini, nor her underlord, nor any of the dreaded beasts, Fireslayer, or Suneater, or Cakgor. It troubled him, but at the same time he felt reassured. The direction was left to the field captains and commanders of the Gorgolac and Worlugh armies. But the sheer numbers alone told him this was no minor skirmish. It had to be something on a major scale. There was too much committed to the action.

He cast his thoughts toward Melodias at Fourthwaite, but no response came, and he wondered what mission his friend was upon that took him beyond reach. He turned his mind to Faragon Fairingay, and faintly felt his young friend, but from very far away. He quickly passed on his present situation, and relayed the distressing news of the great hordes of enemy soldiers, then went on to the rumor of news about the Arkenchest.

When Froghorn learned of this last information, he quickly turned to Urien Typhon. The two friends sat before a small fire on the first of the chain of hills beyond Calix Stay. A great elfin host lay camped about them.

"Greymouse thinks the Chest has been recovered," he said, looking up from the fire into his friend's eyes. "I had hoped it would come about before now, but better late than not at all. And a great army is prepared to attack Thirdwaite. Greymouse seems to think he can stand off the assault, but we'd best prepare ourselves, in case need arises for our aid."

"Will we need Tyron's men?" asked the elf.

"I think we had best save Tyron for an absolute reserve. His service hangs by a thread now, and I think it would be dangerous to risk calling on Tyron, except as a last resort. Greymouse seems to feel unsure about the situation there. He feels no hand to guide the battle, other than the enemy commanders. No sign of Doraki or Dorini, or any of those other foul beasts."

"Could it be a diversion to draw our attention from elsewhere?"

"That's what he wondered," mused Froghorn. "Yet he feels sure the number against him could be spared only for a major attack. And we've seen nothing to say of anything planned for Fourthwaite or elsewhere. After Melodias drove off Doraki, the Dark Queen's armies were in rout, and I dare think, in general retreat all along the borders of Atlanton Earth."

"But they seem to have regrouped for a try at Thirdwaite."

Urien Typhon rose and stamped his booted foot to get his legs awake.

"On the face of it, yes. Yet there seems to have been some build-up in the Dragur Wood even before, as if they'd had it planned this way all along. Perhaps the attack on Fourthwaite was the feint, and Thirdwaite the objective from the first."

"How does Melodias feel about this?"

"I'm not sure. It was a close call at Havamal, right enough. If it hadn't been for Greyfax and the Chest, I honestly think Melodias would have lost his army." Froghorn paused, the bitter thought of what would have occurred had that happened burning in his mind. "But I haven't been able to reach Melodias or Greyfax. They seem to be elsewhere at the moment. So we shall have to lay our own plans, in the case that Thirdwaite is more than Greymouse thinks."

Froghorn stood and whistled a low note, and Pe'lon appeared silently at his side.

"And for now, I think I shall have a look back in the direction of the Dragur Wood. It seems my dwarf has recovered the Chest, and may be in need of some assistance."

"What shall we do in the while?" asked Urien, not quite liking the idea of his friend leaving him with the decision of when or where to move his army.

"Nothing. We must wait before we move. To strike too soon is as loathe as too late. It may be Greymouse will have no need of us at all."

"And if he does?"

"Then I shall be back, and we'll see what must be done."

Froghorn touched Pe'lon gently, and the great horse spun away in a blue-white light, up beyond the cool breath of the wind that roamed across the Fallow Hills, and Froghorn shot through the speed and distance of time, and sought traces of Broco, and Otter, and Bear, far away, and out of his sight beneath the grotesque trees of the Dragur Wood.

Even as Froghorn searched, the comrades were fallen on by a band of ragged assailants.

Strange Meetings

Dwarf peered cautiously over the rough edge of a fallen log. A sudden, angry whine buzzed over his head, followed by the flat crack of a rifle.

"They're still there," he announced, although Bear and Otter had heard the shot clearly, and knew their assailants had not given up the fight.

The three companions lay concealed in a fall of thick black trees, blown over in the windstorm that had just abated. Behind them, they could still see and smell the heavy gray-black smoke that drifted up from the smoldering fire.

Two more shots rang out, and black dust puffed up above the friends' heads.

"Can you make out where they are, Dwarf?" asked Bear, squinting to see through a small chink in their barricade.

"No, but they're in front of us, as close as I can make it. Not too many, either, by the rifle fire."

"Can't we sneak out?" whispered Otter, looking about him for a path of escape.

"When it's darker," replied Dwarf, once more poking his head carefully above his concealment. His eyes caught a brief flicker of movement off to his right. A shadow slipped behind a large, bent tree, and disappeared.

"They're trying to get on our flank," hissed Dwarf, motioning Otter to move to the right side of their position.

Otter nodded, and crawled to face this new threat.

Someone whistled a low, fluttering note, and it was answered by a higher, sliding call.

"There's one behind us, too," growled Bear, whirling and aiming his firearm in the direction of the danger that loomed at their backs.

Another shot whined away harmlessly over the heads of the three comrades, then a silence began to grow that was more frightening than the rifle fire.

Time oozed slowly by, and they heard nothing. The barren wood had no evident wildlife, and only the beating of their own hearts and their breathing broke the stillness. Their eyes strained to detect a movement, but there was only stillness and silence.

When Otter whispered to Bear, the big animal jumped, and triggered a shot into the dirt near Dwarf.

"Be careful, you silly ass. You've almost put a hole in my boot." Broco fumed, forgetting in his huff to keep his voice down.

"Shhhh," warned Otter frantically.

"Oh, shush yourself," ranted Dwarf, working up to a high state of indignant anger.

"Who goes there?" rang out a clear voice in man tongue,

but none of the three friends could tell how close it was, or from what direction it came.

"Don't answer," whispered Dwarf, holding his finger to his lips to indicate silence.

"Are you friend or foeman?" came the voice again.

It seemed to come from all directions at once. The words echoed, then died.

The silence grew deafening throughout the wood.

"They sound like men, Dwarf," said Bear, in a barely audible voice. "Maybe we should answer."

Dwarf pondered, then called out in a mighty voice, "We're followers of the Light."

As his voice died away, a soft laughter drifted slowly to the friends' hiding place.

"Might you be known as Broco, Dwarflord?"

Dwarf was shocked beyond speech.

Bear answered in a thundering voice that made the dead leaves tremble.

"Broco, Dwarflord, he is, and I am Bruinlen, Bearlord. We head a strong force that will destroy you and your ancestors if you be foemen."

A long trill of muffled laughter floated from the brush surrounding them.

"Is an otter among you?" questioned the voice once more.

"Otter, kin of Othlinden, King," shot back Otter, fingering his firearm, the battle fire glimmering dangerously in his eyes.

"By the living gourd, Cranny, we has found 'em again," cried a laughing voice, and Ned Thinvoice stood up not twenty paces from Otter's concealment.

Flewingam and Cranfallow appeared from behind trees near

Dwarf, and the friends stood staring dumbly at their lost companions.

"Well, I would never," stammered Bear.

"Flewingam," shouted Otter, racing to clasp his old comrade's hand.

Bear lumbered heavily along behind him, and Dwarf stood numbly, looking at his two companions of the Battle of Seven Hills.

"Well, we is in the soup, right as not," said Cranfallow, "so we might as soon says hello."

"I didn't think we'd ever see 'em no more, but here they is," agreed Thinvoice, advancing on the still speechless Dwarf.

"We come near on plugging you for them Lughs as what jumped us a whiles back," said Cranfallow, dusting the little man off and shaking his hand heartily.

"They started shooting so's we couldn't makes hide from hair, with the fire and all. And then we's seen some awful funny moving around, and we just thoughts them Lughs had found us sure."

Thinvoice took Dwarf's hand and shook it.

Without warning, Dwarf sobbed and sat down heavily.

"Is you hurt, sir?" cried Cranfallow, leaping to Broco's side.

All the others quickly gathered around the little man, their faces grim.

"No, I'm not hurt, blast you, and good thanks to your poor marksmanship," huffed Dwarf, trying to swallow a sob.

"Then what's done to hurt you?" asked Ned, kneeling.

"I must have eaten something that disagrees with me," blustered Dwarf testily, rising and stalking out of the circle of his surprised friends. He stumped heavily to the fallen trees that lay in front of their hiding place, and wiped his eyes. He turned, and in control of himself once more, walked quickly back to Thinvoice and Cranfallow.

"Hail, and well met," he said, thumping them great thwacks as high up as he could reach. "I've been wondering when you'd find your way back. And it seems you've come just at the moment we could use you most."

"Well, we is glad of it, isn't we, Ned?"

"We is indeed, Cranny."

"And I'm at your service, too," put in Flewingam, extending his hand to Dwarf, who readily accepted it, and shook it briskly.

"Otter and Bear have talked of you," said Broco politely, "and I'm sure I'm at your service."

"But what ever are you doing all the way out here?" asked Otter.

"That's a question we might well ask you," replied Flewingam. "We got set upon and separated from our company. We were a patrol sent out by General Greymouse, but now I imagine we're stragglers."

"Is it hard by with Greymouse?" Dwarf frowned as he spoke.

"It wasn't when we left, but we came upon so many enemy troops, we thought it safer traveling in the wood. Yet it proved just as dangerous here."

Flewingam sat, and drew a rude map in the black earth. "Here, we counted over a full division of Worlughs, moving toward Thirdwaite."

He made a mark to show where they had seen the enemy soldiers.

"And here, two divisions of Gorgolacs."

Another mark.

"There seemed to be a band of Worlughs that were following after you, from everything we could make out."

"I knew it. Or I knew something or someone was back there. It couldn't have been all my imagination," rumbled Bear.

"And we're somewhere near here, not too far from the Cross," finished Flewingam.

"At least that's good news," broke in Dwarf. "If we're that close, we could be there by tomorrow."

"But that road is full of the enemy," said Flewingam. "They've been moving in force since the day after we left Thirdwaite. We couldn't even find a way to get back to warn the general. They have all the road in pickets, and I think probably most of this forest, too."

"Then they won't be watching so closely somewhere they don't fear the Light to be. We can travel easier if they're not looking for anyone to be abroad."

Dwarf moved a line with his finger on Flewingam's map.

"If we move on here, then to the Cross, then up the road that runs through this wood, we'll be on the right way to the Grimm wastes."

"The Grimm wastes?" said Cranfallow, surprise and fear heavy in his voice.

"And then on to Grimm Crossing," finished Dwarf.

"But that would be the other ways what we should be going," corrected Thinvoice. "We is never going to gets no help thataways."

"We can't get back to Greymouse either, Ned. And to cross the Fallow Hills is too long, and I doubt it's safe any longer if the Darkness is moving in the numbers you say."

"There isn't no help in going into them Grimm wastes neither, to my way of thinking. We can't finds no help in them parts."

"The River, Cranny. We're going to cross Calix Stay."

"I ain't never heard no river called by that handle. Has you, Ned?"

Ned shook his head, regretting already the reunion with his strange dwarf witch.

"I knowed it would come to this," he muttered under his breath.

"Come to what, Ned?" asked Dwarf, turning to face Thinvoice.

"Come to no good, that's all. Kit and boodle, all bound for where we was come from."

"I think Broco is right, Ned. We can't get back to our lines through all those lumps behind us. Our only road lies away from here."

Flewingam looked sternly at Thinvoice and Cranfallow.

"We doesn't has no say, nohows. If we is done, then we's done, so no matter whichaways we goes. At least we is with friends," said Cranfallow.

"That's what I says, Cranny. At least we is with friends."

"Good lad, Ned. Now what should we look to first? Arms? Food? Have we any water?"

Flewingam began going over the supplies they would need for their perilous undertaking.

"We have little food, but we've found water. Our arms are adequate," replied Dwarf. "We're not interested in carrying a fight to our good lumps out there, but in getting away with the least trouble possible."

"Then food seems to be our main concern at the moment. We have two days' rations between the three of us, four or five, if we're careful."

"Ugggh," moaned Bear, looking at Flewingam. "We've just barely kept our strength up with these bird's rations we've had. I'm so hungry now I might think Worlugh steak not so bad."

"We'll find something, Bear, without tasting that delicacy." Flewingam stood, adjusting his pack harness.

"There's no use thinking about it, Bear," chided Otter. "It only makes it worse."

"That's right, Otter. Our best move now is to start as quickly as we can. Something will turn up."

Flewingam clapped Bear on his broad back.

"Cheer up, old fellow. We'll stand you to supper at the first inn we come to."

Dwarf picked up his firearm and slung it on his shoulder.

"Let's make a start. The sooner we get on our road, the sooner we'll find its end."

Otter handed Bear the near empty sack Froghorn had given them when they set out, and turned to Flewingam.

"Well met, friend. It's a good wind has blown us together again. I hope we'll find better fare before long, to gladden our reunion."

"It's gladdened already, Otter. But a dram or two of good water and supper wouldn't dampen it any."

"And I don't think a few tote kegs of new honey would hurt so much," added Bear.

Dwarf turned and addressed the small band as everyone stood ready to go.

"I think it must be some sort of wizard's doings that we are all together again, and I know it makes me feel easier to have such good comrades to start out this rather risky business of getting to Calix Stay. I wish there was another way, but there seems only one road open to us, and that leads on through these woods, and to the Grimm wastes. Or at least that's all I can fathom now."

"After that, what?" asked Flewingam.

"I don't know. We have word that we are to reach the River, and that's all I can say. I think, though, that once we reach there our journey will be done, and our errand seen through to its proper end."

"What about them Lughs what was following along, Flew? Them what was tracking our friends here? Do you think we got them lumps in all the ruckus?"

"I hope so, Cranny."

Bear looked at Otter, a faint doubt edging into his voice. "You don't think that could be that Worlugh who escaped us, do you? I mean surely he wouldn't be so foolish as to try to follow us all this way?"

"It might be, Bear. I've felt we were followed, but I just thought it was a band of stragglers trying to escape. Now I don't know."

"I think I know what he has in mind," broke in Dwarf. "If

it's the same one, he'll have a certain object on his mind that we know about. And I don't doubt that if he has followed us all this way, he will have overheard us talking about it. It would make him even greater than all the Dark Queen's underlings. He may have plans of his own."

Cranfallow had opened his mouth to speak, but a hail of bullets burst from the deeper part of the thickets, and the friends fled hastily into the cover of the dark trees, followed by harsh curses and gunfire.

The horrible form of Trag stood out from the gruesome band of Worlugh warriors.

"This way," cried Dwarf, and plunged wildly into a tangled patch of thorns. "This way."

Shots and cries came from all directions, and his heart froze for a moment as he thrashed madly on, but the thickets cleared, and he burst headlong into the deep, slippery bank of the small stream again. Bear followed closely on his heels, then Otter, Cranfallow, and Thinvoice, with Flewingam bringing up the rear.

"Where now?" shouted Otter over the noise of running feet and rifle fire.

"Straight on," screamed Dwarf. "To the waterway. To Grimm Crossing."

His words echoed on over the flash and burst of rifle fire, and the companions, their gladness of their reunion sinking into a black shroud of terror, followed on after the flying form of Dwarf, now ahead and away, running hard, deeper and deeper into the foreboding gloom of the Dragur Wood.

Their long journey to return the Arkenchest to the Circle had begun once more in earnest.

A New Beginning

A New Beginning

Retreat

Raging hordes of Gorgolacs and Worlughs fell shrieking on the defenders of Thirdwaite. The night sky blazed with battle fires, and the fiery tails of angry shells ripped the darkness, lighting the land with an eerie pyre that loomed over the Fallow Hills and cast grisly shadows in the Dragur Wood.

Donark, attacking the flanks of General Greymouse's armies, rolled up the outlying pickets in a vicious stroke that threatened the positions farther up the slopes of the Council Hill, and Thiazi, at the head of fresh Worlugh troops, beat savagely at the outposts of the smaller hill, called Thin Elder.

Beyond, thousands of enemy troops lingered, waiting to be thrown into the attack.

Greymouse, from his command point at the heights of Thirdwaite, studied the exploding bright orange lights going off below him, and ordered his soldiers into an ever tightening ring.

The battle lines swayed to and fro, first giving, then regaining ground, and after the third hour of the assault, the firing seemed to subside, and the enemy hordes that ranged on the slopes of the three hills retired, leaving the bodies of their dead to lie in ragged heaps where they fell. A dull red sun rose slowly over the smoke and dust of the battle, glowing dimly through the clouds, like a distant, malevolent eye.

As the day grew on toward midmorning, an ominous silence spread across the battle camps, and no movement was seen throughout the enemy positions. Great black carrion birds circled and landed on the sprawling heaps of the dead that littered the lower slopes.

General Greymouse searched relentlessly for some sign, some clue as to what the enemy planned next. They had not been driven by force from his defenses, but simply melted into the dawn. Not even a third of their troops had been put into action, he knew, and yet it had taxed his inferior-numbered army to almost its utmost to stem the hordes of the Dark Queen. He realized his defense of Thirdwaite was hopeless.

Having reached this decision, he began gathering his captains to outline his new plans, and to begin the withdrawal from Thirdwaite. It would leave the door open, but his only chance lay in the Forest of Cypher. There, he thought, he would have a natural barrier that would be unfamiliar to the enemy, and their numbers could be dispersed in the thick woods.

By noon, everything was in readiness, and the first companies of Greymouse slowly and methodically began the descent into the dark shadows of the wood.

At an hour past midday, Thirdwaite stood barren and desolate beneath the unwarming, brittle sun.

At dusk, new positions were taken, and General Greymouse inspected his lines.

A tall redhaired man strode beside him.

"Is the 20th in the glen, as I ordered?" asked Greymouse, looking back toward the empty hills of Thirdwaite.

No movement could be seen, and the silence still hung over the enemy camp.

"As ordered, sir. We have the main line along the edge of the wood, with the reserves waiting at intervals, in the backup positions. We can keep falling back, regrouping, and holding as long as we have a need to."

"Good. These woods are deceptive, so be sure to keep close contact with those companies that make up the flanks."

"We have runners, sir, and all the commanders are warned to maintain contact, no matter what the situation."

Greymouse halted, and began sketching a rough map with his boot. In the failing light, the lines seemed to flicker and glow as he spoke.

"If they come tonight, see to it the commanders are all equipped with the signal rockets."

"It's already been done, sir."

"Now. Here is our position. We have the woods' edge blocked to here, and reserves behind us."

He drew in another solid line to show the placement of his troops.

"Should we fail to hold here, we shall fall back upon the reserve line, and so on. Our only chance to turn them is to separate their numbers. We must divert the brunt of their attack, and lump them into smaller bands, if possible."

"I see your point, sir."

"And remember, lad, we have no backup. No one can reach us here in time. We must keep them at bay at all costs. There is no escape for us if we fall. Make sure the men know that."

"They know it, sir."

"Then let's finish our tour, and get what rest we may. We shall need all our strength soon enough. Too soon, perhaps."

"Sir."

The two figures disappeared into the shadowy trees, and from beyond Thirdwaite, an angry swelling was heard, like a flaming heart of fire beating upon iron, and it built in volume, until the very earth trembled and reeled, and a dull orange glow filled the early night sky with dancing tongues of flame, and like a river of molten fire, a wave of enemy troops came rushing down the abandoned slopes of Thirdwaite directly on toward the woods.

An alarm bugle sounded, and the defenders in the Forest of Cypher gripped their weapons and stared in awe at the unbroken tide of Gorgolac and Worlugh hordes racing to sweep them away in the overwhelming, raging flood of fire and death.

General Greymouse, standing beside an officer of his Fourth Army, sent a lightning bolt arching up in green and blue and red lights to burst in a thousand bright arrows that fell into the river of swarming enemy troops, but the light was quickly devoured in that rampaging torrent, and the elation and hopes of the defenders who watched soon vanished, and they waited nervously as the oily fires of the enemy's torches advanced upon them.

Quite suddenly, like a dam bursting, the hordes of Dorini were in their midst, and a roar like the dying of mountains drowned all sight and sound in its terrible maw, and the forest shook with this violent wind, and much sooner than he had expected, Greymouse found his armies forced to fall back upon the reserves.

And to his right and left, he saw the frightened fingers of flares streak up the black wall of heaven, and he realized in his distress that his army was becoming hopelessly broken apart.

There was nothing but the woods and his badly outnumbered forces between the bloodthirsty hordes of Darkness and the realms of Cypher.

In the Halls of Ice

In the frozen halls of Dorini, great stone bells tolled in rolling thunder, and the greenish light shone dimly in the towering throne room.

A yellow hissing cloud ringed the cold seat where the Dark Queen rested, her eyes a chilling shadow flickering in the depths of a black void.

"It is time, my love," rang her voice, dull and cold. "Come forth to me once more. You have dwelled long in my thought, and healed yourself in my hatred and revenge. I bid you come forth."

A trembling sliver of icy light, dulled and pale in the frozen air, began to grow before Dorini. Its phantom shape whirled and writhed into a dim, misty ice form, and there stood before her the bodiless spirit of Doraki, who had been returned to her by Cakgor after his defeat at Havamal by her hated enemy, Greyfax Grimwald.

Doraki's grim eyes opened, and heavy lids revealed the

hollow, glowing sockets that reflected back the nothingness of eternal death.

"I am here, Your Darkness."

"You have another errand, my lovely. This time we shall not fail."

"Your command, Your Darkness?"

"You will return to our armies at the Dragur Wood. We have my cursed sister's Cypher in our grasp. None can hope to hold us from our quest now. And her sniveling daughter is mine."

As she spoke, she opened her deadly eyes wide, and upon a sudden gale of frozen air there came a sheet of solid ice, and within it lay the ashen features of Cybelle, her eyes closed, and her body encased in the unsleeping death of Dorini's mind.

"What of those other foul beasts, Your Darkness?"

"They have no power to stop us, fool. We hold our most powerful weapon here, where they can do nothing against us. And all we need for total control is the accursed Chest. Then all shall be ours forever. Not even the High Lord of Windameir can revoke his own Law. It is written that these lower realms shall be mine. I shall merely make them mine forever, and take them beyond the grasp of the accursed Circle."

"As you wish, Your Darkness."

"And take Cakgor with you. Those wretched souls shall feel the agony of his hunger, and the vengeance of Dorini. All shall be darkness soon. Even now, I hear my warriors cry at the very realms' edge of that stinkhole Cypher."

"We shall have it, Your Darkness, if it is your command. You have my oath upon it."

"And if indeed you succeed, my pet," crooned Dorini, an icy edge in her voice, "then you shall have my sister's brat for your own plaything."

"My thanks, Your Darkness. You are most gracious."

"Now go."

Far below in the grim dungeons of the Palace of Ice, Cakgor set up a wailing howl of rage and hatred and rattled the cold chains that bound him. Doraki hurried to unleash him, and the dark walls parted as the two sped away toward General Greymouse's armies, struggling grimly in the flaming Forest of Cypher.

A frozen wind began to blow across Atlanton Earth as Doraki and Cakgor made their dark way toward Cypher, and the hearts of men quailed and flew in terror at the coming of these terrible foes.

Lorini, watching the embattled defenders backed to her very gates, looked sadly away, and went to her daughter's room, where the cold body of Cybelle lay.

It would soon be time to leave her beloved Cypher.

Sorrow in Cypher

Ashocking change greeted Faragon Fairingay as Pe'lon entered the realms of Cypher. The great horse neighed and tossed his silver mane as Froghorn dismounted. A subtle change was evident in the air, one that he had noticed as soon as he had entered Cypher's borders. At last, an elf he had not seen before came out of the stable and asked him his business.

"Where is Derin?" asked the young wizard, slightly taken aback by the elf's impolite inquiry. He was used to a more elaborate welcome.

"Gone," was the brief reply.

"Derin gone?" repeated Froghorn, somewhat shaken.

"To join Greymouse."

"And Erin, and Frey?"

"Both gone."

Froghorn walked slowly into the stables where Pe'lon had stayed on so many occasions. The stalls had a smell of disuse, and a faint musty odor hung like mildew in the high, once bright tack room.

There was no fresh water for Pe'lon, nor any of the cool, refreshing grass that always grew in abundance in Lorini's realms.

Froghorn turned Pe'lon free in the courtyard below the tower of the swan, so that he might find forage and water in the long meadow that bordered the end of the north gardens.

"I shall not be long," he told Pe'lon. "Stay not too long at your pleasure, my friend."

The huge steed neighed into Froghorn's shoulder, then trotted away.

"You ought not let your animal tear up the walkway," scolded the elf. "I've enough trouble keeping the stable clean, much less having to pick up after a brute turned loose in the garden."

A white-hot sheet of spiraling, billowing flame shot upward from Froghorn's hand, and drumming thunder seemed to move the very earth the young wizard stood upon, and his gray-blue eyes blazed menacingly.

"You won't have to trouble yourself over my mount," he shot at the stunned elf, who simply stood wringing his hands in nervous silence.

For the first time, there was no Cybelle to greet him from the tall white tower of the swan, nor music to soothe his troubled heart. It suddenly struck him there was no sound at all coming from Lorini's halls. A shadow of uneasiness crept over him, and he hurried on to find explanations for surly stable elves and the disappearance of Pe'lon's old friends who used to care for him on his previous visits.

As he entered the tall doorway that led into the main rooms of the north wing, he noticed the sunlight did not dance its

usual bright song on the carpets and tapestries, and his footsteps rang hollow in the long passageway that ran down the
high, airy hall. No voice called out to him, and no cheerful
faces appeared to seek his news or relate the happenings at
Cypher.

As he entered the wing where Lorini kept her study, a fair
elf dressed in golden livery barred his way.

"My lady is receiving no callers," he said shortly, blocking
the door into Lorini's rooms.

Froghorn did not recall this elf, nor approve of his manner
any more than that of the stable elf. His eyes blazed a shooting
shower of stars and golden sparks, and the elf fell back cowering before him. Froghorn strode past, and into Lorini's deserted sitting room. He hesitated, his dark anger replaced by
foreboding. He heard soft weeping from the chamber ahead,
and hurried on.

Lorini sat at her pearl-colored desk, head down, her frail
shoulders burdened with sorrow.

"My lady," murmured Froghorn softly, stunned and dis-
mayed at the sight.

He choked up and dared not go on, lest his voice should
give him away.

The seated figure started at the sound of his voice, and the
weeping subsided.

Lorini raised an ashen face, streaked with tears, and her
eyes were red and puffy from crying. A grief beyond bounds
weighed on her, and she suddenly looked old and defeated.

Froghorn's voice would not come.

For the first time, the lady of Cypher seemed to recognize
him.

"Fairingay," she stammered out, then broke into fresh sobbing. "You should not have come, not just now," she managed.

"But my lady," began Froghorn, advancing toward her.

"No," she cut him off, "you must not see me this way. I'm a mess, and I have to have time to make myself decent. Leave me now. I'll call you when I'm presentable."

Froghorn had to obey, and reluctantly withdrew to her sitting room and sat heavily in a window seat, staring listlessly out over a much changed Cypher.

The fountains no longer tumbled merrily, and the colors had all melted into a single silver-gray hue. Where bright blue sky and soft golden sunshine had been, there now was an overcast gray light, and the sunshine that bathed Cypher had grown colder and more remote.

There was no warmth in Lorini's halls now.

He had pondered these new developments while he awaited Lorini, and did not hear her when she entered.

"My good Fairingay, my light. You've come in bad timing, I fear. I was expecting Greyfax to be here before you."

Although her features were drawn and pale, Lorini looked more her old self. She looked younger, and without the air of despair and defeat that had upset the young wizard so.

"What has happened here, my lady? I find the change quite disheartening."

"It's not so gay, is it?" Lorini's eyes seemed to look through and beyond Faragon. "You may as well know, my dear. I had hoped I would not be the one to deliver such tidings, but it seems it shall be so, after all. Since you have been away, my sister has been to Cypher, in these very rooms."

Froghorn drew breath loudly, and hissed between his teeth.

"You mean *here?*"

"You were all away at your errands, and she knew I am helpless to act against her. She timed it so that there would be none here but Cybelle and I."

He knew what she was going to say next, and a black grief gripped his soul with the unrelenting truth of the terrible change that had burned through the very life of Cypher.

"Cybelle fell under her power," he said, half aloud, his heart frozen within him.

"She is here, in her room, but her spirit is captive of my dark sister. I am powerless. It will take greater wisdom than a grieving heart to win her back."

"May I see her?" asked Froghorn, in a subdued tone.

Lorini beckoned him to follow her, and she led the way to the starlit twilight wing, where he had spent his last time in Cypher.

Cybelle lay on a canopied bed, its headboard in the fashion of the Crown of the Five Secrets. She appeared asleep, yet her features were without a sign of warmth, and a pale halo of fear marred her beautiful face.

Froghorn knelt at her side, and wept into his cape.

Lorini laid a gentle hand on his shoulder.

"Despair not, dear Faragon. All is not beyond hope. We shall have to put aside our sorrow to win her back."

He remained motionless, head hung forward on his chest.

At last he spoke.

"I shall return her, if it's the last breath I breathe. What is my life to hers?"

"We shall call Greyfax now, I think. I have spoken to him on this grave matter, as well as with Cephus Starkeeper. Greyfax says he has tidings, so we'd best wait upon his counsel before we act."

Froghorn rose, and kissed the cold lips of Cybelle. He turned quickly, unable to bear the sight of her lifeless beauty.

"By the Eternal Flames of Windameir, I shall see her safely home," he vowed, his eyes turned a piercing, fiery gray-blue.

A sheet of golden fire ringed his head, and blinding pillars of light reached out from him in dazzling white.

As the brilliant lights dimmed, Greyfax Grimwald entered the room, his face drawn.

Before Froghorn or Lorini could speak, the older wizard had bowed to the lady and kissed her hand tenderly.

"We must move, my friend. Doraki is upon his way, with one of the beasts. Even yet, we may be too late to escape his notice. We are not ready to strike our, blow as yet. We must hurry."

His voice was grave and old.

Without waiting for a reply, Greyfax was gone, striding quickly out of sight.

"Wait, blast you," cried Froghorn, barely bowing to Lorini, and dashing away after the older man.

Froghorn caught up as Greyfax was mounting An'yim.

"Where are we bound? To Dorini?"

"Hardly, my reckless pup. That's exactly what she would wish." Greyfax shook his head wearily. "No, I'm afraid our paths lie away from Cybelle, for the moment."

"Then you go without me," shot Froghorn, whistling for Pe'lon. "I find my path leads only to the Dark Queen."

"Come, come, you bull-headed fellow," said Greyfax, his look softening as he gazed at the young man. "We shall have your Cybelle back, but we cannot bolt in through the front door. I said our paths lead away from your lady, but only because it's the only way we may reach her. But our chances grow dimmer the longer we tarry. Haste, my young friend, sometimes is in order. Even if it appears to some careless and ill-planned."

Greyfax met Froghorn's gaze, and the clear gray-blue eyes had regained their old sparkle.

Greyfax spoke again, gently touching Froghorn's shoulder. "You must gather the forces of the Circle wherever you find them, my friend. I shall be upon the same errand. We have little time to lose." Greyfax stood beside An'yim, and patted the noble animal tenderly.

"But where shall we gather? Surely it is too great a distance to span to be of any help here," said Froghorn doubtfully. "Or to be of any use in freeing Cybelle."

"They can be of no use trying to make their way here. And we shall work on more planes than this. Our allies are to be gathered exactly wherever they are, and to carry the struggle against the Darkness wherever we may. We only find the brunt of Dorini thrown against us in these lower realms. Her forces are everywhere over these worlds of ours. We must stem those tides, too, if we are to succeed in defeating her aims. It is very difficult to dam a river as it enters the sea, but very simple when it is done when it is but a small stream."

"I don't understand, Greyfax. I mean I can see all that, right enough, but I don't see how it will help."

The old man put his hand on Froghorn's shoulder. "Your father and I had foreseen this day ages ago, when we were still unsure of how many things would be. But we saw this clearly enough. We have too long concerned ourselves with only this small space at the realms' edge of Cypher, but it is not the only place where we are needed."

"You mean you would leave here now, with everything in the balance?"

"It is as it must be, my dear fellow. I must seek the forces of Light beyond, and so must you. It is all in the Book. We shall do no more good here, at the moment."

"But Cybelle? What of her? We can't leave her in Dorini's hands."

"That is beyond our powers, Faragon," said Greyfax rather sternly. "She will be saved, but not by your hand or mine."

"Then who?"

"These things are often confusing. The Book says she is to be delivered from Dorini, but it doesn't go into such small detail as to how or why. It is enough to know she will be delivered. That is if we're not caught napping like rabbits here, waiting for Doraki."

"Does the Book say we must make our way elsewhere at this time?"

"It does. It shall pass as it says. The Holders of the Light shall go forth to rally the Circle to do war against the Darkness in all the corners of Creation."

"And what of Mithramuse, and Melodias?"

"Their part to play is where they are, on Atlanton."

Froghorn looked away, to the distant mountains that bordered Cypher.

"We must go now, my friend," said Greyfax more urgently, gazing long into Froghorn's eyes.

"Shall we meet again, Greyfax? Before the end?"

"As surely as we stand here now."

"Then farewell, if part we must. When shall I know if we have won through?"

"When the Star of Windameir shines like a light in darkness."

Greyfax mounted, and with a quick salute, was gone.

Froghorn, torn by a desire to return to Atlanton Earth, turned slowly away at last, and guided Pe'lon's head toward the distant realms beyond.

A sudden loneliness filled him with an anguish so heavy he felt his heart would surely burst, but he urged Pe'lon on, and horse and rider disappeared for a time from the embattled lands of Amarigin.

Spinning away upward, Froghorn saw the older wizard far ahead, above the rising green sky of morning over Atlanton Earth, and Pe'lon stretched out his great neck in a burst of silent speed, and time and distance melted beneath his flashing hooves, until at last he rode beside Greyfax over the darkening horizons of a world at war.

Visions of the Light

While Froghorn rode the wild lands to the west, and Greyfax gathered the forces of Light in the east, the battle for Cypher raged on in merciless savagery. Melodias returned to his armies waiting at Fourthwaite, and began the march to reach General Greymouse, now fighting in the Forest of Cypher.

He could see the black smoke of battle fires rising from far away, and hear the unbroken roar of their death struggle rattling in the still, early dawn.

As he neared, he saw great sections of the once thick wood burned and gutted, and a fine layer of black ash over the countryside around. His armies met little resistance, for the main forces of Dorini hammered on deeper into the woods, in pursuit of Greymouse's dwindling strength.

After a small skirmish near where the Thirdwaite road ran into the Forest of Cypher, his legions encountered no further action until he had marched almost two leagues into the now ruined wood.

The constant din of firearms so confused the senses that his front company had advanced into a well-laid Gorgolac trap before any realized it, and many of those troops lay slaughtered as the company wheeled about to regroup.

Melodias set out his lines and began the advance.

And in the twilight wing of Cypher, Lorini kissed her daughter's icy brow, and gently closed the door to her chamber. She walked slowly back to her sitting room and study, sadly gazing about her halls, empty now of all save a few who had remained with her to the last.

The great hall was in shadows now, the echoes of other laughter muted and lost in the dull carpets and tapestries of long-past occasions and feast days, and the singing pools beyond the tall windows lay silent and still. No elfin voice drifted on the scented air, carrying the old songs of that magic time. Instead, the wind carried the smoke of war, and a fine black dust began to settle on the white towers of Cypher and cloud the waning sun that yet hung in the darkening sky.

Lorini crossed her study and sat at the pearl-colored desk. She sat long in silence, then turned her thought to Cephus Starkeeper, and Erophin, Elder of all Windameir.

Flashing golden lights spun about the room, and a silver dolphin with dazzling green eyes appeared, followed by nine small glowing fish, swimming in a constant halo of brilliant white light. As her mind neared Windameir, a rushing wind of stardust and music enveloped her, and welcomed her home.

A wry, droll old man in flowing white robes greeted her.

"In time, Lorini. You have tarried long on your journey," said Erophin, extending his ancient hand to her.

"Oh, Master," she bowed low, "I have let my desires overcome my wisdom."

Erophin nodded, tugging his long silver-gray beard.

"As I say, in time. It has played out as it will. The act is already done, and not even I may alter it, even if I so wished. We shall wait now. It shall come to pass, as always."

Cephus Starkeeper entered the long, comfortable, airy room.

"My dear Lorini, welcome. We have been expecting you."

"I must ask forgiveness for my tardiness, Cephus. I had hoped to manage things better before I left."

"It was not to be, dear lady."

"I know, but I could not help but try."

"Cybelle shall not linger long in the domains of your dark sister. Even now the bonds are loosening."

"My pride and love as a mother blinded me, Master. I can only ask again for forgiveness."

"It is not mine to say you are forgiven, my child," said Erophin softly. "We must all play out our given roles, for whatever results they may bring."

"And all our roles are changing, Lorini. What has been shall always be, and what shall be is a mere flicker of thought in the mind of the All."

Cephus placed an arm about Lorini, and led her to the long table, and drew back a chair for her.

"Is it mine to know about Cybelle? I mean how it will end?"

"Only that she shall be freed from the Darkness."

Erophin sat opposite her and began arranging a great sheaf of parchment.

"And Cypher?"

The old man sat silent for a time, pulling his beard and staring away into a deep stillness that ranged beyond all things, all planes, or spheres, or dimensions.

After what seemed to Lorini an aeon, he spoke, slowly and carefully.

"Cypher, dear sister, is, and was, a dream, a beautiful dream, given to those lower worlds to remind them of faith and hope, and their True Home. It is given to those whose faith and hope have been lost, or is being lost. Before you went there, a countless number of Cyphers were, and are, and will be, perhaps. To those who have not forgotten the Light of Windameir, Cyphers are not necessary. They know already. Our Council, and others, such as the elves, and dwarfs, and animals of old, have not lost the Secret of Home. But among most of Mankind, the way back is forgotten."

Erophin paused to clear his throat, and his pure blue-gray eyes focused once more on some distant vision.

"In the darkness at times, we may smell the fragrance of some flower that is hidden from us, yet it grows stronger as our senses awaken to its aroma. It colors the very darkness with its beauty. Cypher is like that. And now, it shall be but common ground for all to trample over. It will be conquered, its magic gone, and it is written that it shall pass from its hidden boundaries to nothing more than geography."

Lorini bowed her head in sorrow as Erophin spoke.

"Then there is to be no hope for Atlanton Earth?"

Erophin's features cleared, and he smiled.

"Gold does not become iron because it is made dirty on the outside. You can cover it in mud, yet it is gold, all the same. So, dear lady, Cypher will fall, and for a time the Darkness may think it has won a great victory in its capture. But Cypher, like the gold, will not have changed. It is still Cypher, and its power is mighty. All who enter Cypher will sooner or later feel its pull, whether they are willing to do so or not. And sooner or later, all will be reminded of what Cypher is but a mirror of."

Erophin patted Lorini's hand when he had finished, and turned his attention to Cephus Starkeeper.

"How fares Greymouse, Cephus?"

"At the realms' edge of Cypher. It is almost over. He shall soon give up the fray and retire." A faint trace of sadness flickered across his clear eyes. "But even so, as Erophin has just said, it is but one more step in the direction of the long journey Home."

"And Faragon?" asked Lorini.

The room glimmered and shone with a pale moonlight, and the mounted figure of a man hidden by the folds of his cloak stood out in stark relief. Around him blazed the watch fires for as far as the eye could see, and when the shadowed figure moved to stroke his horse, the cape fell away, revealing the anxious features of Froghorn Fairingay.

Erophin's thoughts touched the young man, and he briefly looked directly at the three seated in the distant room in Windameir.

As that vision faded, another replaced it, and Greyfax Grimwald smiled gravely from the throne room of a great palace. Upon his head he bore a crown, fashioned in the manner of five stars above a field of gold.

Lorini drew in a sharp breath, but could read nothing in the expression on her old friend's face.

And as that vision vanished, another, more distant and remote, came, of a dark wood; filled with low, stunted trees and choking underbrush. Long shadows of pale sunlight filtered weakly into the gloom, making the dim cloak of darkness move in eerie patterns.

Almost imperceptible at first, then growing, Lorini saw a light, glowing faintly, as if from the depths of some fathomless sea. As she looked closer, she realized the light was coming from beneath some form of jacket or riding cape, and that it was worn by a dwarf.

As the vision cleared, she saw Broco and Bear and Otter, in the company of three men, racing through the grim shadows of the Dragur Wood.

And in her heart the answers came, just as Erophin spoke.

"You see, my lady, the Arkenchest is in the hands of the Circle, and at the moment is on the way to cross Calix Stay. It is the Chest which will save Cybelle. It is the Chest, with its Secrets, which is the hope of all Atlanton Earth, and indeed all the lower worlds in the Creation."

Lorini had reached up and touched Erophin as he spoke, and she knew suddenly that it was the Chest which awakened the wild hope she felt in her heart, and the certain knowledge that somehow, some way, the bitter struggle that was being waged by the Light was not lost, and that as long as the Chest remained in the hands of the Circle, the fight to rise up from the Darkness would go on, unceasing and unyielding, until the final victory was won, when the Fields of Light in Windameir illuminated all the planes of the High King's Creation, and all was returned safely once more to the happiness of his unending love.

Orson Scott Card

ENDER'S GAME

Winner of the Hugo Award
Winner of the Nebula Award
An American Library Association
"100 Best Books for Teens"

Ender Wiggin has hardly had a childhood when representatives of the world government recruit him for military training at a facility called Battle School. A genius, Ender is considered a master strategist. His skills will be necessary if the Earth can repel another attack by alien Buggers. In simulated war games Ender excels. But how will he do in real battle conditions? After all, Battle School *is* just a game, right?

"Superb."—*Booklist*

ENDER'S SHADOW

2000 Alex Award Winner
An American Library Association
"Top 10 Best Book"

Life on the streets is tough. But if Bean has learned anything it's how to survive. Not with his fists. Bean is way too small to fight. But with his brain. Like his colleague and rival Ender Wiggin, Bean has been chosen to enroll in Battle School. And like Ender, Bean will be called upon to perform an extraordinary service. A parallel novel to the extraordinary *Ender's Game*.

"An exceptional work."—*School Library Journal*

H. M. Hoover

ORVIS

An American Booksellers
"Pick of the Lists"

Parents Choice Children's Media
Award for Literature

When Toby stumbles upon an abandoned robot named Orvis, she knows exactly how he feels. No one wants her either. With Orvis and her only friend Thaddeus—another lonely castoff—Toby sets off across the vast Empty in search of sanctuary.

"A first-rate adventure."—*Parents Choice*

ANOTHER HEAVEN, ANOTHER EARTH

An American Library Association
"101 Best of the Best Books in the Past 25 Years"

"Superb!"—*The Times Educational Supplement*

Only a handful of residents remain on Xilan from the original crew that colonized the planet centuries before. Including Gareth. When a rescue mission arrives from Earth, however, Gareth must make a difficult decision: accept their help and abandon the only past she has ever known . . . or cling to the past and risk extinction.

"A real blockbuster of a novel. As readable as it is wise."
—*The Junior Bookshelf*

David Lubar

HIDDEN TALENTS

American Library Association
"Best Books for Young Adults"

"Wondrously surprising, playful, and heartwarming."—*VOYA*

"Sure to be popular."—*Kliatt*

Martin Anderson doesn't like being called a loser. But when he ends up at Edgeview Alternative School he has to face the truth: Edgeview is the end of the line. But he discovers something remarkable about himself and his friends: each has a special . . . *hidden* . . . talent.

IN THE LAND OF THE LAWN WEENIES
and other Misadventures

"Four stars!"—*Chicago Tribune*

"Really off the wall stories. They're funny thrillers that scare you out of your seat, but have you laughing all the time."
—Walter The Giant Storyteller

"Clever, creepy, and full of surprises."—James Howe

Kids can be *such* monsters. Literally. From the award-winning author of *Hidden Talents*, two remarkable short story collections—*Kidzilla* and *The Witch's Monkey*—together for the first time. Each hilarious and harrowing.

Roderick MacLeish

PRINCE OMBRA

"Reminiscent of Bradbury's *Something Wicked This Way Comes*."
—*Publishers Weekly*

"Highly recommended."—*Library Journal*

"Whirls the reader along."—*Chicago Sun Times*

Bentley has secret powers. And he's going to need them. Bentley is a hero—the thousand and first to be exact—in a long line of heroes that has stretched all the way back to antiquity. Heroes like Arthur and Hercules. And now: Bentley. One day when Bentley is grown he will be that hero. What Bentley doesn't know is that his "one day" is today.

Caroline Stevermer

A COLLEGE OF MAGICS

"Strikingly set, pleasingly peopled, and cleverly plotted."
—*Kirkus Reviews* (pointer)

"Delightful!"—*The Washington Post*

Teenager Faris Nallaneen—heir to the dukedom of Galazon—is shunted off to Greenlaw College so that her evil uncle can lay claim to her inheritance. But Greenlaw is not just any school as Faris—and her uncle—will soon discover.

Joan Aiken

THE WHISPERING MOUNTAIN

Winner of the Guardian Prize for Fiction

"An enchanting, original story."
—*The Times* of London

In an effort to recover the magical Harp of Teirtu, Owen and his friend Arabis are plunged into a hair-raising adventure of intrigue, kidnapping, exotic underground worlds, savage beasts . . . even murder.

THE SHADOW GUESTS

"Writing seems to be as natural to Joan Aiken as breathing; her imagination is as untrammeled as ever, the precise construction of the astonishing plot lends conviction, and her style is as witty and sparkling with images."
—*The Horn Book*

After the mysterious disappearance of both his mother and older brother, Cosmo is sent away to live with his eccentric mathematician aunt. But things take a weird twist when Cosmo is visited by ghosts from the past. Ghosts who claim to need his help fighting an ancient deadly curse!

THE COCKATRICE BOYS
Illustrated by Gris Grimley

VOYA "Outstanding Science Fiction, Fantasy & Horror Books of the Year"

A plague of monsters has invaded England and Dakin and Sauna come to the rescue! A rollicking comic masterpiece.

Patricia C. Wrede

MAIRELON THE MAGICIAN

"Delightful . . . Wrede's confection will charm readers."
—*Publishers Weekly*

"A wonderful fantasy/mystery. Highly recommended."
—*VOYA*

When street urchin Kim is caught in the act stealing, her accuser surprises her by suggesting she become his apprentice. An apprentice to a magician!

THE MAGICIAN'S WARD

"A sure bet for fans of Philip Pullman's *Ruby in the Smoke* series."
—*VOYA*

Several wizards of Kim's acquaintance have mysteriously disappeared. And it's up to Kim to find out why.

Isobelle Carmody

OBERNEWTYN
Book One in The Obernewtyn Chronicles

"A major work of fantastic imagination."
—Lloyd Alexander

"A brave, multi-talented girl, her interesting friends,
and animal characters with minds of their own—this book
is a dream date for me."
—Tamora Pierce

For Elspeth Gordie freedom is—like so much else after the
devastation of The Great White—a memory. Feared because of
her mysterious mental powers, she and others like her are hunted
down like animals.

Tanith Lee

RED UNICORN

"Lavish, whimsical dreamscapes reminiscent of Lewis Carroll.
Lee's charming exuberance is everywhere in evidence,
no more so than in Tanaquil's familiar, a wonderfully
comic, cavorting beasty."
—*Publishers Weekly*

In this enchanting novel, sorceress Tanaquil is lured by a red
unicorn into a mirror world where she encounters Tanakil, a
diabolical version of herself.

Neal Shusterman

THE DARK SIDE OF NOWHERE

ALA Best Book for Young Adults
Texas Lone Star Reading List
YALSA Top 10 Quick Picks for Young Adults

"A tense thriller. Shusterman seamlessly combines gritty, heart-stopping plot with a wealth of complex issues."
—*Kirkus Reviews*

Ever have one of those days when you just don't feel like yourself? Jason is having a day like that. Only for Jason, he really *isn't* himself. At least . . . not any more.

H. M. Hoover

THIS TIME OF DARKNESS

"With detail and suspense the author tells an exciting futuristic survival story which comments on power and class-ridden social structures."
—*Horn Book*

"A highly readable story that, while frighteningly powerful, ends on a comforting note."
—*Booklist*

Having lived all her life underground, 11-year-old Amy is intrigued when she befriends a strange boy named Alex who claims to have been . . . *Outside*. Can such a place exist? Amy is determined to find out.